T0191165

Praise for

Elizabeth Bass Parman

"First-time novelist Parman delivers a twisted tale of small-town drama. Fans of gothic tales or Southern novels will enjoy this."

—*LIBRARY JOURNAL*

"Get ready to laugh! Elizabeth Bass Parman is a true Southern storyteller. I couldn't have loved *The Empress of Cooke County* more."

—FANNIE FLAGG, *NEW YORK TIMES*
BESTSELLING AUTHOR

"Funny, fast-moving, suspenseful, with unforgettable and deeply drawn characters, *The Empress of Cooke County* will rivet readers."

—LEE SMITH, *NEW YORK TIMES*
BESTSELLING AUTHOR

"You won't simply read *The Empress of Cooke County*, you will fall into a world we all long for: sizzling small-town life in the American south with its secret history, vivid characters, and juicy dramas. If the complicated Jezebel and the feisty women of *Steel Magnolias* had a baby, it might be Posey Jarvis. Put on a pot of coffee, cut yourself a wedge of chess pie and dive in."

—ADRIANA TRIGIANI, *NEW YORK TIMES* BESTSELLING
AUTHOR OF *THE GOOD LEFT UNDONE*

"*The Empress of Cooke County* gives you a juicy taste of small-town Southern life at its best! Be prepared to laugh out loud as you race through pages full of secrets, high drama, and an unpredictable ending!"

—LISA PATTON, BESTSELLING AUTHOR OF
WHISTLIN' DIXIE IN A NOR'EASTER

"The Empress of Cooke County is, at its core, a tale of connection. Parman examines both the small acts of kindness that nourish connection and the selfish impulses that starve it. You can't help but root for this tender celebration of community, would-be empresses, and big dreams."

—MARY LIZA HARTONG,
AUTHOR OF LOVE AND HOT CHICKEN

"Elizabeth Bass Parman dazzles in The Empress of Cooke County, a lush, 1960s Southern charmer brimming with wit and whimsy. Join the unforgettable Posey Jarvis and her daughter as they navigate the twists and turns of small-town Tennessee with gin-soaked escapades, a possum-infested mansion, and enough peach cobbler to make your mouth water."

—HOPE GIBBS, AUTHOR OF
WHERE THE GRASS GROWS BLUE

"As someone who often fantasizes about a simpler way of life, stepping back in time to Queen Bee Posey Jarvis's colorful world was a slice of literary heaven. A delightful 1960s southern charmer on every level. What a stunning, poignant debut."

—REA FREY, #1 BESTSELLING AUTHOR OF
DON'T FORGET ME AND THE OTHER YEAR

The Empress of Cooke County

The Empress of Cooke County

a novel

Elizabeth Bass Parman

HARPER MUSE

The Empress of Cooke County

Copyright © 2024 by Elizabeth Bass Parman

All rights reserved. No portion of this book may be reproduced, stored in a retrieval system, or transmitted in any form or by any means—electronic, mechanical, photocopy, recording, scanning, or other—except for brief quotations in critical reviews or articles, without the prior written permission of the publisher.

Published by Harper Muse, an imprint of HarperCollins Focus LLC.

Scripture quotations are taken from the King James Version. Public domain.

This book is a work of fiction. The characters, incidents, and dialogue are drawn from the author's imagination and are not to be construed as real. Any resemblance to actual events or persons, living or dead, is entirely coincidental.

Any internet addresses (websites, blogs, etc.) in this book are offered as a resource. They are not intended in any way to be or imply an endorsement by HarperCollins Focus LLC, nor does HarperCollins Focus LLC vouch for the content of these sites for the life of this book.

Library of Congress Cataloging-in-Publication Data
Names: Parman, Elizabeth Bass, 1961- author.
Title: The Empress of Cooke County : a novel / Elizabeth Bass Parman.
Description: [Nashville] : Harper Muse, 2024. | Summary: "Posey Jarvis knows she's the rightful Empress of Cooke County . . . she just needs to make everyone else realize it too"—Provided by publisher.
Identifiers: LCCN 2024005833 (print) | LCCN 2024005834 (ebook) | ISBN 9781400342594 (paperback) | ISBN 9781400342563 (epub) | ISBN 9781400342570
Subjects: LCGFT: Novels.
Classification: LCC PS3616.A75698 E47 2024 (print) | LCC PS3616. A75698 (ebook) | DDC 813/.6—dc23/eng/20240212
LC record available at https://lccn.loc.gov/2024005833
LC ebook record available at https://lccn.loc.gov/2024005834

Printed in the United States of America

24 25 26 27 28 LBC 5 4 3 2 1

This book is dedicated to the memory
of my father, Robinson Neil Bass,
who always knew this day would come.

Chapter 1

Posey

POSEY JARVIS SNATCHED the newsletter from her mailbox and rushed inside. Maneuvering around a pair of cloisonné lamps, she entered her bedroom, crammed full of ornate furniture that looked as out of place as a ball gown at a square dance. She nodded at the renewal reminder on the envelope: "1966 Membership Fee Due by February 1." If receiving updates on Frances Ryan meant ponying up annual dues to the Nashville Garden Club, she would gladly siphon the money from her grocery allowance and send it in.

She sat at her vanity, digging under her datebook and scarves for the silver flask stolen long ago, a memento from the happiest week of her life. As she unscrewed the cap, she wondered again if CJ had ever noticed it was missing. And why he stayed married to Frances. On her darkest days, she berated herself for not being enough to trigger their divorce, but most of the time, she blamed either CJ or Frances.

After a long pull of gin, she scanned the newsletter. The headline announced "Garden Club Gathers at President's Coventry Circle Home to Discuss New City Garden," with a photo of Frances on her sofa holding a sketch, surrounded by fawning club members peering over her shoulders. Posey read, "Eighteen years ago I traveled to New Zealand on a horticultural tour. Recently I came across a souvenir from that time, which brought back vivid memories. I used my notes and photos from that trip to re-create the gardens here in my beloved Nashville."

Posey smiled wistfully as she recalled what had transpired while Frances was on the far side of the globe. Before Frances's plane had even reached cruising altitude, CJ had whisked the then nineteen-year-old Posey Burch from her dumpy apartment and into his stunning home for seven whole days of uninterrupted passion.

CJ had downshifted the white Jaguar as he turned into the driveway that day, the growl of the engine thrilling her with its power. She gasped as the three-story house came into view, silently vowing to live there as CJ's wife one day. *"My God, it's a mansion."*

"Yep. She calls it Eden Hall."

The last day of their weeklong rendezvous, CJ had been tense. He yelled up the stairs, *"Damn it, Posey, hurry! Her plane lands in twenty minutes."* A lovestruck Posey lifted the flask from his dresser and tucked it into her suitcase before slamming the lid. Impulsively, she dropped one of her monogrammed earrings among the hand creams, pens, and bookmarks in Frances's nightstand. Her mother had saved for over a year to buy them, but to get what you want to get, you have to do what you have to do.

Sure of her future with the man she was so obsessed with, Posey gave the earring three full weeks to get the ball rolling. When she realized her plan had failed, that there would be no announcement from CJ that he was divorcing, she was equal parts furious and heartbroken. In an effort to lessen the sting, she vowed to possess a house even finer than Eden Hall. How to accomplish that goal was unclear, but if Frances could get a mansion, so could she. And once CJ saw her as a successful hostess in her own magnificent home, it would be only a matter of time before he came to his senses and married her.

Shaking herself from her memories, Posey wondered why Frances was writing about that week now. She frowned at the newsletter. Surely Frances hadn't just found the earring after almost two decades. Even if she had, how would she know it was left there while she was in New Zealand?

Posey was alerted to the arrival of her daughter and husband by the rumble of her husband's truck. Ordinarily she would object to such a jarring sound and insist the engine be fixed, but the distinctive throb served as a warning toll and had proven itself useful on more than one occasion.

She tucked the newsletter and flask in her drawer and covered both with scarves, flinching as Vern called for her. After a quick swipe of her signature Scarlet Scandal lipstick across her thin lips, she stepped into the kitchen, first smiling at her daughter and then addressing her husband, whose deeply lined face appeared particularly pale. "You're home early."

He set a hummingbird cake onto the flecked Formica counter. Posey rolled her eyes. Vern was well-known in town for helping out his neighbors, and they were always repaying her already-portly husband with sweets. If she didn't know better, she would worry about the motives of the ladies so intent on impressing him with their baked goods. And didn't they already have half a cake left over from her birthday celebration?

With a pained squint, Vern looked at her. "I have one of my migraines and Callie Jane feels puny, so we closed up early."

Posey crossed the tiny kitchen and placed a hand on her daughter's forehead. "It's probably just excitement from getting engaged yesterday, but you do feel a little warm. Why don't you lie down until dinner?"

Callie Jane shrugged off her wool jacket, a sixteenth-birthday present from her mother she had worn every cold day for the last two years, and, without a word, headed for her bedroom.

The scent of Aqua Net filled the room. Vern gestured to Posey's beehive, asking, "Since when do you go to the Curly Q on a Thursday?"

"Queenie moved my appointment up a day—something about training a new employee." Posey scowled. "The whole point of a standing appointment is that it doesn't change. She *knows* I like fresh hair for the weekend." Gesturing to her calendar hanging on the wall, she added, "You would've known my plans if you'd bothered to learn my color-coding system." She stabbed the date, January 6, for emphasis. "Periwinkle for me and cobalt for Callie Jane. Family activities are in fuchsia."

Vern glanced at the calendar, massaging his temples through his dark hair. "What color am I?"

"You have no color because you never do anything."

"That's not true." Vern removed his jacket and hung it on a hook by the door. "I work every day, bowl on Tuesday nights, and go to church. And don't forget taking flowers out to the cemetery on Sunday afternoons."

Vern visited his parents' graves every week, bringing homegrown daisies from the first blooms until the killing frost.

"Do you need me to write down 'Vern: Cedar Hill three o'clock'?"

"Maybe so. Then at least I'd know you cared where I was at."

"Bringing bouquets to live people instead of dead ones makes more sense. And store-bought, not from your scraggly mess of a garden."

Vern's voice was low. "There's lots of ways to show love."

"All cheaper than a real bouquet, I bet."

His broad shoulders stiffened. "Black."

Posey's hands dug into her bony hips. "What's that supposed to mean?"

"My ink pen color for the calendar. I want black."

She heaved an exasperated sigh. "The color has to start with the first letter of your name, like vermilion."

"What the hell color is that?"

"Bloodred." Her face brightened. "The exact hue of my latest purchase for the Emporium." She waved her arm toward the pair of lamps standing tall on the den's faded rag rug.

He flipped over the tag and whistled. "Way too high for what we sell. The Nashville crowd might pay those prices, but my customers won't."

"You said if I found something I like I could get it for the Emporium. Remember? Or has our arrangement changed?"

They had forged the deal before Callie Jane had cut her first tooth. Posey could buy inventory for the Emporium at her beloved estate sales, but Vern was in charge of the store.

"There's been no change," he answered, rubbing his neck. "I need to lay down. My head's killing me." He paused on his way to the bedroom. "But I'm cutting your budget."

"If we don't have new inventory, people will stop coming in," she snapped to Vern's back. He shut the door as she whispered, "You're not cutting my budget."

Without her Emporium allowance, what excuse could she give for driving into Nashville so often to shop at estate sales?

She delighted in prowling through the luxurious Belle Meade homes of the recently departed, particularly when the decedent had been a size four. Standing five foot two, with dark hair, emerald eyes, and orchid-white skin, Posey was proud of her good looks. She wasn't as tall as Jackie Kennedy, but she made sure she was as elegantly dressed as her idol. Posey's mother had always bought Posey's Goodwill clothes two sizes too big, telling her mortified daughter she would grow into them, but once Posey started buying her own outfits, she made sure every piece fit her perfectly.

The Belle Meade ladies favored Gucci and Chanel, so she was able to keep her closet stuffed with barely worn designer outfits she bought for next to nothing during her forays into Nashville. Every excursion ended the same way—with a slow cruise down magnolia-lined Coventry Circle to gape at number 229, a stately Colonial with green shutters she would have painted black.

Her own house was an abhorrence. It had belonged to her in-laws, and they had thought it a palace, but to her, the two-bedroom, too-small ranch screamed middle class. The narrow windows were better suited to a medieval fortress, and the closets couldn't hold the belongings of a nun sworn to poverty. When Vern's mother passed away less than a year after his father's death, Vern insisted their little family of three move in. Her cheeks had ached from the effort it took to smile her way through the compliments offered by the townsfolk on her new home, "the cutest house in Spark," much as they had from all the congratulations on her marriage: "The Lord has never made a sweeter man than Vern Jarvis."

Posey walked down the hall and tapped on Callie Jane's door. After hearing a soft "Come in," she sat beside her daughter, who was on her bed, curled under a blanket. Posey stroked her head. "How are you feeling, sweetie?"

"Lightheaded and queasy, like I might throw up."

Posey brushed a strand of long blonde hair from Callie Jane's pale cheek. "It's probably just nerves. Getting engaged is a pretty big deal."

"I didn't know he was going to propose. It was so awkward, with his family there and all."

"The whole town's known for years you two would end up together. I'm not sure how it could be a surprise."

"Trace and I are friends. I love him, but not like that." Callie Jane struggled to a sitting position. "You and Daddy were friends before you got married, and I'm not sure you all—"

"I adore your father." Posey picked up a pillow, fluffing it. "If you love someone, hang on to them, no matter what." She gently tucked the pillow beside her daughter's head. "You'll have plenty of time to warm up to the idea while we plan the wedding." She smoothed her skirt and smiled. "Let's start with your gown. You're not obligated to wear Opal Humboldt's dress, no matter what she said."

"Mama, I'm not sure I want to marry Trace. He's been my best friend forever, but the truth is, I don't think I want him for my husband. Getting married was always just a *someday* idea we'd talk about while we were doing homework together or watching for shooting stars in his backyard, but now that we're engaged, it feels wrong."

Posey studied her daughter's troubled face, at a loss for an answer. Her own mother's advice, *"The truth is overrated,"* sprang to her mind. Marriage was for security, not for some fairy-tale happily ever after, but Callie Jane was too naive to understand that. Instead, Posey responded, "He gave you the highest compliment a man can give his future wife. He said he needs you by his side to be truly successful." She twisted her thin gold wedding band.

Callie Jane was the one thing she had done right with her life, despite the rocky start. Vern loved Callie Jane because she was smart, capable, and creative. He told anyone who would listen that she spent her first Emporium paycheck on a yard sale doghouse, repurposing it for the feral cats she fed behind the BuyMore grocery store. Posey loved Callie Jane because she was quiet, obedient, and polite. Everyone in town gave Posey credit for raising such a fine young woman, and she always accepted the compliments with a smile. What she kept to herself was what she was most proud of: Callie Jane was the spitting image of her father.

Posey had probably faded from CJ's memory long ago, but she had an unforgettable reminder—his child, something Frances had never provided. Callie Jane was the best of herself and CJ blended together, flesh-and-blood proof that he had risked everything to be with her. Each time their daughter looked at her with eyes the color of a still summer lake, a rush of both love and pride washed over her.

She studied the shadow box on the shelf containing the Miss Tiny Tennessee sash and fifteen-year-old *Gazette* article about Callie Jane participating in the Caney Ridge toddler beauty pageant. Her daughter was perfect, a blonde version of herself she could manipulate, carefully steering her away from the mistakes that had ruined her own life.

"Do you love Trace?"

Callie Jane nodded. "He's always taken care of me and makes me feel safe, like the big brother I never had."

"All brides get cold feet." She frowned. "Although not usually this early." Standing, she said, "You'll get over it." Pulling the curtains closed, she added, "I'll get dinner started." She paused by the bedroom door. "I hate to think of you grown and gone, but being the wife of the man you love is every woman's dream."

"But, Mama, what should I do about not wanting to marry—"

"You'll be so happy," Posey said as she shut the door.

The enormous hummingbird cake Vern had deposited on the kitchen counter was swaddled in cling wrap. She'd have to take the remnants of her own cake out of the ancient fridge to make room. Sliding it from the wire shelf, she studied the remaining holes in the chocolate frosting— Callie Jane had formed a 3 and an 8 with candles—and recalled her three wishes, the same ones she made on every eyelash, double rainbow, and white horse: to be loved by her daughter, to live in a mansion, and to one day call CJ her husband. One down, two to go.

She closed the refrigerator door and pressed her hand along its side to assess the throb of the motor, like a nurse checking a pulse. Steady. *Damn it.* No Foodarama fridge for her anytime soon.

Earlier that day at the Curly Q, Barbara Ricketts had been crowing about how she was headed to Nashville to buy a Foodarama, the most expensive refrigerator sold at Sears. With a dramatic flourish, Barbara had pulled out an ad from her purse depicting a beaming woman gesturing to an enormous refrigerator, doors wide open, laden with enough food to feed their whole town of Spark for a week. "Ring in 1966 with a New Kelvinator Foodarama," the ad blared. *"What color should I get, Queenie? Mike says he can't eat anything out of a pink refrigerator, so maybe yellow."*

Posey knew Barbara didn't want Queenie's opinion. That holier-than-thou heifer's only goal was to make Posey jealous. Barbara had never forgiven Posey for an incident their senior year of high school involving her then-fiancé and now-husband, Mike. If Mike had been dumb enough to pull her into the dark cloakroom with Barbara nearby, no matter how much Posey had been flirting with him, well, that wasn't *her* fault.

She began making dinner, glancing out the window as she worked. A white envelope resting on the ground by the mailbox caught her eye. In her haste to read the garden club news, she must have dropped it.

Hunching her shoulders against the biting wind, she hurried to the road and lifted the letter from a muddy puddle. It had her full name on it, Posey Burch Jarvis, with a return address of Dawkens, Smith, and Sievers, Attorneys at Law. *What the hell?* She clawed open the letter. Could she come to their office in Nashville in two weeks for a meeting? *Why on earth would a lawyer need to speak with me?*

Had someone seen her switch price tags at that estate sale? Even if they had, how would they know her name? She nibbled a nail. Had some sharp-eyed IRS employee realized her tax return proved she had shaved a few years off her real birthdate? Did it somehow involve Frances and that trip to New Zealand?

Her head cocked at a new thought. Was her father dead and had he finally acknowledged her in his will? Doubtful.

She pushed back the memory of the day she turned five, crying after she made her single wish on her birthday cake.

"There's still more I want," she'd sobbed.

Her mother appeased Posey by saying, "You were born on the third, so instead of one wish, you should get three."

"Light them again," Posey demanded. "I'm making two more wishes."

After blowing out the candles a second time, Posey dashed out the front door of their Stadler Court home, shouting, "Daddy's coming to get me!" She plopped herself on their cracked cement stoop, shivering in the January air.

Her mother tried for over an hour to coax her inside. "He's not coming," she said, and later, "Honey, it's getting dark."

"But my extra wishes. He's taking me to the circus and then coming to live with us."

Posey bit her lip. How appropriate that her earliest memory of her father involved his absence, not his presence.

She returned the letter to the envelope, making a mental note to record the appointment in her private datebook. This was certainly *not* going on the family calendar. *They probably want to thank me for my suggestion to the governor that he declare Spark's downtown district a historic site.* Tourists would flock to Spark, spending big-city dollars in her husband's shop.

She tucked the letter in her purse, planning to call the lawyer's office as soon as Vern and Callie Jane left for the Emporium the next morning. She went back to preparing dinner, counting out the days until she would make the hour-long drive into Nashville. Thirteen. A bad omen.

Chapter 2

Callie Jane

CALLIE JANE GRIPPED the steering wheel of her father's truck until her knuckles whitened as she recalled what had happened two days earlier around the Humboldts' oak dining table. After Wednesday night church, she'd eaten dinner at the Humboldts' as usual. As they were sitting down, Trace had suddenly dropped to one knee and asked Callie Jane to marry him. Stunned, she had only managed to squeak out, "Oh, Trace," when his mama shot out of her chair with a scream and started hugging Callie Jane. Deep against Mrs. Humboldt's ample bosom, she was unable to articulate the rest of the sentence formed on her lips: "I'm not ready."

With tears in her eyes, Mrs. Humboldt had said, "I love all four of my sons, but I have always asked the Lord to send me a daughter." Callie Jane squirmed in Opal Humboldt's embrace, not fully sure what was happening. "I can't wait for the babies. Please let the first one be a girl, or maybe even twin girls. They *do* run in my family on my father's side." Mrs. Humboldt released Callie Jane and gasped, then said, "We'll do it on Mr. Humboldt and my's twenty-fifth anniversary, August 20. You can wear my dress." Mrs. Humboldt then grabbed a photograph from the sideboard and presented it to Callie Jane. "It's a beautiful gown."

Callie Jane had been too dumbfounded to respond. She had always assumed that she and Trace would marry, everyone did, but having the engagement move from an abstract possibility to a concrete reality sent a chill through her soul.

Mrs. Humboldt had dashed to her bedroom, returning with a velvet box. She handed it to her eldest son. "It was your grandmother's. Put it on her finger, Trace."

The ring, a delicate gold band with a small diamond solitaire, dug into Callie Jane's skin. "It's too tight."

Mrs. Humboldt grabbed Callie Jane's hand to inspect her finger. "It needs to be secure so it won't come off. You'll get used to it." She hugged Callie Jane. "A daughter at last."

Once Callie Jane had recovered from Mrs. Humboldt's outburst, she wanted to correct the misunderstanding, but she couldn't bear to embarrass Trace in front of his family. She thought she and Trace could sort it out later, but the whole thing had snowballed. Before the banana pudding had even been served, Mrs. Humboldt had called her sister, advised her other sons to find a wife as suitable as Callie Jane, and begun planning the wedding. "I'll phone your mama first thing in the morning."

In shocked silence, Callie Jane had walked the short distance with Trace to her home along the worn, slick path between their backyards. Once at her kitchen door, he kissed her on the cheek, smiled shyly, and said, "May I speak to your father?"

Trace had explained his intentions. "I will always take care of her and be a good provider. My daddy said the first son to get engaged will be assistant manager, so I'll be gettin' a raise, plus I have some money saved up. My plan is to expand the BuyMore and open three stores in the next five years." He beamed at his bride-to-be. "With Callie Jane by my side, I'll be the grocery king of Cooke County in no time."

Her daddy had asked only one question. "Do you love her, Trace?"

His voice had been strong. "Yes, sir." He looked at Callie Jane. "And I always will."

"If Callie Jane has accepted you, then I will too. Welcome to the family, son."

She had not slept that night.

Her friendship with Trace had begun when they'd toddled toward each other at a Fourth of July town picnic, delighted to find a same-sized friend, and they had remained pals from that day on. As kindergarteners, Trace found Callie Jane sobbing in the cloakroom because she'd lost her lunch money, so he'd slipped her his own, saying he wasn't hungry. In third grade, Bubba Alcott had called her ugly, and Trace slugged him hard enough to bring tears to Bubba's eyes. And when Trace and Callie Jane were the last two contestants in the Cooke County High School spelling bee, he purposefully misspelled *colonel* so Callie Jane could advance to the state championship.

Was the fact that Trace was a good man—someone she genuinely cared for—a good enough reason to marry him? Or was the knot in her stomach signaling that the knot she might tie was a bad idea?

She switched on the radio, rolling the dial from her daddy's country station to her favorite, with their Beatles-heavy playlist. The Fab Four's "Think for Yourself" spilled from the speakers. Ever since that night in February two years prior, when she had stood mesmerized in front of a tiny black-and-white TV listening to "All My Loving" on *The Ed Sullivan Show*, she had been crazy about the Beatles. Her classmates had all fallen in love with Paul that night, flashing that innocent yet wicked smile as he bobbed his head. For her, though, the experience had not been about identifying a future, albeit unlikely, husband but about realizing her universe had irreversibly tilted. Those boys had knocked her breathless, with an energy and urgency that seemed fully misplaced in her world. She had vowed that night she would one day see them for herself, not through a television screen but in person, where she could experience every note and beat firsthand.

Traffic was light, so in less than an hour she was driving by the sign that proclaimed "Welcome to Nashville's Greatest Flea Market—Open Year-Round." She parked and climbed out of the truck.

Her father had given her advice when she started purchasing Emporium inventory. *"Wait 'til right before the vendor is closing for the night, so's he's interested in making a deal."* He handed her a stack of dollar bills. *"Carry only ones. We treat our customers like gold, but most of those fellas don't. They'll say they don't have change when a whole wad of singles is stuffed in their pocket. Ask about the history of the item. What we all care about in life is the stories. Our customers could find their bacon presses or sewing needles anywhere, but they come to the Emporium for what they get, not what they buy."*

Phil Brody, a neighbor of the Jarvises, was loading his truck. His booth was always popular, overflowing with handmade goods. Raw honey jarred with a piece of comb from Dixon King's hives was his bestseller, and whenever he displayed one of Mrs. Simpkins's double wedding ring quilts, it was sold before the day was out.

"Hey, Callie Jane," he called. "You'uns doin' all right? Ever'body's closin' up early because of the snow comin'. Roads'll be slick by this evening. Don't want you to get stranded."

She waved. "Hey, Mr. Brody. I'm not staying long."

"Nice to see another generation of Jarvises gettin' into the junk business, with your daddy fixin' to retire and all."

Pulling her jacket close to her thin frame, she mustered a weak nod. Her father was older, having married for the first time at age forty-seven. Retirement was on his mind, and she was his logical successor. She had worked alongside her father since she'd stood on a peach crate to reach the counter, and just like with marrying Trace, everyone assumed her path, that she would one day take her place as owner.

She had delighted in being close to her daddy in the early days. As she grew older, though, the sameness wrapped around her like a shroud. Her father reveled in the minutiae of rolls of wire and bags of marbles, but she found the tedium of the static walls and shelves of inventory stultifying. She had no better ideas of what to do with her life, though, so for now, she dutifully pushed the register's timeworn black keys and bagged her customers' purchases.

Turning toward the vendor booths, she sighed as she wandered over to a sign promising "Oddities." A heavyset man in grimy overalls greeted her as he hefted boxes onto the back of the battered pickup parked at the rear of his stall. "Closin' up, girlie, 'fore the snow hits. I'll make you a good deal. Better to sell something than carry it back home."

She frowned. She had been eighteen for over a month, hardly just a girl.

The booth was filled with the detritus of people's lives: a dented aluminum Jell-O mold, a Roy Rogers cap gun in a battered cardboard box, and a coffee mug declaring the owner to be the "World's Greatest Grandpa." Turning to move to the next booth, she spotted a banker's box.

Drawing closer, she felt warmth envelop her, despite the raw day, like she was basking in May sunshine. As she tugged open the lid, wavy from some long-ago encounter with water, excitement flooded her body.

Her eye fell on a museum postcard of a painting depicting a naked woman standing on a clamshell floating in the ocean, with a man in a cloud blowing her across the waves. "*The Birth of Venus*, by Sandro Botticelli, circa 1485, Uffizi Gallery, Florence, Italy," the caption read. "Venus rides a scallop shell across the sea as Zephyr guides her to shore."

A misfolded map of California with worn edges was next, partially obscuring a hardcover book entitled *California: America's Eden*, with an odd pendant tied to a leather cord dangling from one of its corners. A card peeking from a tattered paperback grabbed her attention. She drew it from the book and knew she had to have that box.

The card's golden-yellow sky glowed like a summer sun. A beautiful young woman with finely sketched features and flowing blonde hair gazed serenely back at her. She was dressed in opulent robes sprigged with red flowers, with a pearl necklace gracing her neck and a crown of stars adorning her head. Holding a scepter, she reclined on vibrant red and orange cushions in a field of wheat. Resting at her feet lay a heart-shaped shield depicting a symbol Callie Jane did not recognize. The Roman numeral III was written at the top, while *The Empress* was scripted across the bottom. An empress, just like the one from her childhood tales.

"You wanna buy that?" the booth owner asked. She hastily tucked the image in its book and glanced at the title, *A Guide to Unlocking the World and Wisdom of Tarot Cards*, before returning it to the box.

"Yes," she answered. "How about two dollars?"

"Make it three and you got yourself a deal."

"Three it is." Remembering her father's instructions about getting a good story, she asked, "Can you tell me anything about this box? How did you come by it?"

"A lady in East Nashville up and left town," he answered. "She had wrote her daughter, saying she was moving to India, or maybe it was Italy—one of those *I* countries—and to sell whatever the daughter didn't want."

Callie Jane contemplated being brave enough to leave everything behind and take off for an *I* country as she peeled three ones from her pocket. Joggling the ill-fitting cardboard lid back on, she hauled her treasure to the Ford. She nestled the box onto the seat beside her and then extracted the Empress card, placing it beside her to ride shotgun on the drive home.

Her friends heard stories of Cinderella and Rapunzel, but Callie Jane's mother, who had an abhorrence of any fairy tale, took a different approach. Callie Jane was fed accounts of Princess Victoria of England, growing up in a palace and being waited on hand and foot.

"People remember Victoria as only a queen, but she was an empress, which is the only thing better than being a queen," her mother would say as she settled dime-store crowns on both her head and Callie Jane's. *"When you're a queen, you rule the country, but when you're an empress, you rule the world."*

Her mother had once caught her daddy telling Callie Jane about Goldilocks and had exploded. *"No fairy tales! We need to teach her about the real world so she can learn to survive in it."* He had asked how stories of a long-dead European monarch would prepare Callie Jane for a life in Spark, but his only answer had been an icy stare.

Callie Jane had spent more time than she would ever admit believing her mother was a real empress. When she was four years old, one of her parents' many fights had woken her up and she'd stumbled toward her parents' bedroom, listening as an argument wafted through the partially closed door. *"The Cadillac's a good deal, and we should buy it. I can't impress Cooke County with a beat-up truck."* Her mother had noticed her tiny daughter and guided her back to bed. Once settled back under her quilt, Callie Jane had fallen into a fitful sleep, turning over in her mixed-up brain the news that her mother had to "empress" the whole county.

Registering Callie Jane for kindergarten offered her mother an entrée into the world of elementary school politics. Power suited her mother, and her reign soon spilled over into all areas of daily life in Spark, like when she told the owner of Honeybelle's dress shop that a geranium-pink door was unacceptable for the town's historic district. When Callie Jane had corrected Fayelene, the daughter of Honeybelle's owner, saying her mother was not bossy but was just performing her duties as an empress, things took a dramatic turn. Callie Jane was set straight by Fayelene about how Callie Jane's mother was nothing more than a housewife who pushed a buggy around the BuyMore and carried her child to the pediatrician for booster shots, the same as every other mother in Spark. Callie Jane was humiliated to realize she had confused *impress* and *empress*, and refused to join her classmates on the playground for a solid week to avoid the relentless teasing.

The teenage years hit, and she realized how fitting the moniker was for her mother: the Empress of Cooke County. Nothing was ever good enough, and appearances were valued way more than the truth. At first, Callie Jane had assumed all mothers were like her own, but after spending the night with Cheryl Ann Tisdale one Friday night, somewhere between Mrs. Tisdale's kiss good night to *both* girls and the waffles prepared for breakfast because they were the guest's favorite, Callie Jane began to realize a mother's love was not typically transactional.

Once back on Market Street with the banker's box in tow, Callie Jane turned into the alley behind the Emporium. She pulled into her father's parking spot under the maple and let herself in the back door, lugging her flea market find. After a scary incident where her father had lost his breath as he moved a table, Callie Jane had insisted he see the town doctor. It had taken weeks of nagging for him to make an appointment with Doc Grisham, but he had finally agreed and was there that afternoon. Callie Jane sent up a quick prayer that the visit was going well as she checked her watch. Twenty more minutes until closing time. She unlocked the front door, flipped the sign to "Come In, We're Open," and returned to her flea market purchase.

The bell of the Emporium's door jingled as she lifted the box's lid. Dixon King's rawboned frame slipped through the wooden door. "Hey, Callie Jane," he called. "You holding down the fort today?"

"Hi, Mr. King." She smiled at one of her favorite customers. "Daddy's not here, so it's just me. What can I help you with?"

"I need some licorice whips for my niece. She's got an upset stomach and they'll fix her right up."

A farmer and beekeeper, Dixon King could tell you the very day the spring's first crocus would be spotted and could coax the sweetest honey in Cooke County from his bees. His ability to predict the weather was legendary. Tall and still handsome, he had sparkling brown eyes the color of a perfectly cured tobacco leaf. His wife had died years ago, and he had never so much as looked at another woman, much to the dismay of the eligible ladies of Spark.

Callie Jane carefully transferred lines of the black candy into a paper sack, using a pair of ancient tongs. She gave an expert twist to the top. "That'll be ten cents. I hope Rennie feels better soon." As Callie Jane dropped the dime into the register, she asked, "Is the weatherman right about us getting six inches of snow tonight?"

Mr. King shook his head. "Nope. Just a dusting." He turned up his coat collar. "But an ice storm's comin' 'fore too long that'll catch ever'body off guard." He clutched the sack to his chest. "Tell your daddy I said hello." He paused. "I know Sheriff Ricketts is doing his best to catch that Peeping Tom, but it's gonna come to a bad end. I can feel it." He took a single step and then stopped, adding, "Be careful, Callie Jane."

Barbara Ricketts had rung the first warning bell about the Peeping Tom back in November, telling a spellbound group of ladies at the Curly Q how her husband had been called to a home because of a man looking through a young woman's window as she undressed for bed. Dewey Prichard, editor of the weekly *Gazette*, had dubbed the man "the Creeper" and replaced his usual headlines about a five-pound squash or a resident's trip across two time zones with offerings like "Creeper Stalking Spark!" And "Crime Wave Terrorizes Town!"

All of Spark suddenly realized they needed locks to secure doors that had always stood open. The hardware store had run out of key blanks and had to send to Nashville for more to keep up with the demand. By the time the third Creeper headline had appeared, taking your trash to the dump at dusk instead of mid-day was enough for previously friendly neighbors to give each other the side-eye. That stranger at the feedstore *claimed* he was in town visiting Beb White, but had anybody checked that story with Beb? And since when did Tiny Hendricks do their family's shopping instead of his wife at the BuyMore, where every lady of Spark could be found on a weekly basis? Was Tiny really shopping for his next victim?

Callie Jane turned the shop sign to "Sorry, We're Closed" and walked to the alcove that served as the office, thinking over Mr. King's warning to be careful about the Creeper. His accuracy predicting weather events was renowned. Did his abilities extend to knowing how the Creeper issue would end? She shook the thought from her head. That was impossible.

Grabbing the tarot book, she settled into the worn recliner sitting just outside the small room that served as the office. A shiver crossed her body. Something was about to change.

Chapter 3

Posey

THE CURLY Q'S door trembled from the force of Posey's entrance. No time for chitchat today. Her appointment with the lawyer was later that afternoon. They were probably expecting a hayseed, but she would set them straight, with her best only-one-season-old Chanel suit and the tallest beehive she could bully out of Queenie.

Queenie glanced up as the doorframe rattled. "We have a new girl I want you to meet. Evangeline is Arden's niece and just moved to town. She'll be shampooing you, then watching me fix your hair." She called to the back of the shop, "Evangeline, come meet Mrs. Jarvis."

A young woman emerged from Queenie's office, and Posey did her best not to gasp. Evangeline's blonde hair was shorter than Vern's. A flowy white top billowed from her slim frame, and her tan corduroy skirt stopped well above her knees. Posey had seen similar outfits in a magazine article on the latest London fashions but had assumed such outlandish garb would never infiltrate Spark.

"I'm glad to meet you, Mrs. Jarvis." Evangeline's nasal accent rocketed Posey back to her visit with Vern's cousins in Scranton,

Pennsylvania, a side trip tacked onto their Niagara Falls honeymoon. She hadn't wanted to go, but Vern insisted on introducing his bride to his only kin. Her new husband's relatives kept asking her to say words like *reckon* and *y'all* before bursting into laughter. That had been her first visit with Vern's cousins, and it would be her last.

"Ohio," Evangeline said in response to Posey's stare. Evangeline grinned, which made her nose wrinkle, highlighting a spray of light freckles. "Yep. A Yankee. Come this way and I'll get you shampooed."

Mesmerized by white boots shiny enough to reflect the sun streaming through the front window, she followed Evangeline to the washbowl. The boots had zippers up the calves, and what were they made of? Posey squinted. Patent leather. *This new girl will be shaking up Spark for sure.*

Instead of Queenie's efficient wrist-flicking unfurl and snap of the shampoo cape, Evangeline gently tucked the plastic sheet around Posey's neck, careful to fold her suit's powder blue collar out of harm's way. As Evangeline wet and lathered Posey's hair, the tension in her neck dissolved under the soothing bubbles and gentle thumb pressure.

"Is the water temperature to your liking?" Dangly earrings swayed hypnotically as Evangeline leaned toward the faucet. "I can adjust it if you'd like."

Posey shook her head and sank back against the bowl with a dreamy sigh. Queenie had a no-nonsense scrub-and-get-on-with-it approach, but Evangeline addressed every knot and kink she encountered as she massaged Posey's scalp and neck.

She practically purred as Evangeline combed her hair and cocooned it in a towel. If this girl styled as expertly as she shampooed, Posey might be compelled to cross the hairdresser Mason-Dixon line. The death of the out-of-favor stylist was usually the only way to move chairs without starting a blizzard of gossip or, even worse, being blackballed. She adjusted the terry turban encircling her head for a better view of Queenie, who looked as sleek as a blue-ribbon sow at the Cooke County fair. *Damn it.*

As Queenie ran her comb through Posey's wet strands, she motioned for Evangeline to join them. "Notice the similarity to both the cut and color of Jackie Kennedy. Mrs. Jarvis has dark hair already, which is a good start, but we've been able to match the shade perfectly."

"It is by coincidence the First Lady and I have the same shade and style," Posey said. "I copy no one." That statement was not true, but hairdressing information was strictly confidential, like with doctors. She would speak to Queenie later about the sanctity of the styling chair.

After most of the curlers were in place on Posey's head, Queenie snatched up the newspaper on her station. "Did you see the latest *Gazette* article about the Creeper?"

Posey read:

CREEPER SPOTTED ON HOLT ROAD!

A local family reported to Sheriff Mike Ricketts that a woman heard a rustling sound outside her window Monday night. Her husband rushed outside with his shotgun, but the Creeper had fled. The homeowner called the sheriff, who with his son, Deputy Sheriff Billy Ricketts, responded immediately and searched the area. No clues were found.

Queenie pinned a final curler into place. "I hope they find him soon."

Posey's voice was clipped. "If we're counting on Mike Ricketts to apprehend this lunatic, we're in for a long wait. The points on his badge are sharper than he is."

Queenie settled Posey under the dryer and held up two magazines. "True crime or Hollywood gossip?"

"Let's go for true crime. It's always fun to see what people think they can get away with."

After her hair was backcombed and teased into the highest beehive gravitationally possible, Posey paid her bill and glanced in the mirror for a quick check of her lipstick. Satisfied with her appearance, she stepped onto the sidewalk and moved purposefully toward her Cadillac, parked in front of her husband's shop next door.

Jarvis Emporium offered Vern the opportunity to visit with all the townsfolk who stopped in for cheese graters or flowerpots, and Posey always suspected he'd rather commiserate over a customer's arthritis or cluck about a mother-in-law's old-timer's disease than make a sale.

One night over dinner Vern had told Posey about a woman who had come in with a newborn. *"I love all my shoppers, but my favorites are the ones with babies. I always tuck an extra something in for the new arrival and tell them, 'Blessings to you and the little one.' I picked a little doll for this one. Sure hope she likes it."*

"It's hard to turn a profit when you're giving merchandise away," Posey had answered.

Driving down Market Street, Posey passed Strickland's Drugstore, whose front window was already plastered with an explosion of red hearts for Valentine's Day. Next was Honeybelle's, showcasing a trio of pink dresses that matched the too-bright door Posey loathed. As she drove past the Buy-More, she nodded in approval at the full parking lot. Trace Humboldt would be a rich man one day.

Posey was much younger than Vern, but he counted every soul in Spark as a friend, young or old, and knew each one by name, including Posey. One of Posey's earliest memories of Vern was when she was a girl and had gone into the Emporium to buy her mother a Christmas present. She had chosen a box of embroidered napkins, but the set of four was too expensive. She had asked if she could buy two napkins from the set, as it was only herself and her mother at home. Vern told her that she was in luck, that all napkins were half off that day.

As she passed the church, she grimaced at the sight of the white lattice gazebo, the scene of the tear-filled proposal Vern had made to Posey almost twenty years ago. She hadn't neared the wisteria-canopied structure since that night, and the smell of the daggerlike blooms still nauseated her.

She chewed her lip for most of the drive. The notion that her letter to the governor asking for a historic marker required a visit to a lawyer's office was fading faster than remnants of the lipstick clinging to her mouth. Equally unlikely was the idea that her father's conscience had kicked in, including her in his will to make up for a lifetime of abandonment.

She scanned her memory for the worst of her infractions, settling for a moment on a scene from *Peyton Place* she had watched the day before. A villainous hussy was being sued for alienation of affection by a wronged spouse. Posey's affair with CJ had been nearly twenty years ago, and alienation of affection wasn't even a real thing. She tilted her head. Or was it? Even if it was, the statute of limitations had surely run out.

....

The gleaming brass sign on the brick building read "Dawkens, Smith, and Sievers, Attorneys at Law." Posey's stomach fluttered as she opened the massive mahogany door.

An efficient-looking woman behind an elaborately carved desk looked up, her eyes flicking over Posey's bouclé suit and alligator handbag. "May I help you?"

Shifting her purse from one arm to the other, Posey tugged at her jacket. "I have an appointment with Mr. Sievers," she croaked. "I'm Posey Burch Jarvis."

"Have a seat, Mrs. Jarvis. I'll let him know you've arrived."

She swallowed, her throat scorched. "I need to visit your little girls' room."

The woman pointed down the hall. "Second door on the left." Posey followed her directions and opened the bathroom door.

Standing in front of the sink, she extracted the flask from her bag with shaking hands. *Only a splash.* A shot of gin rolled down her throat, offering a welcome burn. She screwed the top back on and fished a mint from her bag. *Better make it two,* she thought as she peeled back the foil wrapper. She twisted up the crimson bullet of her lipstick and carefully rimmed her thin lips. Patting her cowlick, she squared her shoulders and left the bathroom. Once back in the reception area, she spotted a man by the desk, tapping his foot.

His suit was exquisitely tailored. She had rummaged through enough estate sale clothing tables to recognize his tie as Hermès. "Mrs. Jarvis, I'm Albert Sievers." He extended a hand, and she weakly shook it. "Will you join us in the conference room?" *Us?* Through the glass wall, she spied a gray-haired woman already seated in one of the massive chairs around the wooden table.

She'd seen enough pictures of Frances in the *Nashville Banner* to know she was still a blonde. And this frowsy woman's lined face told of a rough life lived country miles from any debutante balls or country club mah-jongg tournaments. Posey exhaled as the gin kicked in, loosening her limbs. *That's not Frances.*

Mr. Sievers pulled out a chair for her, which left her facing the woman whose long braid snaked down her arm.

Slipping on a pair of wire-rimmed glasses, Mr. Sievers shuffled a stack of papers. "Mrs. Preston, may I introduce Mrs. Jarvis? And, Mrs. Jarvis, this is Mrs. Preston." Posey nodded across the table. "This meeting is highly unusual, but I am following the wishes of my client, Milbrey Sullivan Harris."

Aunt Milbrey? What in the world? When Posey was five or six, her mother had dragged her to Aunt Milbrey's house on Creekside Road. "We're just distant cousins, but it's our Christian duty to visit a shut-in," her mother had said.

Posey had pouted. "Why do you call her Aunt Milbrey if she's a cousin?"

"Honey, this is the South. We make up relations right, left, and center. And it takes too long to say second-cousin-once-removed Milbrey."

"I still don't want to go."

Posey's cooperation had been secured when her mother had dangled the promise of playing with Milbrey's cats. Posey remembered gaping at the dozen or so peony bushes blossoming along the expansive porch and then looking up at just as many gleaming windows and asking her mother, "Is this whole place all for one person?"

"Yep. It's good to be rich."

Once inside the enormous house, Posey had asked, "Where are the kitties?"

Milbrey pointed to the hallway. "They're in the catio."

Posey popped one hand on her tiny hip and sassed, "Silly goose. There's no such thing as a catio."

Her cheeks flamed, recalling the humiliation that coursed through her body as the woman hooted with laughter.

Milbrey's tone was stern, but Posey could hear the amusement in her voice. "She who owns the house names the rooms. If you want to see the cats, you need to go to the catio."

Her mother scolded her on the way home as Posey defended her position. "I was just trying to be truthful."

As they bounced down their rutted driveway, her mother said, "Mamas are supposed to teach their daughters about life, so here's a pearl of wisdom for you." She threw the rusted Rambler into Park. "The truth is overrated." She slammed the car door. "Remember that."

Mr. Sievers cleared his throat, snapping Posey out of her reverie. "I am sorry to inform you both that Mrs. Harris has passed away in Florida and was buried there. She asked that you both be present as I conclude the settling of her affairs." The lawyer pulled the glasses from his face. "This is a little Hollywood for my taste, but it was her wish."

Mr. Sievers nodded to the woman opposite Posey. "I am sorry for the loss of your sister."

"No loss to me." The woman picked at a snag on her dress. "I have a long drive back to Alabama. Can we get on with it?"

"This meeting concerns her will." The *tap-tap* of the upright papers against the conference table was amplified in the silent room. *"Milbrey's got a sister in Alabama, and it's her and her kin who'll be inheriting,"* her mother had bemoaned. Posey shot a look across the table at Mrs. Preston. *Lucky old coot.*

"The majority of Mrs. Harris's estate was left to a Tampa cat sanctuary, but there remains the matter of her Tennessee holdings." Mr. Sievers extracted a handwritten letter from the stack. "She asked me to read this with both of you present."

> *Dear Posey,*
>
> *The day you back-talked me about my catio was one of the highlights of my life. If I had been blessed with a daughter, she would have been exactly like you. Without children of my own, I am left to decide how to dispose of my Spark assets. I leave to you my house on Creekside Road, all its contents, and a savings account at Tennessee Farmers Bank.*
>
> *To my sister, Anita Sullivan Preston: You took something I thought was mine—Jimmy Preston. Now Posey will be taking something you thought was yours—my house and money.*
>
> *Sincerely,*
> *Milbrey Sullivan Harris*

Posey's jaw did not quite drop to the mahogany table, but it came close. Posey's mother had told her about Milbrey's tragic life, and she had heard the stories about how her aunt's ghost still roamed the mansion, but none of that mattered now. The house was huge, and it was hers.

A frosty silence settled over the room as Anita Preston asked one question: "Can she do that?" Upon hearing that Milbrey could, indeed, do that, she snatched up her dime-store purse and stalked across Mr. Sievers's Persian carpet. With her hand on the doorknob, she paused to address Posey. "May you never have a happy day with that house or that money."

After the door closed behind Anita Preston, Mr. Sievers regained his voice. "Shall we proceed?" The next few minutes were a swirl of signatures and legal jargon she didn't fully grasp, but the one thing she did comprehend was that she now owned the finest house in Spark and a bank account that was sizable enough to pay for little touches to spruce up her new home. After keys, congratulations, and handshakes, she was on her way.

She didn't recall driving to Milbrey's house, but she found herself parked in the weed-choked pea gravel driveway about an hour later. In her dreams, her mansion would manifest when CJ happily signed over Eden Hall to Frances in the divorce settlement, then presented a house twice as big to Posey as a wedding gift, but here it was. She had her second wish.

The two-story clapboard structure was elegant and stately, the polar opposite of the dumpy cottage Vern had been so proud to carry her over the threshold of all those years ago. Though overgrown shrubs obscured it, she could spy a wrap-around porch encircling the front. A Juliet balcony extended from the second story, similar to the one at Eden Hall, although this one sagged a bit to the left. Sun-faded shutters framed the dozen or so windows visible from the expansive lawn, and a chimney sprouted from the shaggy, shingled roof.

Did it have a ballroom? The first night at Eden Hall, CJ had brought her into the elaborately decorated ballroom and picked up his saxophone from a stand, saying he needed to practice a song for his all-doctor band, the Swinging Sawbones, that played dance music on the weekends. A friend with the unforgettable name of Dr. Payne had formed the group so he and a few hospital buddies could blow off some steam playing gigs around town.

CJ had played a sultry version of Tommy Dorsey's "Green Eyes." When the satin-soft notes floated through Eden Hall, her heart swelled to almost bursting. He had chosen a song about her to celebrate their first full night together.

She had given him a green bow tie with a distinctive paisley pattern that night, saying, *"Every time I see you wearing it, I'll know you are thinking of how much you want me."* She had hoped he would murmur, *I'll also be thinking of how much I love you.* He hadn't, though.

Sharp pea gravel dug into the leather of her soles, and Posey shifted her feet. Why couldn't Milbrey have given her the house simply because Posey deserved it and not dragged her sister into it? All those years Milbrey had lived alone, with only cats for company, had she been concocting her revenge, using Posey as part of her scheme to punish her sister for the poaching of a beau?

The thought of stealing a man caused Posey to look at the house with new eyes. *CJ will see what I can do with a mansion.* She took a step forward as the electrifying thought crystallized. *I can be a socialite.*

As she took the silver flask from her purse, she recalled how it had been responsible for bringing CJ and her together. She and the handsome, thirtysomething doctor had both reached for the flask at a Belle Meade estate sale, and when their hands touched, her life was changed forever.

His voice was deep, with a fine whiskey drawl. "I believe you are in possession of something I want."

"Then take it from me."

"I'm keen to add this to my collection." His blue eyes reached into her very soul.

"And it would make me at least five dollars in my booth at the antique mall." When Posey first began planning to leave Spark, she knew she wanted to be her own boss but recognized opportunities for women were limited. She and her mother had always been regular Emporium shoppers, and she had seen Vern Jarvis's success. She had peppered him with questions about running a resale shop, which he had always patiently answered. Vern emphasized providing popular goods at fair prices, but her business model was buy low and sell high.

The man bowed gracefully. "I could never deny a beautiful woman her right to turn a profit." He flashed a dimple. "I'll be in next week to buy it back from you."

CJ and Posey's affair kindled that October night over cocktails, and by the time the first snow fell in the new year, they were both fully engulfed. When the drunken revelation that he was married finally emerged, she was past caring. And when CJ's wife left for New Zealand during a mid-March sleet storm, they sipped gin martinis in front of Eden Hall's library fire and skinny-dipped in the heated pool, turned to the maximum temperature against the spring chill. While CJ was seeing patients at the hospital, she explored every room of the antique-filled home. Her tours always ended in the conservatory, lush with Frances's award-winning orchids, each nestled in a silver bowl. The largest one was engraved.

Awarded to Frances Vanderbilt
Senior Class Golf Champion

On the thirteenth of May, when she called CJ to her run-down apartment complex in a sketchy part of town to announce her pregnancy, she had been certain he would jilt his childless wife for her and the baby growing in her womb. CJ had no such plans.

"This was just for fun," a stone-faced CJ had claimed. When she protested, first crying and then screaming, he responded, "You knew going in all I wanted was a fling." When she shouted that he had led her to believe he would marry her, he shook his head. "I need someone who can throw elegant parties for hospital board members and help me climb the rungs of the social ladder." He had dropped a wad of cash on her bed and careened out of her life in his Jaguar, top down, blond hair blowing behind him. She had crumpled to the floor of her efficiency unit, sobbing through the night.

She squinted at her new house, shining like a beacon in the sun. It didn't matter how or why she got it; it was hers. Her position in society would be as secure as the enormous brass knocker bolted to the front door. She would reign over the finest parties, and invitations to her soirees would be treasured like jewels. Queenie would never give her the side-eye again, and the likes of Barbara Ricketts would weep at being excluded from the elite gatherings. Her circle would widen to include Nashville's blue bloods, with Frances blackballed from every event.

A thrilling thought washed over her. The *Nashville Banner* would cover the parties, and CJ would see the photos. He'd realize Posey had become the socialite he wanted, divorce Frances, and marry her, claiming both her and his long-lost daughter at last.

Elated, she took a step forward as she scanned the house. After two decades of prowling through estate sales in rich neighborhoods, Posey could recognize a house's good bones.

With a little fixing up, this one could rival any mansion in Belle Meade. She'd see to it that her home would have a resplendent library, an orchid-filled conservatory, and an enormous heated pool. Her first event would be Callie Jane's wedding reception in August, where her daughter would be celebrated like royalty.

Chipped paint on the wooden columns caught her attention as she mounted the sagging stairs. *I'll be dipping into that bank account sooner than I thought.* To her right was a plaque affixed to the wall proclaiming *"Amor Vincit Omnia."* She recognized it as Latin, but could only guess at its meaning. She shrugged at the fragments of glass from the broken sidelights littering the porch. *A little cleanup should be expected.* Her hand shook in anticipation as she inserted the key. Swinging the door wide, she triumphantly crossed the threshold, tripping on a stone lying on the heart-of-pine floor.

She staggered from the smell. The air was thick with years of ancient mildew. Wallpaper drooped in fly-speckled sheets from the entryway walls. *A roof leak must have let a little moisture in. The rest will be fine.* She spied a massive fireplace to her right. *That will be my library.* At the first step into the room, dark from heavy drapes pulled tight against decades of sun, she was already imagining herself lounging by a crackling fire, a gin martini in her manicured hand, without a care in the world.

Movement from within the library brought her out of her daydream. Posey fled as a possum reared up from its nest in a tattered velvet wing chair and hissed at the new owner of 1480 Creekside Road.

Chapter 4

Callie Jane

THE OLD BELL on the Emporium door jingled, drawing a sigh from Callie Jane as she pulled open the desk drawer and dropped in the tarot book. She'd been trying to read it for days, whenever her father wasn't in the shop, but each time she had picked up the worn paperback, a customer had come in. The book on California was on her nightstand, her new nightly bedtime story, but she couldn't risk taking the tarot book home, as her mother would declare it satanic and summon Brother Cleave for an exorcism, so it stayed in her desk at work, waiting for Callie Jane to steal a moment to read.

She rose from her chair and paused, hit by a sudden thought. Were the constant interruptions the universe's attempt to shield her from the book's contents? Sweat prickled her armpits. She really didn't know what tarot was. Could it be witchcraft? Would she need that exorcism? Was she dabbling in a dark world that would bring on some dreadful curse? Callie Jane rolled her eyes. Her life was already a mess. How could a few cards make it worse?

Looking down the central aisle of the Emporium, she spied Hannah Neal hesitating by the door. "Hey, Hannah. Come on in. I was in the back."

"I wasn't sure you were still open."

"We don't close for another twenty minutes. Can I help you find something?"

"Okay if I just look around?" Hannah asked softly.

"Sure. You never know what you might find in here. Daddy and I have been on the lookout for yarn, but we haven't had much luck."

"I've used up all I have, so if you come across any yellow or white at a really good price, please get it for me. Cotton would be best, but I can make any thin kind work."

Dust motes floated through the late-afternoon sun, illuminating a smudge on a glass picture frame. Callie Jane wiped it with her shirttail and asked, "Are you going to knit a baby blanket for the county fair again this year? You always win the blue ribbon."

"Not this year." Hannah blushed. "I'm knitting for myself now." She rubbed her belly. "Well, for my child. We have a little one coming in August, due on our first wedding anniversary."

"Congratulations!"

"Thank you." Hannah's smile was strained. "Expectin' changes everything, of course." She stood transfixed by a Moses basket, then gently touched the braided handle. "I thought I might get some ideas for what the baby needs." She tentatively flipped the price tag and then turned it back. "Of course, it's early yet."

"Grady doin' okay?"

"I don't think he's suited to factory work, though he never complains. His hours has been cut, but he tells me not to worry, that he'll provide for us." Hannah sighed. "It'll be too crowded in my parents' house when the baby comes, but we'll never find anything cheap enough to rent with less money comin' in, even with my job at the bank." Her voice quavered. "We'll find some way to get by." She rubbed her neck, wincing as she kneaded a spot. "I'm sorry to burden you with my troubles."

"Sharing what's on your heart is never burdening someone." Callie Jane patted Hannah's arm. "I bet you'll find a great place to rent, and maybe Grady can find a better job right here in town, something he likes."

"Thanks for being my friend." Hannah's face brightened. "How's your wedding plans comin'? Are you gonna have one of Arden's Scripture cakes? Have you picked your colors?" She smoothed her hand over her belly. "Before you know it, you'll be expectin' too."

What was a Scripture cake? What did you need colors for? Callie Jane sagged against the Emporium counter as the room spun. *Your body is trying to tell your brain something. Better listen.* Every other girl in her orbit was a boy-crazy mess, ruled by hormones, focused on bagging a husband and starting a family. Why wasn't she? The thought of marrying Trace should have brought joy, not signs of coming down with the flu.

Hannah opened the door. "I'm glad you're so happy, Callie Jane."

Helpless regret and exasperation throbbed in Callie Jane's temples, made worse by thoughts of being Trace's bride or doing with him what it took to end up in Hannah's condition. The realization hit her as swiftly as those sickening feelings. She couldn't marry Trace.

Glancing at her watch, she reached to flip the sign to "Sorry, We're Closed." The door flew open, hitting her in the chest. A redheaded boy of about sixteen lumbered into the Emporium, his boots trailing mud. He wore a dirty wool coat with a torn pocket, a scowl across his face. "Ain't closing, are you?"

She sighed. "No, *Wasp*," she said, emphasizing the nickname his mama had given him at birth because of both his copper hair and his foul temperament. "What can I help you with?"

"It's Linda's birthday, and I need a present right quick." Linda was his sister, who had been in Callie Jane's class until she dropped out in eighth grade to work at the Humboldts' grocery store. On their first day of kindergarten, Callie Jane had tried to befriend Linda, whose arm was in a grimy cast. When Callie Jane asked how she had gotten hurt, Linda had snapped at her to mind her own business, so she did.

"Do you have anything in mind? Notepaper? Maybe a book?" She cringed. It was doubtful Linda had any friends to write to, and none of the Fentresses could read much past *Tip and Mitten*. Maybe she'd like to smell good. "Perfume?"

"Naw." He grabbed a ceramic angel off a shelf and checked the price tag. "This'll do. Wrap it up."

Girls swooned over Wasp's six-foot frame and farmhand muscles, but she didn't see the appeal. The only thing worse than his temper was his reputation.

Callie Jane swaddled the angel in tissue paper and added a pink bow. "That'll be seventy-five cents." Wasp threw a filthy dollar bill on the counter and held out his hand for the change. She tried her best to avoid touching his skin as she dropped a quarter into his palm. "Thank you for your business." She felt sorry for Wasp—everyone did—but he'd snarl at anyone who tried to be kind, so Callie Jane just steered as clear of him as she could.

After Wasp swiped the package off the counter and left, she flipped the door sign and turned the key. She recorded the sale in the spiral notebook by the register and grabbed the tarot book. Settling in the lumpy recliner, she felt her pulse quicken.

The drawings were both strange and beautiful, reminiscent of legends and quests. An old man in monk's robes, surrounded by snow, held a lantern aloft in one hand and grasped a staff in the other. Another entry depicted a blindfolded woman posing on a stone bench by a blue ocean, two enormous swords crossed in front of her. A horned half man, half beast clutched a fiery torch, towering over two chained, naked humans. She shivered. The Devil.

Her hands shook a little as she turned to her Empress.

THE EMPRESS

The Empress in the upright position is one of tarot's most powerful cards. Ignore the message of this magnificent woman at your peril.

The Empress is the feminine archetype. The life of the Empress is full, rewarding, and overflowing with all the good things the world has to offer. She is unconditional love, new life, harmony, and peace.

The red pattern of her flowing robes references the theory it was a pomegranate, not an apple, that Eve ate in the garden of Eden. The twelve stars in her crown represent the signs of the zodiac. The pearls around her neck symbolize the planets in our solar system. Her shield bears the symbol of femininity, the sign of Venus, which resembles the Tree of Life.

She studied the symbol on the Empress's shield. Why did it look familiar? With a start, she realized she had a pendant with that same design waiting for her on a leather cord in the flea market box. Struggling out of the recliner, she retrieved the necklace and examined its intricate design before slipping it over her head and returning to the chair to continue reading.

> Her round scepter mirrors the round Earth over which she rules. She rests on luxurious cushions of ruby red, the color of passion. She brings a happy life, realized dreams, and success in all pursuits. The Empress is associated with the number 3, standing for the past, present, and future.
>
> When the Empress is drawn from the deck upside down, or reversed, the opposite meaning of the card is true. The reversed Empress is equally as powerful as her upright counterpart.

Callie Jane thought back to the moment she opened the box, recalling with relief that the Empress had been right side up.

> A reversed Empress is self-centered, incapable of meeting the emotional needs of others, even as she is emotionally demanding. Her life is a superficial one, and she is vain rather than beautiful. Not an evil figure, willfully withholding what is needed, she is instead empty, incapable of providing what she herself lacks.

Though she sat motionless in the recliner, her mind spun. She hadn't planned on receiving a message, and had never heard of tarot until a few days ago, but she understood the call of the Empress had lured her to that flea market stall.

The sharp *yap* of a horn snapped her back to the Emporium. She blinked at the display shelves, jam-packed with bath mats and cookie sheets, as if seeing it all for the first time. She had spent practically every Saturday of her life in this shop, helping her father stock shelves and greeting customers. They patted her head when she was little, remarking how she was growing like a weed. Later, they asked her how school was going, and then in her teenage years, they wanted to know if she was dreaming of her wedding to Trace Humboldt.

Curled in the recliner, she studied the Empress as she stroked the pendant around her neck. Could she relate to the figure on the card? The Empress embodied abundance and success. What Callie Jane had was an unfulfilling life orchestrated by her parents, her fiancé, and even her future mother-in-law, all of whom had more ideas for her life than she had for her own.

"'Ignore the message of this magnificent woman at your peril,'" she whispered. But what was the message?

The answer began to emerge from its eighteen-year-old chrysalis, unfolding fledgling wings within her soul: *Choose your dreams and then do all in your power to conjure them into being, before someone else does the choosing for you.*

Now she just had to figure out what those dreams were.

Chapter 5

Posey

THE NEXT DAY Posey returned to the old mansion, determined to finish her exploration. Wary of possums, she crept into the library, then sprang back with enough force to fall against an antique secretary. *Dear God. Is that a cow?* She squinted. A hickory limb, as big around as the drum of a dryer at the Wishee-Washee, jutted through a shattered window, resting on the remains of a side table split in two from the impact. Among the branches and sticks lay splintered glass, which appeared, for a moment, to be diamonds scattered across a forest floor. Cold air blew through the gaping hole, which had served as a not-so-secret passageway for Spark's wildlife.

She turned to examine the piece of furniture that had bruised her hip. Sentinel-like, the enormous walnut secretary spanned the distance between two library windows. Its arched glass doors appeared as eyebrows, raised disdainfully as they silently observed Posey gaping. *Even Frances does not have such a magnificent piece.*

She moved away but then returned her gaze to the secretary. What was that on the shelves? Narrowing her eyes, she hardly believed what she was seeing. Row after row of her beloved

Gordon's gin. She slipped one of the bottles from the secretary and grinned as she studied the familiar golden-yellow label, glowing like a summer sun. She and Aunt Milbrey had something in common.

Across from the library stood an opulent dining room, whose claw-foot double pedestal table appeared to crouch, ready to rear up if awakened, like a dragon under a spell. Two chandeliers hung over the table, with a brown blotch blooming on the ceiling between them. *A little water damage, easily fixed.* Over a handsome sideboard hung a massive portrait of a beautiful woman dressed in a scarlet ball gown. Posey squinted at the picture. The gorgeous figure bore no resemblance to the eccentric old woman who had mocked her during her visit so long ago, but who else's likeness would be hanging in the dining room?

Next, she moved down the wide hallway, where she spied the room that had secured her the gift of this house.

She had remembered the catio as larger. Glass walls rose from the limestone floor, creating a greenhouse-like space ideal for enticing orchids into bloom. A cat tree listed forlornly in one corner, and a felt mouse lay corpse-like in the doorway. *"She who owns the house names the rooms."* The catio was now the conservatory. She sniffed, wrinkling her nose in disgust. *What is that odor?* No worries. One good cleaning and the smell would vanish.

The kitchen was her next stop. Posey crossed the black-and-white tiled floor and opened the door of the slim refrigerator on her left. A lone jar of olives sat on a wire shelf. Once the electricity was on, would it run? Milbrey's savings account money was a bonus, but she still had to be careful. Ever since the sanctimonious Barbara Ricketts had taunted Posey with the Sears ad, she had been desperate for a Foodarama. Maybe she could buy one if the repair list quit growing.

Next to the fridge stood a wide, paneled door. Cautiously, she cracked it open and peered inside. A pantry, filled with boxes and cans dating to the Truman administration. Could Milbrey not have been bothered to even clean out the food? She grasped the handle of an ancient stove, enameled in white, resting against the adjacent wall. Would a Thanksgiving turkey fit inside? The oven door yawned open, squeaking in protest. *Two* holiday birds could easily roast the day away in the cavernous opening.

Three bedrooms graced the upstairs. Posey smiled. Three people, three bedrooms. Perfect. She had endured sharing a bed with Vern for almost twenty years, but now she would finally have her own room.

The backyard, already dubbed *the grounds* in her mind, was the final point of interest on the tour. She scrutinized the overgrown landscaping by the house. An army of machete-wielding gardeners would be needed to defeat the tangled mess. Boxwoods as big as a Mercury space capsule anchored the corners of the house, and thick ropes of ivy meandered through weed-filled flower beds before hiking up the clapboard walls.

She studied the flagstone terrace that spanned the back of the house, edged by a low wall. The terrace would serve as the ideal setting for Callie Jane's wedding reception. Was August 20 far enough away to get everything done in time? She pursed her lips. It had to be.

A vine twisted across the arched gate leading to the driveway. *Dear Lord, not wisteria.* The smell was inextricably entwined with her memory of Vern's proposal. She squinted. *Damn it.* Yanking out the noxious vine by the roots catapulted to the top of her list.

Visions of soirees and magazine photo shoots swirled in her brain as she drove home, with Posey the star of every event. Once back in her kitchen, she took a swig from a gin-filled vinegar bottle, her secret weapon for both good days and bad, as she began preparing dinner. Hearing the rumble of Vern's truck in the driveway, she hastily tucked the bottle back into its hiding place behind the steak sauce.

Callie Jane came inside and swatted a spiderweb from Posey's collar. "Were you digging around in a barn today?"

Sprinkling potato chip crumbs over the tuna noodle casserole, Posey answered, the lie coming to her easily. "The man running the estate sale I went to had some silver in the attic, so I poked around up there."

Posey's head never touched her pillow that night. As Vern snored softly in their bed, she perched at the edge of a chair at their kitchen table, notebook and pencil in hand, sketching room layouts and crafting the announcement to her family. The list of chores was daunting, but she shooed them all away. She just had to apply herself, one project at a time, to create her own Eden, more dazzling than Frances had ever dreamed of, with a very workable deadline of August 20 to keep her motivated.

The next evening the aroma of roasted chicken filled the house on Poplar Avenue. Cloverleaf rolls rose under a tea towel, and a pot of rice simmered on the stove. Posey sprinkled an extra spoonful of orange drink mix over the Tang pie, a ladies' magazine favorite since John Glenn's recent Gemini space missions. Pouring a generous portion from the vinegar bottle into a glass, she toasted herself, humming as she snapped the green beans into a colander. She'd had twenty-four hours to construct her battle plan, and it was time to launch the attack.

Vern and Callie Jane arrived home to find dinner already on the table. After savoring every bite, Vern pushed away his scraped-clean plate. "Delicious."

"I'm glad you enjoyed it." She rose and brought the pie, a midweek shocker, to the table. "We're celebrating."

His brow furrowed. "What's the occasion?"

The first volley of her attack was a calm yet intriguing description of the inheritance. *Sell it like you've never sold anything before.* "I have been given a wonderful gift."

He blinked at her. "Who from?"

"My beloved aunt Milbrey."

He cocked his head. "You hated her 'cause she made fun of you when you was a girl."

"You are not recalling correctly. She loved me deeply."

"Okay, Posey. What's going on?"

Callie Jane rose from her chair. "May I be excused?"

Vern said yes just as Posey said no. Callie Jane looked from one parent to the other and dropped back in her seat.

Posey fought to keep the jubilance from her voice. "Aunt Milbrey has sadly passed away, and she has left me her home and a small bank account as tokens of her love."

Vern's face beamed. "That's great! We'll sell that house and I can retire. Callie Jane can start her married life as the Emporium's owner." He clapped his hands. "Fantastic news."

Time for the second prong. "A field bordering a charming thicket of woods is simply crying out to be a garden, big enough to grow every flower and vegetable in your catalogs. You'll be knee-deep in produce."

"I love the garden I already got."

The failure of the first two prongs did not bode well for the third, a simple statement of fact. Posey straightened her shoulders. "We're moving."

The typical red of Vern's face became mottled with purple. "I'm not going anywhere."

Redouble your efforts and remain firm. "Yes, you are."

"This is our home."

Posey tried to steady her voice. "This was *never* our home. It was your *parents'* home, and you were just too cheap to buy us one. I have always wanted a house to call my own, and now I have one. We. Are. Moving."

Vern's voice shook. "Leave my parents out of this."

Posey countered, "How could I? You've made this crackerbox a shrine to their memory. Meanwhile, you ignore your wife and what she wants. This inheritance means we finally have somewhere to go." She glared at her husband. "Vern Jarvis, you are leaving this house."

He stood, throwing his napkin onto the table. "You know what?" He strode to the kitchen, puffing from exertion, and grabbed the key ring hanging on its peg. "I *am* going to leave this house." The slam of the door shook the walls of their tiny home.

· · · · · · · · · ·

The pink fingers of sunrise were stretching over the sky as Vern's truck pulled into the driveway. Posey sat with her gin-laced coffee in the kitchen, pretending not to hear as Vern let himself in. Where had he gone? And who was he with? Twice Posey had to stop herself from quizzing her husband about his whereabouts that night, but she managed to hold her tongue in a valiant effort to say nothing to him until he agreed to move.

She was confident the logjam would loosen with prong four of the campaign. She'd tell that busybody Queenie the news at her next appointment, which would ensure the whole town would be up to speed by the time the dinner dishes were cleared from their tables. As word spread of the gift, prong five would be activated, sitting back and letting Vern's beloved townsfolk congratulate him, compelling him to accept Posey's decree and pack up for Creekside Road.

....

The Spark gossip mill did its job. For several days, news of the inheritance bumped the latest Creeper sighting from the first topic of conversation at the Curly Q, Honeybelle's, and the BuyMore. With every good wish, Posey was closer to her goal.

A week after Posey told Queenie about Milbrey's gift, Darlene Prichard, a high school classmate of Posey's, called. "I have a big favor to ask about our reunion. Can you meet me at the Blue Plate for lunch at noon on Monday?"

"I'd be glad to."

The smile that snaked across Posey's face as she returned the receiver to its cradle told it all—Darlene had just handed her an unexpected sixth prong.

....

Popping open her compact, Posey applied another layer of lipstick outside the diner. She checked her watch. Twelve twenty. Perfect.

As she reached for the door, Mike opened it from inside and stepped onto the sidewalk. "Hey, Posey. Congratulations on your new house."

"Thank you. Vern, Callie Jane, and I are all thrilled to be moving."

"I remember driving out there years ago when the delivery boy from the BuyMore called me about her groceries being left out on the service porch." He chuckled. "He didn't mention the liquor store order, but I remember bottles of gin too. Couldn't find any sign of her, but there was no evidence of a crime either." He turned up his coat collar against the sharp wind, then opened the door for Posey. "Have a good lunch."

She walked through the door and spotted Darlene, waving vigorously from the corner booth. "Over here."

Posey shrugged off her mink and slipped her sunglasses into the pocket before hanging the jacket on a coatrack. The air was heavy with the diner's holy trinity: fried chicken, turnip greens, and biscuits. She approached Darlene, who was nervously smoothing her blonde hair, styled in a Gidget flip.

"Your call sounded urgent," Posey said, sliding across the vinyl bench of the booth.

Darlene blushed. "Not exactly urgent, but I've had a brilliant idea."

"An idea?" Posey raised one perfectly stenciled eyebrow.

Darlene's lip trembled. "As head of Spark High's twentieth reunion committee, I want to make the event unforgettable," she said. "We need elegance, so, of course, I thought of you."

Posey's smile was somewhere between an acknowledgment of the truth of Darlene's statement and a warning that she was aware she was being buttered up and to get on with it.

"Our committee has already met twice. We're printing up copies of our Senior Superlatives, which are a hoot. Dewey and I were voted cutest couple. You were most likely to leave Cooke County." Darlene's face reddened, and she rushed to add, "Which, of course, we are all so glad you did *not*, because we love having you here with us in Spark." Darlene tugged at her Peter Pan collar as the words spilled out. "We need the perfect location for such an important event."

Arden, the Blue Plate's owner, approached their booth, pencil poised above her pad. "Ladies, what can I get you?"

Posey handed her unopened menu to Arden. "Tuna in half a tomato, no crackers. And Tab with a slice of lemon."

Arden turned to Darlene. "And you?"

"The same."

After Arden left the table, Darlene marveled, "I've been coming here my whole life and never knew tuna in a tomato was on the menu."

"It's not, but it should be, so I keep ordering it. Eventually Arden will get the message." She smoothed a nonexistent wrinkle on her sleeve. "Now what's this about my involvement in the reunion?"

"I am so sorry about your aunt Milbrey passing away, but how fabulous that she left you the most glamorous house in Cooke County." Her face darkened. "My boys used to say her place was haunted, that the Creekside Crone wandered the property looking for her dead gangster husband, but they were just being silly, trying to scare themselves. I'm sure you don't have a single ghost." She smiled. "Are you almost ready to move in?"

Posey's mind ticked back to the possum nesting in the wing chair, the limp wallpaper, and the oddly pungent catio-now-conservatory. She rubbed her aching back as she answered, "Our workmen have a bit more to do, but they should be finished soon."

Arden placed their food and drinks on the table.

"Thanks, hon," Darlene said to the diner's owner. Turning back to Posey, she sighed. "Living in the only two-story house in

Spark, how divine." She clasped her hands together as if praying. "The reunions are always on the second Friday in May. Everyone will want to see your new home, and if you think you'll be settled in by then . . . um, well, could we have the party at your house?" Darlene gulped her drink so fast an ice cube hit her lip, causing a dribble of soda to cascade down her chin. She grabbed a wad of napkins from the chrome dispenser in a futile effort to save her blouse from the brown stream.

Posey wound the crown of her diamond watch, one of her very best estate sale finds. Hosting the dinner and dance would be the ideal way to show off her grand house. She took a delicate bite of tuna and looked at Darlene's anxious face. She'd say yes, of course, but first she'd play with her lunch companion the way Milbrey's cats toyed with their catnip mouse. "Callie Jane's wedding is August 20, and the reception will be on the terrace. I'll be quite busy planning."

Darlene's face fell. "Oh, I understand. I shouldn't have even said anything. We'll have it at my house instead. Dewey'll clean out the carport and—"

"You have so much on your plate already, being the chairman and all." Posey gave a solicitous pat to Darlene's hand. "I could try to have the wedding plans finalized early."

Relief crossed Darlene's face as she sawed at her tomato. "Thank you for considering it. I know Dewey would love to put you on the front page of the paper." Darlene shrugged one shoulder and smiled. "Being married to the editor has its perks."

Picking up her fork, Posey asked, "Does Dewey have any connections in Nashville? We need a write-up in the *Banner*."

Darlene frowned. "I don't think he knows any *Banner* people, but I can guarantee you'll be in *our* paper." Her face brightened. "And speaking of the *Gazette*, did you see the latest headline? Somebody thought they caught a glimpse of the Creeper by their back porch. They took a shotgun out there, but he was long gone." Darlene took a careful sip. "Dewey tells me all the good stuff he can't print." She looked around at the customers. "He'd have my hide for gossiping about the case, so don't tell anyone, okay?" She leaned forward and whispered, "It was more than a glimpse. They have a partial description. Mike asked Dewey to keep it out of the paper so the Creeper doesn't find out the sheriff has some details about his appearance."

"Oh, I won't breathe a word, I promise. How thrilling to have the inside story. What else does Dewey say?"

Darlene glanced around her again and then scooted closer to the edge of the table. "He's real tall and can run like a jack-rabbit, so he's young."

Posey sipped her Tab as her brain twirled around this new information. *Hmm . . . young.* Popping open her silver compact, she freshened her lipstick and waited for Darlene to pick up the check.

As Darlene helped Posey into her mink jacket, she began prattling again. "I can't thank you enough for even thinking about hosting the reunion. And don't you worry about the decorations or the food. If you agree to us using your house, the only thing left is finding a band who knows all the hits from the year we graduated."

"Tell the committee I am considering it. You'll have my answer in a few days." Stepping into the biting February air, Posey pulled on her kidskin gloves. "Ask Dewey to work on a *Banner* connection. The Nashville paper needs to cover this."

Slipping on her sunglasses was a gesture meant to dismiss Darlene, who continued to shout her thanks to Posey's fur-clad back. Posey allowed herself a congratulatory smile as she sauntered back to her car.

An idea struck her with such force that she had to steady herself on the Cadillac's hood. *My God.* Could she pull it off? She opened the door and sank into the seat, shaking. *This could change everything.*

Chapter 6

Callie Jane

THE SEED CATALOG lay on her father's desk spine down, its numerous dog-eared pages resembling an accordion. He glanced at his calendar, smiling as he tapped the day's date, February 15. "In exactly two months, Callie Jane, we'll put the tomatoes in. Planting day always takes away the sting of tax day."

He picked up the catalog. "I'll plant my signature Big Boys, of course," he said, patting his belly. "But I'm looking to try some new ones." He thumbed through the catalog. "These Mortgage Lifter tomatoes are named for a fella who got through the Great Depression selling the seedlings when his repair shop went bust." Perusing the catalog, he murmured, "There's one called Perfection." He shook his head. "That's aimin' too high for me. Better move on." Licking his thumb, he turned a page. "And here's one called Abraham Lincoln. Seeing what happened to him, maybe not." He shifted in his seat. "Hey, how about these Brandywines? 'Each fruit can be over a pound,' it says." He grinned. "They say knowledge is knowing a tomato is a fruit, and wisdom is not putting it in fruit salad."

"Sounds like we'll be busy," Callie Jane said with a smile, even as she worried how the move her mother was demanding would affect his planting.

"Being in my garden is like a moment in Eden. Working in the sunshine, tending to the sprouts as they grow, soothes my soul."

"Mine too." She touched her blonde hair. "Maybe I don't *look* like you, but I *think* like you, and that's more important."

"It is. Never forget the peace caring for God's green earth can bring."

She looked around the empty shop. "I think I'll sit outside a few minutes before lunch."

Tennessee weather was unpredictable, especially in February. One day would be freezing cold, spitting snow, and the next would be sun-filled, balmy enough for any optimist to leave their coat behind. On a morning as fine as this one, you could believe spring was around the corner, ready to hug you like a long-absent friend.

Breathing in the fresh air helped clear Callie Jane's memory of what had transpired the day before in Nashville at the alterations shop. Within a week of the engagement, Mrs. Humboldt had hauled her wedding gown out of her attic and dragged it to the Jarvises' house for Callie Jane and her mother to inspect. As Callie Jane stood miserably in the den, with Mrs. Humboldt's veil pinned to her hair, her mother told Mrs. Humboldt that the dress was both out of fashion and much too large, but when Mrs. Humboldt suggested that the dress be altered, her mother had hesitated.

"I don't want Opal Humboldt to misunderstand who's running this show, but altering a dress is a lot cheaper and easier than buying one,"

her mother had later said to Callie Jane. The two mothers had compromised, with her mother in charge of the new design and Mrs. Humboldt granted bragging rights that Callie Jane was wearing her dress, all while Callie Jane sat on the sofa in yards of frothy lace, shell-shocked.

The dressmaker had taken one look at Callie Jane in the gown and shaken her head. "It can't be done. She's too skinny."

"You must try. My daughter is counting on wearing this dress."

"You're a good customer, Mrs. Jarvis, so I'll give it a shot, but I can't guarantee anything."

She pinned and trimmed, gathered and smoothed, until her mother was satisfied. The dressmaker asked twice for Callie Jane's input, but each time Callie Jane just shrugged. "Probably just nerves," the dressmaker whispered under her breath. Callie Jane had taken to bed as soon as they had gotten home.

Now, as Callie Jane turned her face to the sun, Barbara Ricketts and Darlene Prichard stepped onto the sidewalk from the Curly Q, deep in conversation. Barbara spoke loudly. "Somebody phoned in a tip that Tiny Hendricks was walking through people's yards at ten o'clock a few nights ago. Tiny told Mike he and the missus had a huge fight, and he was just tryin' to cool off 'fore he did something he regretted, but it sure seems suspicious."

Darlene nodded. "Mike said the Creeper was tall, and Tiny's, what, six five? He could easily see into any window he wanted. I've had my doubts about him ever since he bragged all around town about being drafted by some fancy professional baseball team." She snickered. "But he wound up back here in Spark not a year later, and is *still* salty about getting cut."

As Darlene passed the Emporium, she spotted Callie Jane and squealed, "There's our bride." She bent down and hugged her. "Being engaged is the best time of any girl's life. All the fun without any of the housework." She winked. "Or the *man* work. Lord knows I love Dewey, but his smelly socks could practically walk themselves to the Wishee-Washee."

Callie Jane clawed at the blonde strands that had slipped from her ponytail, as if being suffocated by Trace's fetid socks.

"I'd better scoot. Barbara and I are meeting Mike and Dewey for lunch." She gave Callie Jane another squeeze. "I can't wait for you to be Callie Jane Humboldt."

Callie Jane Humboldt. The words smothered her soul like a blanket being wrestled off a clothesline in a downpour. She gulped. *Why is every woman in town so focused on my wedding? Is a ring on your finger and a baby in your belly all a female can hope for? Neither is even close to the top of my list.* She grimaced. *What list?*

She needed one, but what should she put on it? She had no idea, but her soul screamed it wasn't Trace, BuyMore ribbon cuttings, or babies. She rubbed her throat. Escaping this life sentence without hurting anyone, most of all herself, seemed impossible. Her mother would eventually get over the loss of the grocery kingdom and the tills full of cash that would follow. Mrs. Humboldt had four sons, so her chance of getting grandbabies was pretty secure. The worry constricting her soul was Trace. Breaking his heart was something she was loath to do. He had always taken care of her, and now she was thinking of hurting him. Trace had been made assistant manager the morning after the proposal, and he had swelled to the size of a prize-winning pumpkin at his promotion. He chattered on to Callie Jane about milk suppliers and the benefits of weekly newspaper advertising, to the point she had tuned him out, unable to hear another utterance about store traffic patterns or why the grocery world's future lay in the frozen food aisle.

Trace's brother Robert, only a year younger, was already serious about a girl from nearby Marshall County. If they became engaged, would Robert replace Trace as assistant manager? His father said the first son to get engaged would get the job, but would Mr. Humboldt really take the position away from Trace? She nervously bounced a knee. Maybe.

She shifted on the bench, its metal slats suddenly sharp against her spine. A cloud covered the sun, instantly lowering the temperature. She shivered and went back into the shop.

Her father glanced up from his ledger when the bell announced her return. "Hey, hon. Ready for lunch?"

"Sure."

"Wonder what we're having?" He laughed softly at his joke. "Just kidding. Tuna for me, pimento cheese for you, same as always."

He snapped open the lunch box and unwrapped their sandwiches, placing two rectangles on each of their plates, then sprinkled a few pretzel sticks alongside before adding a large dollop of potato salad. Callie Jane poured sweet tea from the thermos into their cups. They performed this same ritual every workday afternoon. Sighing, she looked at the bland food that brought to mind one of her beloved Beatles songs, "Eight Days a Week."

"Did I tell you I found another mealworm feeder for my bluebirds last week? Bought it for a nickel."

He became animated as he explained his plan. "Once you're running the shop, I'll focus on my garden and my birds full-time. There's a lot I still have to learn about bluebirds, and once I'm retired, I'll have time to study up. Did you know some stay put in the same place all their lives?" He nodded. "Like me. But some migrate. They go all the way to Mexico in the winter, and fly as far north as Canada in the spring." Frowning, he added, "But how do those ones know when they're home? If you're always on the move, how can you ever feel settled?" He gazed out the Emporium window. "I'll plant more of their favorite berry bushes, and have birdbaths too, so at least they'll feel at home when they're in Spark, like you and I do."

But I don't feel at home here. Maybe I'm one of the ones that need to migrate. "I bet they like moving around, not staying in one place their whole lives. Their home could be a feeling instead of a place."

"I like that—a bluebird does what its heart wants and flies to where it's happiest." His eyes darkened. "A good lesson for both of us."

She nodded slowly, thinking over the advice. After a sip of tea, she asked, "Any news on Aunt Milbrey's house?"

A thundercloud rolled across her father's face. "Your mama says we're 'getting rid' of our house and moving right after she gets Milbrey's place all fixed up." He drained his tea, and she rose to refill his glass. "That tour she took us on was horrible. It's way too big, cold, and empty feeling." His voice lowered. "I was raised in our house, and you was too." He glanced out the tiny window overlooking the gravel parking lot. "Living in that house is as close as I can get to still having my parents. Every inch, inside and out, has a precious memory."

Although nodding her head was signaling her agreement, she knew her father would lose this fight. She respected her father's determination to stand up for what he believed in, but she also knew the consequences of opposition.

A few days earlier Callie Jane had tried in vain to have a heart-to-heart talk with her mother, a recommendation to another fearful bride she read about in a Dear Abby column, but had ended up with a lecture about obedience and servitude.

"Abraham Lincoln outlawed slavery a long time ago," Callie Jane had snapped, showing a rare moment of irritation.

"All your teachers said how smart you are, but there are days I just don't see it."

Callie Jane had bitten back her answer, *There's a lot you don't see. Maybe all that gin is clouding your eyesight.* Callie Jane had discovered her mother's vinegar bottle secret years ago after ruining a batch of coleslaw she was making for a third-grade home economics project, but even as an eight-year-old, she knew not to mention it. Things were tense enough without adding gasoline to the fire.

After Callie Jane cleared the lunch dishes away, she pulled the C volume of the *World Book* from the Emporium shelf. Her father had bought the encyclopedia set years ago, but it had never sold. *Apparently every soul in Spark already knows everything.* Ever since she found that book on California in her flea market box, she hadn't been able to get the Eden-like images and descriptions out of her mind.

She flipped to the state's entry and began to read about Southern California. The weather, the agriculture, and the lifestyle were all foreign to her, so different from Tennessee. Year-round warmth, vineyards brimming with grapes, majestic groves of avocados, an endless ocean in your backyard—it all sounded perfect. She smiled at the notation explaining that *pacific* meant "peaceful." A photo of sunflowers caught her attention. "Crops of sunflowers growing in California," read the caption beneath a field of yellow blooms. She tilted her head as she considered how flowers could be crops.

A notion took root in her soul. Her father wanted to live *in* Spark, her mother wanted to rule *over* Spark, but she wanted to be as free as a migrating bluebird—to fly *out* of Spark to wherever felt like home, wherever her heart was happiest.

Chapter 7

Posey

WAITING TO MAKE the call to Darlene was torture. She was desperate to activate her plan but couldn't appear too eager. She glanced at her datebook again to confirm that a full week had passed. It was time.

"Oh, Posey, how nice to hear from you. I hope you've had a chance to think about allowing us to use your home for the reunion."

"I will be delighted to host the reunion on the sixth." She underlined the periwinkle *Reunion* a third time on the Friday, May 6, square as she spoke. Her heart thumped as she thought of what would transpire that night if everything fell into place. She sketched a periwinkle heart and added an exclamation point.

Darlene's words rushed out. "Oh, Posey. There's been a misunderstanding. The reunion is May *13*. It's always on the second Friday in May. I'm certain I said that."

Blood pounded in Posey's temples, and she stretched the phone cord to its limits to reach a chair before her knees gave out. *No, no, no, no, no.* May 13 was the worst date on the calendar, the day she told CJ of her pregnancy. The day he dumped her.

Though she tried to keep an even tone, her voice was strained. "If it's at my home, it will be on the sixth."

"The class president will be out of town 'til the eleventh babysitting her grandkids. She told me yesterday at the Curly Q," Darlene wailed.

Posey's throat tightened. She *had* to host the party for her plan to succeed, but any thirteenth was unlucky, and May 13 was the unluckiest day of all. "If you prefer the thirteenth, I believe you mentioned your home would be available." That ought to do it.

Darlene's words tumbled over each other. "She'd snatch me bald-headed if we held the reunion without her." Darlene's despair gushed through the line. "I'm so stupid. I thought I told you the *second* Friday." She sighed and in a quavering voice said, "We'll have to have it at my house."

Posey tuned out Darlene's babbling and stared at her date-book. If the reunion were held in Darlene's carport, her whole plan would be ruined. Maybe it was time to get over that superstition about the number 13, and that dread of May 13. She had convinced herself CJ had abandoned her because she'd revealed her pregnancy on the thirteenth. *If only I had waited a day, or told him twenty-four hours earlier*, she had castigated herself. She eyed the 1 and 3 that had haunted her since that day. Maybe she could change her luck. *Maybe this May 13 will bring him back to me.* "You know what, Darlene? The thirteenth will be fine. But you did say the *first* Friday at our lunch. I don't want any more errors."

Relief was palpable in Darlene's voice. "Oh, how generous. And I apologize for my goof-up. I am such a ditz." She added, "You're sure everything will be finished, right? Because we can't have the reunion in the middle of a construction zone."

The mile-long list of repairs had no chance of being completed in time, but she couldn't worry about that now. "Of course. We're just finalizing a few details."

"I'm so glad! Now the only thing left is finding a band who plays music from the '40s."

The intro she had been waiting for. "I have an idea for the music. Let me make a call and I'll get back to you."

"Oh, how wonderful. Thank you."

Posey hung up the phone and silently congratulated herself. The plan was brilliant. Genius, even. But she didn't want to tip her hand before everything was ready. Her first moments reuniting with the man she loved had to be picture perfect, under the moonlight by her manicured garden, at the height of her success, and not a minute before. CJ couldn't get even a whiff of what was going on until the stage was set.

Her hand shook as she dialed the hospital's number. Everything depended on this phone call. "This is Darlene Prichard calling. I'd like to leave a message for Dr. Payne. Would his band, the Swinging Sawbones, be available on May 13? Our party is in Spark, about an hour outside of Nashville." She paused. "Yes, I'll hold." As she waited, she pulled out a photo from her datebook cut from a recent *Banner* society page of the Swinging Sawbones playing a party, with CJ front and center. Just one thing left. They had to be available.

"Mrs. Prichard? May 13 will be fine for the Swinging Sawbones to play at your event. They book pretty far ahead, but nobody wanted Friday the thirteenth, so it's open. Dr. Payne will mail you a contract and you can send him all the details."

The gin sloshed as she poured herself a celebratory glass from her hidden stash. She would see CJ again. And he would see her. If she played her cards right, that third wish was about to come true. She would marry CJ.

Posey had endured her marriage long enough to have raised Callie Jane, but now it was her turn to be happy. She looked around her cramped kitchen, reviewing her strategy. Before she could divorce Vern, she needed to make sure she had an engagement ring coming to replace her current wedding band. She would handle the husband switch the way Callie Jane had crossed Flat Rock Creek on a dare during a town picnic, not leaving the safety of one midstream stone until she'd found another.

But was it realistic to think CJ had been pining for her for almost twenty years? She frowned. Or that he even remembered her? She drained her glass. She was beautiful—elegant and refined outside the bedroom, and an insatiable wildcat in it. Why *wouldn't* CJ remember her? And then when their eyes locked at the reunion, all those memories would come flooding back to him and he'd confess his love.

Setting the empty glass in the sink, she twisted the faucet. A geyser of water spewed from the now-loose tap listing into the sink. Water shot to the ceiling, where a dark circle of damp plaster was already forming. Posey shrieked and grabbed a dish towel, fruitlessly trying to stem the gushing faucet. A separate stream sprayed a mist of droplets, dampening her like some kind of deranged perfume atomizer. Vern claimed to have fixed the faucet months ago, but of course he hadn't. Water now dripped from the ceiling light. Would she be electrocuted in her own kitchen? She grabbed the phone.

"Thank you for calling Jarvis Emporium. This is Vern."

"Come home right now!" Her voice was an octave higher than her usual measured tone. She slammed down the receiver and dashed to the bathroom for towels.

With her Curly Q hairdo dripping on her shoulders, she watched for him from the front window. When Vern's truck finally pulled into the driveway, she rushed to the door. "Get in here!"

Vern stood in the doorway as water spewed from the sink with the strength of an oil strike. "What happened?"

"I turned on the water. That's what happened. I wanted to call Bill Horton to come repair the faucet last time it broke, but you said Horton's prices were too high."

"I thought I had it good as new. I'll cut off the water, then try to rig something up 'til we can get Horton out here." Vern went back outside.

Posey stewed in the bedroom as she listened to the *clink* and *bang* of Vern's tools striking the pipes. She slipped her flask from her vanity, took a long drink, then lay on her bed. The tension had just started to uncoil from behind her eyes when a new sound, pinging, caught her attention. She moved to the window. Tiny pellets were striking the glass panes. She dashed to the kitchen. "Everything's icing up."

Vern started. "Callie Jane! She'll be stranded if I can't get to her." He threw down his wrench and ran out the door. His foot touched the glass-slick stoop, and his body launched, airborne. After one vertical moment, he became horizontal and then began his descent, resembling the *Hindenburg* as it fell to earth. Gasping, he struggled to an upright position. Inside, the phone was ringing.

Posey gripped the receiver in her hand, listening intently to her daughter.

"I'll close up the shop and walk home, Mama. I'll be fine."

"No, stay there." Posey looked out the window. "The sleet's really picking up. Your father's coming for you."

The Jarvises' power went out the same instant the phone went dead. In the distance, an ominous *pop* turned both their heads toward the electrical pole near the street.

Vern gingerly inched his way down the ice-covered steps and race-walked to the truck. Tugging against the now-frozen door, he wrested it open. Roaring the engine to life, he sped away. About fifteen minutes later he came limping back.

Posey's eyebrows shot up. "Well?"

"Slid into a ditch." He bowed his head. "I can't get to her. I'm not fit enough to walk all that way. 'Bout did me in just to make it a half block home."

"Dr. Grisham and I have both been telling you to lose weight." She glared at her husband. "Actions have consequences."

"A moment of kindness wouldn't kill you." He rubbed his back, grimacing. "Callie Jane's a smart girl." His voice shook. "She'll be all right."

The room was darkening around them. "I've got a flashlight in my toolbox." Vern made his way to the utility porch and returned with a small cylinder pulsing out a thin beam of light. "Shoulda checked these," he muttered to himself, shaking the batteries into his hand. Reversing their order, he replaced the top and toggled the switch back and forth. Nothing.

She blew on her fingers. "Can you at least light a fire?"

He knelt by the hearth, wincing as he reached for an old copy of the *Gazette* in a brass basket. He wadded it beneath the logs stacked crisscross in the grate and scratched a match. A flame spluttered as he touched the fire to the paper. Posey watched an orange finger curl around the word *Creeper* as a shaky light flicked across the room. Vern struggled to stand. "A few blankets and some dinner and we'll be all set."

"And what do you think we're going to eat? No electricity to cook, remember? And thanks to you, no water either."

"At least we won't have to wash the dishes." Posey refused to acknowledge his weak smile. "You go put on some dry clothes and I'll fix us some cereal. I'll pull this side table by the fire and we'll have a candlelight dinner."

Without a response, Posey marched to the bedroom. When she returned, pulling her heaviest cardigan around her, he had set the table for two and added a blanket by her chair. Two bowls of cornflakes awaited, along with two tumblers of juice.

She stood and lifted her full glass. "Just need a little more OJ," she explained, heading to the kitchen. The increasing cold stung her nose as she reached into the cabinet. Before she returned she swirled her drink with a finger.

"So how was your day before Old Faithful erupted?" He smiled at his joke, but she did not.

"Busy. I've agreed to host the class reunion at our new home."

He continued to eat his cereal without acknowledging her statement. Her shoulders tensed as Vern's spoon hit his teeth with a metallic *ting*. Over sixty years old and he didn't know how to use a utensil without practically knocking his fillings out.

He urged the last now-limp flake onto his spoon and into his mouth before he spoke, the sharpness of his tone amplified by the quiet of the dark, frigid room. "This house was my parents' home, and now it's my home." He paused and then added, "It's your home too, if you'd only realize it."

"Well, I don't."

Vern sighed. "I love it here and don't want to leave. The upkeep on Milbrey's house would cost a fortune, and I don't even want to think about the heating bill. Lord, the insurance alone would kill me. It makes so much sense for us to sell."

She interrupted. "Aunt Milbrey left her home to *me*, not to *us*, so I am not sure why you think you should have an opinion. If you hadn't noticed, this dump is falling apart." She gestured toward the drenched kitchen, Exhibit A. "We are moving, so you can hush." She slipped the blanket around her shoulders and drew the covering tight across her body, burrowing deep into her wool cocoon. "I've lived here almost twenty years because it's what you wanted. Now it's my turn. I'm going to have a library and a conservatory. I've even thought of the perfect name: Cold Spring."

Vern rose from his chair and tossed another log on the fire. A spray of embers arced from the grate. "Why does the house need a name?" He jabbed an errant piece of wood back into place. "Milbrey lived there just fine without having to call it anything. There's cold springs all around here, so it's not even special. And what the hell is a conservatory?"

"A conservatory is like a greenhouse. Once I get it cleaned up, it will be perfect for my orchids."

"You don't have any orchids."

"Not yet," she snapped.

After a moment of tense silence, he spoke. "We're not moving."

She repeated the words her husband had said to her years earlier as she argued against moving to his parents' home. "I love that house. We're moving."

He took her tiny hands in his enormous ones. His fingers were so thick they'd had trouble finding a wedding ring that fit, a problem solved only by special ordering one from an expensive jewelry store. "I can't leave. This house holds my memories." He gestured toward the doorframe of the water-soaked kitchen. "Every pencil mark means so much more to me than just how much Callie Jane grew that year. I was measuring our life together." His eyes brimmed with tears. "Every line meant I'd been blessed with more time to be with my baby, the one I thought I'd never have."

"Why don't you dry those tears of yours and remember who gave you that baby. When you proposed that night in the gazebo, you promised to do everything in your power to make me happy. You gave me a sob story about a farm accident when you were a teenager, said the doctors told you that you could never father a child. You said having a wife and child, a *family*, was all you ever dreamed of, and that if I married you, you would do your best to make all *my* dreams come true." She crossed her arms and delivered the coup de grâce. "I thought you were a man of your word." She choked out a small cry and summoned a few tears.

Despite the loss of power, the air in the room was charged, crackling between them. He lowered his head for a moment and then looked up. "Is this what you really want, Posey?"

I knew that'd do it. She suppressed her victorious smile. *Stupid cluck.* "Yes."

Chapter 8

Callie Jane

GRABBING A FAT candle from a display case, Callie Jane reached for the ashtray that held the bits and pieces of shop life: a rubber band, a nub of chalk, a couple of rusted paper clips. And, thankfully, a book of matches. She struck a match and a momentary flare pierced the darkness. The dim light spitting from the candle cast shadows around the long-familiar room that now seemed like something reflected in a funhouse mirror.

She shivered. The heat had been off only a few moments, but the Emporium was already as cold as the BuyMore's walk-in freezer. Picking her way to the back of the shop, she slipped into her jacket and buttoned it to the top, then tugged a blanket off a shelf and settled into the recliner that would serve as her bed for the night. Pulling on her mittens, she briefly considered walking home, but on a good day her house was thirty minutes away, and this was definitely *not* a good day. Like it or not, she would be sleeping in the shop that night, with half of a leftover sandwich for her dinner.

The Creeper! Would he use the cover of a blackout to slink around the town? *Sweet baby Jesus.* Both the front and back doors were unlocked, leaving her completely vulnerable. She trembled, partly from the stinging cold penetrating the room and partly from the thought of the man who had been skulking around Spark. Should she start with the front door or the back one? How could she have been so stupid? She started for the back of the shop and then pivoted, rushing to the front to twist the metal lock.

As she hurried down the center aisle, she stubbed her toe on a suitcase between the towel display and the notions table. A bottle teetered for a moment and then crashed to the floor. Wincing, she limped to the back. Reaching for the key, she spotted a pale face in the window above her father's desk.

She screamed, and the head jerked back from view. Heart in her throat, she peered through a pane. To her relief, she spotted not the Creeper but a young woman bundled in a puffy coat, a heavy scarf swaddling her throat. She was stamping her feet on the rubber mat. Callie Jane grabbed the key and swung open the door.

"I'm Evangeline from the beauty shop." She tilted her head toward the Curly Q. "When I saw your light, I thought I'd better check on you."

"Sorry I yelled."

"No problem. It's as cold as a witch's tit in here." She brushed bits of ice from a fringe of bangs peeking from beneath a tie-dyed cap. "Why don't you come to my place for the night? I live on the other side of those woods," she said, pointing behind her. "There's a big fireplace, so we can stay warm and heat up some soup." When Callie Jane hesitated, Evangeline smiled and held up her hands in surrender. "I know we haven't really met, but at least I'm not the Creeper." She grinned. "Just a hairdresser from Ohio." Evangeline wrinkled her nose. "You wearing Shalimar?"

Callie Jane gave her a sheepish look. "I, uh, broke a bottle in the dark," she said, gesturing down the aisle. "And thanks. I'll take you up on your offer. I'm hungry and cold, and no way could I sleep here tonight. I just need to leave a note for my father in case he comes for me." After scribbling a message and taping it to Vern's chair, she blew out her candle and followed Evangeline out the door.

Shards of ice pelted their bodies and needled their exposed faces. They slipped and slid their way along the path through the woods, their lungs aching as though they had walked two miles, not two minutes. A distant limb crashed to the ground, startling them both. "Holy shit," Evangeline said. After another ten minutes of struggle, a modest house on Stadler Court came into view.

No one needed a street sign to know they were on Stadler. Sofas sat molding in the yards while dogs patrolled the chain-link-fence perimeters of the quarter-acre lots, lunging at anyone close to their property. *This is where Evangeline lives?*

A jagged panel of corrugated metal roofing dangled from the corner of a carport housing a faded blue sedan.

Evangeline patted her car's trunk. "She's beat up but paid for. I drove her to work when I was still at Aunt Arden's, but with living so close now, I walk. Saves on gas. Her name's Lady Liberty." She grinned. "It's bad luck not to name your cars."

She unlocked the wooden door to the duplex and held it open. "Let me grab the candlesticks so we can get some light in here. Hang on." With a satisfying *scritch*, a flame leaped from the match. Evangeline touched the fire to the wicks of the candles.

Enough light filled the room for Callie Jane to see that Evangeline had made the shabby house a cozy home. Knotty pine paneling covered the walls, and though the linoleum had decades of scuffs and tears, it was dotted with brightly colored rag rugs. Evangeline knelt before the massive hearth and twisted open the flue. She struck another match, and soon welcoming flames jumped from the kindling waiting at the base of the logs. "You take the rocker, and I'll get another chair from my bedroom."

She returned, hoisting a wooden armchair, with an ancient Lab hobbling behind her. "Hope you don't mind dogs. This is Muse."

"Oh, I love dogs. My mother never let us have one, though. She says she's allergic to all animal fur." Callie Jane rolled her eyes. "Except mink."

Muse, a black dog with a grizzled face, approached, her toenails clacking softly against the floor. She snuffled Callie Jane's thigh and wagged her heavy tail. Evangeline's eyebrows shot up. "Whoa, she's usually skittish around people she doesn't know."

Callie Jane bent to rub the dog's ears, amazed at their velvety softness.

"She can't see well," Evangeline said fondly, "but she can hear about anything." Evangeline ran her hand along Muse's graying snout. "Yeah, you can, sweet girl."

Callie Jane spread her fingers in front of the fire. "Thank you for saving me tonight. I know I'm basically a stranger."

"If Muse thinks you're all right, then so do I. She's even letting you pet her." Evangeline smiled. "Do you smoke grass?"

Her throat was full of cotton. *Drugs?* "I, uh, haven't had the chance yet." She paused, then added, "But this seems like a good night to start."

"All right, later. But first, a glass of wine to warm us up." She padded across the room to the kitchen and returned with two mismatched glasses and a bottle. "California Cabernet," she said as she poured. Callie Jane took her glass as Evangeline raised her own drink and said, "A toast to my first friend in Spark."

Lifting her glass, Callie Jane gave a wobbly smile, then took an unfamiliar sip of wine. She closed her eyes as she swallowed, the wine warming her throat. "This is really good." She took another, longer sip and then set her glass on the mantel. "Delicious." Using both hands to pick up the bottle, she scrutinized the label. "I've never heard of Sonoma. Sounds nice, peaceful."

"It is, from what I remember. One summer my parents sent my brother and me to stay with a cousin there so they could get us out of their hair for a couple of months. I've never seen such a beautiful place. When it was time to come back, my brother said he was staying, and he's been there ever since." She shrugged. "Can't blame him. I'd have stayed too, except I'd met someone back home I was interested in."

Tiny flashes of light caught Callie Jane's eye—firelight dancing off the dozen or so safety pins holding the sofa's tattered brown slipcover more or less in place. "How long have you been in Spark?"

"Not too long. I got my cosmetology license in November and came here to work at the Curly Q after Christmas. I visited Aunt Arden—she owns the Blue Plate—one summer for a couple of weeks as a kid, and I liked it here. I spent hours chasing lightning bugs and playing in the creek, hunting for crawdads. I thought that shit was just in movies." A charred stick of wood split open, throwing embers into the air. "So I decided Spark might be the right place for me. My aunt helped me find this house to rent, already furnished." She snickered. "It's early Goodwill style, very sought after."

How wonderful to have your own place and get to live your own life. "It's perfect."

"I wouldn't go *that* far, but it's okay. So what's your story?"

Callie Jane had done nothing interesting enough to fall into the category of *story*. "I don't have one." She frowned, realizing the truth of it.

"I've heard there's somebody named Trace in your life. I imagine there's a good love story in there somewhere."

That would have to be some kind of imagination. "We, um, Trace and I have known each other since we were kids. We're more buddies, really."

"Lucky you, engaged to your best friend. I wish I could be."

Evangeline's words sharpened the point of her guilt, now jabbing her gut. Trace deserved better.

After a quiet moment, Evangeline stood. Muse struggled to her feet to follow her, but Evangeline patted her head softly and said, "You stay here, baby. I'll be right back."

Muse settled back to the floor but kept one ear cocked in Evangeline's direction. "Hey, I offered you some soup, so let me get that going. I've got tomato. Will that do?" she called over her shoulder. Callie Jane followed Evangeline into the tiny kitchen. She watched as Evangeline ran a bar of soap first under the water and then around the outside of the pot, coating the exterior with a thin white film. "I'll set it over the coals and it'll be hot in no time. And with the soap on there, the soot washes right off."

"Were you a Girl Scout?"

"Nope. A friend of mine, Becky, taught me that trick when her power got cut off one winter. It saves a lot of scrubbing if you have to cook over logs."

They returned to the fire, Callie Jane with two mugs and Evangeline with the pot of soup, which she nimbly situated among the glowing coals. After they'd eaten, draining the last drops from their mugs, Evangeline reached for a small tin box on a shelf. "Ready to get high?" Evangeline asked. "After a day like this one, we deserve it."

"It's been a doozy. Thanks." Her companion lit the marijuana cigarette and took a long drag before handing it to Callie Jane, who inhaled gently. A skunky-sweet smoke filled the room, and she waited expectantly, closing her eyes. To her disappointment, nothing happened. "Am I supposed to be feeling something?"

"Breathe it into your lungs and hold it for a second," Evangeline explained. Callie Jane inhaled, and as she held her breath, a rare sense of well-being filled her body.

"Leaving your family to come to a new state by yourself was a brave thing to do," she said as the smoke left her lungs. The California entry in the encyclopedia came to mind. *Could I do the same?* "Were you scared?"

Evangeline added a log to the fire and stabbed the others with an iron poker. A chill was back in the air, despite the roaring blaze.

"I didn't mean to pry." Callie Jane rubbed Muse's soft ears. When Muse lowered her head into Callie Jane's lap, she gently scratched the dog's neck. "It's none of my business why you came here."

Evangeline took another long drag from the joint and answered. "I needed to leave, so I did. I took my cosmetology license, Muse, and that blue Dodge." She jerked her thumb toward the carport. "Those were the only things that were truly mine. I earned the license, paid for that car, and rescued my sweet Muse."

"Rescued?"

"I went for a walk one day down a dirt road near my house. A man in a truck pulled over, got out with a dog in his arms, and went about ten feet into the woods. He threw her into a ditch and drove away. She chased after him for at least fifty yards before she stopped. I called out to her and she came right to me. We've been together ever since."

"What a horrible man." Callie Jane picked up the wine bottle and studied the label depicting the California vineyard as the marijuana filled her mind with wonder. "Mind if I have another glass?"

"Go right ahead. Pour me some, will you?" Evangeline rubbed under Muse's gray chin. "I told her never to chase after anyone who doesn't want her. A good lesson for her and me both." Evangeline watched the smoke from the joint curl around the room. "My parents ordered me out of their house on my eighteenth birthday, so here we are."

"Why did they kick you out?"

Evangeline stared into the fire for a long moment. "For who I am."

"They didn't approve of you being a hairdresser?"

Her laugh was as cold as the ice shell coating all of Spark. "Oh, they were fine with my career. Their problem was a *who*, not a *what*. That best friend I'll never be able to marry. She's a woman, and our being together, according to my parents, is an abomination to God."

Evangeline is a lesbian. Callie Jane had only learned that word during an incident in high school when a rumor about a teacher ran like a brush fire through the halls. Evangeline was just a normal person—kind and funny, not at all like what the classroom whispers had described. "They said that to you?"

The flames dancing around the log seemed to entrance Evangeline. "Yep," she answered softly. "They said I was no longer their daughter." Her voice caught in her throat. "So I'm not." She ran her fingers through her short hair before taking the last hit from the joint and tossing it into the fire. "But I have Muse, Aunt Arden, and Becky, my girlfriend. She'll be coming to Spark one day. She takes care of her mother, who has dementia. We agreed it would be too confusing to move her mom from the house she's always known, so Becky's staying in Ohio for now."

Evangeline took a photo of a smiling woman with curly brown hair from the mantel and handed it to Callie Jane. "I knew I was in love with her about two years ago when I saw her spreading a bag of leaves her mom had raked up back over their lawn. Her mama loved yard work and cried when the leaves were gone, so Becky made sure the leaves were never gone."

"That's the sweetest thing I've never heard." Callie Jane giggled. "I mean the sweetest thing I've *ever* heard."

Evangeline joined her in the giggle. "That's Becky. She'll stay with her mom until she passes and then come here. I'm not sure how people will feel about that, but I don't care."

"I'm glad you have Becky, but I'm so sorry about your parents. You were brave to tell them."

"The truth part was pretty easy, but the honesty part was rough."

Callie Jane cocked her head. "What do you mean?"

"Truth is not telling a lie, like in a courtroom, but honesty is part of your character, your integrity."

Callie Jane surveyed her new friend as an unfamiliar knowingness filled her soul. "I get it. Through honesty comes peace." Where did *that* come from?

"It's why I can sleep at night." Evangeline poked at the fire. "I'm happier here anyway. I've got my pad, such as it is, my dog, a job, and now a friend." Evangeline looked at her companion and said quietly, "I *hope* I still have a friend. If you want to split after what I've told you, that's cool. I can give you a blanket so you won't freeze and some food if you'd rather go back to your store."

"Why would I leave? You could've walked right past the Emporium, but you didn't. You offered to help me."

"Well then, I'm glad I knocked on your door when I saw your candle, even if I did scare the shit outta you." Evangeline rubbed her hands together. "You know what? I'm starving. I think I have a bag of cookies squirreled away somewhere. It's either those or dog biscuits. What'll it be?"

"I don't want to deprive Muse, so cookies it is."

Evangeline languidly danced into the kitchen as if swaying to music only she could hear. She returned with a bag. "They're probably stale."

"Don't care." Callie Jane popped a cookie into her mouth.

Evangeline scooped two cookies from the bag and pulled a blanket around her. "So tell me about yourself."

Callie Jane started talking, hoping it would sound better in words than it did as thoughts in her head. "Well, I'm eighteen. My daddy is the sweetest man in the world, but I'm worried about his heart. He's overweight, and if he tries to carry something even slightly heavy, it wears him out." She took a sip of wine. "My mother wants me to marry Trace Humboldt because he's going to own a chain of grocery stores and be rich. She's obsessed with my wedding. Yesterday she spent thirty minutes on the phone with the florist, explaining the exact shade of pink she wants for the spray roses. She loves me in her own way, but she thinks love means following her rules and never having an opinion different from hers. I figured out a long time ago to keep my head down and my mouth shut."

Callie Jane walked to the window and studied the ice pelting Evangeline's tiny yard. She debated telling the next part, but it seemed to be a night for truth-telling. "Mama drinks. A lot. I found her secret stash of gin in the kitchen when I was a kid, but it's something all three of us ignore."

Evangeline was listening intently. "Man, that sounds awful. We were always fighting in my house, but at least we could all say what we were thinking." She snorted. "Even if that thing was 'get the hell out of this house.' My brother couldn't handle all the stress. That's why he wouldn't come back to Ohio when it was time for school to start. He's happier in California, and I'm happier here, so it all worked out."

"What's your brother's job?"

"He's really into nature and works in a nursery, growing flowers for the fancy hotels."

Callie Jane had spent the last few weeks studying every page of the California guidebook as she lay in bed at night, and the California encyclopedia entry during downtime at the Emporium. The sun, the lush landscape, the ocean, all mesmerized her, and every time she read about them, she became more convinced that was where she belonged. One night after staying up past midnight to read about the Santa Barbara flower festival, she fell asleep with the book on her chest, dreaming she was a bluebird flying among field after field of flowers, wearing a crown of daisies. And now, right in front of her, was someone who had lived there. "What do you remember about California?"

"The weather was always great, and the plants and trees were beautiful. Flowers grew wild all over town. The people were so laid-back, and what I remember most was how they all acted like living there was just so normal."

"Do you think your brother would talk to me about California?"

"Sure, I'll get you his address and you can write to him. Why?"

"I think I want to live there." She shrugged. "Great idea, huh? Move to California with no plans, no money, and no way to get there. I'm supposed to marry Trace and run the Emporium." She sighed. "I'd be letting everyone down." Gazing into the fire, she whispered, "But there's something about that place that feels so right to me, like I might belong there."

Chapter 9

Posey

BEFORE TURNING DOWN the driveway, Posey stopped her car, squinting in the March sun to admire her new mailbox. The street address was handsomely printed on the side of the black metal, "1480 Creekside Road," but the showstopper was the "Cold Spring" nameplate swinging gently from S-hooks above the box.

She smiled as her tires crunched the pea gravel of her driveway, reviewing the tremendous progress she had made in the last six weeks. The tree had been hauled out of the library, the broken windows had been replaced, and the Nashville handyman she had hired was rivaling a whole churchyard of saints for miracle working. There were only two projects that stumped him: the furry wall of the hidden office and the stench of the catio.

"Ma'am," the worker had said, "I've tried everything. That mold has a tighter grip on the wall than Sherman had on Atlanta. And that pee smell has sunk into the stones on the floor. You'll have to rip up the whole thing to get rid of it."

Posey had missed the existence of the office altogether during the first few walk-throughs. Only a too-linear crack in the paneling clued her in. When she pressed on the wall, a door had popped open, revealing what she guessed was a secret lair for Mr. Harris as he conducted his nefarious business dealings. She had jettisoned a decaying box of cigars she found on a shelf, thinking they were the source of the dank odor, but had realized the mold growing up the wall was the culprit. She made a mental note to ensure the door was tightly closed on reunion night. *It'll be fine. No one will even know it's there.*

The catio smell worried her, though. She'd ask Vern to bring home some fans to run during the party. Surely that would make the smell dissipate.

As she approached the front steps, she marveled at the existence of such a grand structure, so out of place in Spark. The story went that a stunningly beautiful seventeen-year-old Milbrey Sullivan was jilted by her fiancé, Jimmy Preston, who then married her sister, Anita. Milbrey ran away to New York City to be a stage actress, met a man named Miles Harris in a Manhattan speakeasy during Prohibition times, and eloped a few weeks later. Milbrey discovered the only thing she hated more than acting was city life and was so homesick that Mr. Harris built her a house on the outskirts of Spark just to quell her crying. He lived there too, at first, but the charms of counting bullfrog croaks on a rainy summer night and watching hawks wheel over lush tobacco fields eluded him.

The old-timers of Spark concluded Mr. Harris was either a mobster or a bootlegger. Some thought he was both. His trips back to New York became increasingly frequent, and eventually he never came back. A few Spark residents maintained he had been gunned down Al Capone–style on the Lower East Side of Manhattan, and others claimed he was serving time in Sing Sing, but who really knew?

Rumors swirled, embellished with each retelling, eventually spawning the legend of the Creekside Crone, much to the delight of teenagers bent on daring each other to touch the front door or break a window with a well-thrown rock. No campfire ghost-story session was complete without the tale of the old woman wearing a tattered wedding dress who cried as she roamed the halls, searching for her husband. It was said anyone brave enough to enter the abandoned house and call out, "Milbrey, my beloved," three times at the stroke of midnight would be rewarded with an icy hug as the Creekside Crone claimed the intruder as her own.

Posey steered her Cadillac around to the back of the home, parking it away from anyone intent on snooping. The house was a good hundred yards from the road, but she suspected lookie-loos had ventured down the rutted driveway to catch a glimpse of what was being done to the old Harris place. She didn't need any nosy Nellies figuring out she, not a painting crew, was wielding the brushes and rollers.

She popped the trunk and hauled out a gallon of bleach and a gallon of white paint, pausing for a moment to gaze across the lawn to envision the heated pool that would one day be installed, an homage to the midnight skinny-dip she and CJ had taken at Eden Hall.

As she walked toward the house, she surveyed a boxwood her equal in height, wondering how she could manage to trim it back into submission. Eventually the garden would match the vision in her head, but years of work would be needed to transform the overgrown jungle. She frowned. Years she didn't have.

The flagstone terrace, bordered by an elegant low wall, was breathtaking, larger than their whole house on Poplar Avenue, and would be the focal point of both the reunion and the wedding reception. She imagined her guests, mingling and laughing, some sitting on the wall for a private chat. The rest of the house could be in transition, but the terrace had to shine, picture perfect. She scowled at vigorous bindweed choking the liriope grass. *Concentrate your energy on what will be most visible and let the rest of it go.*

"*Are you sure it's going to be done in time?*" Darlene had asked only a day earlier. "*You said it was almost ready, but that was at least a month ago. I swung by there over the weekend and peeped in the windows. It was kind of a mess.*"

"*We're almost finished. Don't you worry.*"

Darlene sounded doubtful. "*If you say so. But it's no problem to move it to my house.*"

"*No need for that.*" There's no way I'll be ready at this rate. "*You have my assurance everything will be perfect.*"

The thought of CJ holding her in his embrace spurred her forward. She'd had to give up sleep and her weekly estate sale forays, her family had to accept their new chef was named Swanson, and every fingernail she had was either chipped or broken to the quick, but all the sacrifices would be worth it the moment she and CJ had their own private reunion at the Spark High reunion.

Her work clothes were waiting for her right where she left them, hidden in the secret office. She slipped her Lilly Pulitzer dress onto a waiting hanger and shook out of her shoes, silently blessing Jackie Kennedy for bringing Jack Rogers sandals into style after a trip to Capri. High heels were painful, but Posey was willing to suffer for beauty. Thanks to Jackie, she only had to endure her pumps during church and winter months. Tying the bandanna around her beehive, she slipped on an old pair of pants, dingy Keds, and one of Vern's stained shirts. After snapping on rubber gloves, she grabbed an old toothbrush and headed to the conservatory. Replacing the floor was way too expensive. She'd have to work on the smell herself.

Bleach glugged out of the bottle and splashed into a corner. She knelt, scrubbing away at the porous limestone. *How many cats did that woman own?* Surely to God, straight bleach would eventually conquer the stink that wafted from the stone, made worse by the western sun whose springtime rays burned through Milbrey's glass panels.

The downstairs wallpaper had been easy to remove, barely adhered to the plaster walls beneath it. Although the space screamed for expensive grass cloth, paint would be its replacement. The staircase, though, was the centerpiece of the house and needed to be exquisite. The bloodred carpet she had ordered would arrive the following week, and the white walls had to be finished before installation. After covering the wall flanking the steps with two heavy coats of paint, she was satisfied with her work. She washed her brushes and rollers, then changed back into her dress and rushed to beat Vern and Callie Jane home.

Letting out a heavy sigh, she settled into the Cadillac. Refurbishing Cold Spring and running a household at the same time was exhausting.

Once back at Poplar Avenue, she extracted three frozen dinners from her ancient freezer and popped them in the oven. She grimaced as she pulled out three ugly plates to serve the aluminum trays on, thankful she had a mansion full of china and silver to dine on once they moved.

At Callie Jane's suggestion, Vern would be renting the house fully furnished to Hannah and Grady Neal, and they were welcome to every piece of furniture, along with each bowl, plate, and glass Vern's mother had collected as premiums in boxes of Duz detergent. The only pieces she'd miss were the Louis XV bedroom suite she'd snagged at an estate sale, but Milbrey's furniture was of better quality, so no real loss. And, of course, her vanity was coming with her. She made sure Vern told the Neals they couldn't have it.

The rumble of Vern's truck snapped her from her reverie. When he came in, he dropped a stack of newspapers on the kitchen counter. "Furnished or not, I'm takin' my bowling trophies. I'll wrap 'em up after dinner." He glanced at his watch. "Trace's mama has had Callie Jane at their house all afternoon talking wedding plans. They've been at it for hours, but Callie Jane said she'd be home for supper."

Posey was about to comment on Opal Humboldt's rudeness in excluding her when she sniffed. The unmistakable scent of fried chicken, heavy with grease and pepper, clung to Vern. "Have you eaten yet?"

Vern looked startled. "No."

"So you didn't go by the Blue Plate to get a break from all these frozen dinners?"

Vern's voice was wary. "I've been at the Emporium all day."

Her husband was lying, but why? He was too cheap to buy a meal at the Blue Plate, and anyway, he'd have had to stand right beside Arden at the fryer to reek the way he did. "Then why do I sm—"

Callie Jane slammed the door. "Trace's mama has lost her mind. She had me over there for four hours talking about taffeta and china patterns and bouquets. I wish she'd just renew her own vows and leave me out of it." She looked at her mother. "Can you please try to talk to her? She wants *three* flower girls." Callie Jane took the silverware from the counter and began setting the table. Glancing at her mother's arm, she said, "I hope you didn't give the painters too hard of a time today."

Posey furrowed her brow. She hadn't told anyone she was going by Cold Spring. "How did you know I was there?"

Pointing to a smear of paint on her mother's wrist, she said, "That."

Her hand flew to her arm. A paint splotch, big as life. How had she missed that swath of white? Time to redirect her daughter's attention. "After you've finished with the table, will you bundle up the folders in the file cabinet? I don't want any of my papers to spill out in the move. There's a box of rubber bands on the top."

Posey emptied the now-cooked frozen dinners onto plates, scraping each aluminum compartment clean in an effort to make the dinner appear more homemade, although she knew she wasn't fooling anyone. As she filled their water glasses, her daughter approached with a small piece of paper in her hand and a frown across her face. "Why do I have a Nashville Fine Arts identification card giving my address as 229 Coventry Circle in Nashville?"

Posey blanched. "I'm . . . I'm not sure what you mean." *Oh Lord. How did she find that?*

"This little card fell out of a folder. It has my name on it, with the address of 229 Coventry Circle. And there's a check mark by Davidson County, with someone's signature."

"Oh, that," she answered weakly. "That's for the children's enrichment activities from the Nashville Fine Arts program." She'd had to flirt furiously with the young man behind the desk as she presented her Cooke County license as proof of Davidson County residency. Leaning forward in her low-cut blouse had paid off, though, and he signed the card without ever confirming her address.

"We've never lived in Nashville." Callie Jane eyed her mother suspiciously.

"It's nothing to worry about." She plastered on a smile she hoped would distract her daughter from the surely audible sound of her pounding heart.

"This makes no sense. Maybe Daddy can explain it to me."

As Callie Jane took the first step toward her father, who was in the other room watching television, Posey grabbed her arm. Callie Jane flinched, and Posey released her grasp. Struggling to keep her tone light, she answered, "Oh, all right. You caught me in a little white lie. If you live in Davidson County, you're entitled to enroll your children in the Nashville Fine Arts activities free of charge. Out-of-county residents aren't eligible. You were always wanting to try ceramics or ballet or acting, and we didn't have the money, so . . ." Her voice got stronger as she became more comfortable with her lie. "I fibbed and said we lived in Nashville so you could participate."

Callie Jane read the card again. "So how did you come up with 229 Coventry Circle?"

Posey had driven past CJ's house dozens of times over the years. On one of her most recent forays, she had wanted to get a closer look at a newly constructed fountain near the front door, so she drove up the driveway through the opened gate, nearly colliding with Frances, who was pulling away from the house. Their eyes had locked for a moment, and Posey had nearly vomited as she backed up to allow Frances to exit. She couldn't resist still driving by the house, but she never left the relative safety of the street again.

"Oh, I made it up," she replied with a wave of her hand. "I just thought it sounded pretty. The whole point of the program was for the youth of Tennessee to be exposed to the arts, so it's all fine." Her tone softened. "Speaking of wanting the best for my lamb, I've given you the room overlooking the terrace at

Cold Spring. It has a lovely view of the grounds and is the far-thest from the other two bedrooms. When you and Trace visit, you will have your privacy."

"Mama, I don't think I can—"

Posey interrupted her daughter. "Will you tell your father dinner is ready?" she asked, slipping the paper into her pocket and silently cursing her carelessness.

As she moved the stack of Vern's newspapers to clear a place for the dirty dishes after dinner, a photograph from the *Nashville Banner's* society pages sent her pulse racing. Frances was shaking someone's hand, with CJ beside her. Posey snatched up the paper and gasped. He was wearing the bow tie she had given him. She had bought it partly because of the unusual paisley pattern, but mostly because the tie's color matched her green eyes perfectly. "Coventry Circle Home the Scene of Festive St. Patrick's Day Party," the newspaper caption read. Posey clutched the paper to her chest as she remembered whispering to CJ as he unwrapped her gift, *"Every time I see you wearing it, I'll know you are thinking of how much you want me."*

She tossed the newspaper in the trash, not wanting to risk Callie Jane spotting the Coventry Circle street name. He probably had a dozen bow ties, and it was just a coincidence he had chosen that one to wear. She looked at the garbage can. Or maybe CJ knew exactly what he was doing.

· · · · · · · · · ·

Later that night, once Vern and Callie Jane were asleep, Posey padded into the kitchen and emptied the vinegar bottle into a tall glass. Fishing the newspaper from the garbage, she wiped off the coffee grounds and studied CJ's face. *Dozens of bow ties,* she told herself. After draining the glass, she looked one more time. *But only one was given to him by the dazzlingly attractive sex kitten he adored.*

Drifting off to sleep back in her bed, she settled on an answer. The green tie was no coincidence. The message was as loud and clear as the saxophone notes that had rolled through the cavernous ballroom at Eden Hall that night. He wanted her.

Chapter 10

Callie Jane

TRACE STUCK HIS head through the Emporium door. "Can I take you to lunch today, baby? I have a surprise for you."

"Nine, ten." Callie Jane looked up from the place mats she was counting. "I guess that's all right, if Daddy can spare me." She glanced at her father, who nodded.

"Great. Meet me at noon at the Blue Plate." He grinned and shut the shop door behind him.

"That was mysterious," she said. "I wonder what's up."

"You'll find out soon enough, I guess." He set the newspaper on his desk and rose. "I left some merchandise in the truck."

"Is it heavy? I'll get it for you."

"It's just a blanket." He opened the door. "Be right back."

The front doorbell shook with Wasp's entrance. Clutching the angel he had bought for his sister's birthday back in January, Wasp said, "Want my dollar back." He set the angel on the counter. "She didn't like it."

"You bought that almost three months ago. She just now decided she didn't like it?"

Wasp scowled. "That's right. Gimme my dollar."

Callie Jane flipped through the sales log, where she and her father dutifully recorded every Emporium sale. "Here it is. The price was seventy-five cents."

"I paid a dollar."

"You paid *with* a dollar, and I gave you a quarter in change. I am glad to offer you a store credit of seventy-five cents, or I can give you a refund." She spoke slowly. "Of seventy-five cents."

"Cheatin' your customers is no way to run a business." Wasp watched her father approaching. "All right, gimme the money."

As Callie Jane dropped three quarters into Wasp's waiting hand, her father asked, "Do we have a problem here?"

She was quick to answer. "No. Just giving a customer a refund."

Wasp stalked out of the Emporium, pocketing the quarters.

She vigorously wiped the angel with a rag. "I bet Linda didn't say a word about not liking her gift, and Wasp stole it from her so he could get his money back."

"Wasp's got a tough row to hoe, with both his parents alcoholics. He's likely raised hisself and his sister both. Hatch Fentress stays on the wrong side of the law, with a temper that'd scare the devil, and his missus is no better. Someone with those burdens needs compassion, not more conflict."

"Do you ever worry about—" Callie Jane stopped talking. Her mother's love affair with gin was a taboo topic, like her maternal grandparents or why she was an only child. No one had forbidden her to bring up these subjects, but some things you just knew. "Never mind. Did you see where Mr. Strickland painted the front door of his shop?"

"What were you going to say? What are you wondering if I worry about?"

"Forget it. Sometimes I just run my mouth before my brain can catch up."

His voice was low. "Callie Jane. Tell me."

She sighed. "Okay. It's Mama's drinking. She tries to hide it but doesn't do a very good job." She looked at her father. "I've known forever, and I bet you have too."

"She thinks her life is hard, even if we don't see that." Her father's face hardened. "People cope in different ways. I've tried talking to her, but you can imagine how well that went." He smiled sadly at her. "She's gonna suit herself, no matter what I or anybody else says." He shrugged. "Let's change the subject."

Callie Jane grabbed her purse. "Is it okay if I head into Nashville to do a couple of errands this morning?"

"Sure, but let me walk you out to the truck. This Creeper business is really worrying me. I heard at the hardware store somebody took a shot at him and mighta nicked him."

After assuring her father she'd be mindful of her surroundings, she hopped in his truck and headed for Nashville. Her mind turned to her future as she drove. The thought of moving across the country was scary but exhilarating. Could California be where she belonged? She shook her head. Maybe she *wanted* to go, or even *should* go, but she couldn't just drop her real life and chase after some fairy-tale life she had dreamed up.

The Nashville library had always been one of Callie Jane's favorite destinations. When she was a child, her mother had brought her to the library weekly, not only for the magnificent puppet shows but also to while away hours in the endless stacks of books. As Posey leafed through fashion magazines, Callie Jane read to her heart's content, first the easy readers in the children's area, then advancing to chapter books, and finally the classics like *Heidi* and *Little Women*. The library had always been the first stop for discovering new information, and on this day she had a whole state to learn about.

As she approached the library's front door, she smiled at a bench nestled in a meticulously maintained garden bed that was bursting with early tulips, hyacinths, and daffodils, recalling one afternoon when she was about seven. She had tried to read the dedication plaque affixed to the bench and had easily deciphered *Nashville Garden Club* and *President*, but had to ask her mother for help sounding out a word with a tricky *c* sound. She still remembered how strained her mother's voice had been when she choked out through clenched teeth the word *Frances*.

When Callie Jane opened the library door, she was greeted by the familiar smell that always reminded her of a combination of woods after a rain and vanilla cupcakes. She scoured the card catalog, searching for information on California. As she thumbed through the cards, her heart rate rose. *So many titles, so many possibilities.* Gathering books in her arms, she walked to a chair tucked into a quiet corner. She stopped in her tracks at the slanted periodicals rack. "California's Emerging Music Scene" was splashed across the top of a magazine. Below that were the words "Flower Power, Peace, and Love—Is It for You?" She grabbed the magazine and set it on top of her pile.

As she read through the magazine, her pulse quickened. The topics thrilled her—people like Joni Mitchell and Bob Dylan, and places like Carmel-by-the-Sea and Laurel Canyon. A whole world was revealing itself.

Checking her watch, she grimaced. Almost time to meet Trace. She rose from her seat and placed the books on the reshelve cart. Reluctantly, she returned the magazine to its spot and headed for Spark, even as she was already in California in her mind, wandering through fields of sunflowers and walking the shoreline of the Pacific Ocean.

When she turned the engine on, "California Dreamin'" by the Mamas & the Papas flowed from the truck's speakers. She didn't know if she should laugh or cry. The song was about a dream, not reality. Was the universe giving her a sign to go, or a reminder that her idea was unattainable?

She parked the truck behind the Emporium and walked to the Blue Plate as she planned her order—a vegetable plate with white beans, turnip greens, and squash casserole, along with some of Arden's corn sticks.

Trace was in a booth, chugging a tall glass of iced tea. "There you are. I was beginning to worry." He placed a chaste kiss on her lips as she absentmindedly bent down to greet him. He gestured to the platter between them. "Arden's brought the chicken, and she'll be back with our sides in a minute. Mashed potatoes, lima beans, and coleslaw for me, green beans and fried corn for you. Biscuits for both of us, of course." He interlaced his fingers and stretched his arms. "I love knowing what to order for you." He grinned. "There are advantages to marrying someone you've known since you were three years old."

The smell from the towering platter of chicken, usually so appealing, nauseated her. The more she stared at the golden skin, the more she wanted her vegetables. *He should have waited and let me choose for myself.*

Arden set down their plates, loaded with the rest of their food. "Be right back with your biscuits. They're comin' out of the oven now."

"Could I have corn sticks instead?"

"Sure, hon. Anything for our bride."

Trace cocked his head. "Since when do you turn down a hot biscuit?" He peered into her face. "Are you feeling all right?"

"Can't I order what I want?" she snapped.

His voice was low. "I'm sorry. You can have whatever you'd like." He bit into the chicken, studying the platter as he chewed. "Arden's cooking is fine, but Mama's is better. She's handwriting you a recipe book with all my favorites." He smiled. "I told her you were already a good cook, but she wants to give you something special for our wedding."

She took a bite of food, instantly regretting it. The beans, shiny with grease, coated her mouth with a thin film of bacon fat. She put down her fork.

"Don't tell Mama you know about the cookbook, 'cause that's supposed to be a surprise. Soon as we finish lunch, I'll show you *my* surprise. Here's a hint. It involves our future together." He pointed to her plate of uneaten food. "Are you finished with that?" When she nodded, he downed the last of her beans and started on her corn.

As Trace paid the bill, Arden asked, "Y'all get enough to eat?"

"Yes, ma'am. Good as always." He turned to Callie Jane. "Come on," he said, guiding her to his truck. "You're gonna love this."

Trace's patter quickened as he drove to the outskirts of town. Despite her efforts to listen, her mind was in the front row of the Trips Music Festival she had read about in the magazine.

"Hey, Trace. Have you ever heard of the Grateful Dead?"

His baffled look answered her question. "Who in their right mind would be grateful to be dead?" Trace reached over and tucked behind her ear a strand of hair that had escaped her hasty ponytail. "I've 'bout busted a gut tryin' to keep this secret."

Her stomach twitched. Something was up.

After driving for about twenty minutes, passing first the retail buildings of Spark, then the houses, and finally farmland, Trace pulled the truck into a gravel drive. A plywood sign was propped against a tree, with orange spray-painted letters spelling "HUMBOLDT." *What in the world?* He navigated around the ruts in the drive, stopping by the frame of a building under construction, whose pine boards stood like a forlorn forest of denuded trees. Throwing the truck into Park, he said, "Stay right there. I'm comin' to get you."

Opening her door, he scooped her into his arms and carried her toward the structure. He took an exaggerated step over the framed-out threshold.

"Where are we?"

"Can't you guess?" he asked, setting her down.

She frowned. "A new BuyMore?"

"It's our house."

She took a step back. "Our *what*?"

"It's my wedding gift to you." He grabbed her hand, guiding her farther into the structure. "Let me show you around. We're in the living room. It's going to have a big picture window here." He waved his hands, forming a six-foot rectangle. "Come on down the hall," he said, taking her hand again. "The first bedroom is over here, and the second one is right beside it. They'll share a bathroom over here."

"Who?"

His eyebrows rose. "Our kids."

Next, he led her to the back of the house, turning bright red as he added, "This is our bedroom." Then he ushered her to the far side of the building. "You're in your kitchen, which goes from that wall to this one," he said, pointing to rows of pine boards. He smiled shyly as he gestured to a structure off the carport. "And here's my special surprise. A greenhouse with a potting shed, so you can grow plants all year long."

Callie Jane bit her lip. "That's really sweet, Trace."

He beamed. "None of it will be as fancy as your family's new house, but it will be all ours. What do you think?"

Her legs were as wobbly as the green Jell-O on the diet plate special at Arden's diner. "Where can I sit down?" she croaked.

He gently led her to a set of three stairs. "These go to the carport. We can sit here."

Her racing heart whirled the bacon grease in her stomach like an egg beater. "What is all this?"

"Haven't you been listening to me? It's our home." His face clouded. "What's wrong?"

"Didn't you think to ask me where I want to live?"

"How can it be a surprise if I ask you? My daddy did this for my mama as his wedding gift to her, and now I'm doing it for you."

Callie Jane stared in horror at the two-by-fours reaching skyward in the two-sectioned kitchen, reminding her of a poster drawn for a long-ago science project of the two lobes and spiky blades of a Venus flytrap. The house stood poised to snap closed and swallow her whole. Sweat formed in the bends of her knees, and she became acutely aware of the rising humidity as she tried to draw sticky air into her lungs.

Trace's face was tense. "It's your dream house."

"You don't know anything about my dreams." She looked away from his wounded expression and rubbed her neck. "I have a terrible headache. Please take me home."

As he backed out of the driveway, Trace switched on the radio, and the Beatles' "Run for Your Life" blasted through the speakers. He immediately twisted the knob. "I hate that song."

The farms and houses rolled by, each identical, like having a song on repeat. *Run for your life.*

Chapter 11

Posey

CHURCH STARTED AT nine o'clock sharp, and although Jesus forgave personal shortcomings such as tardiness, Brother Cleave did not. Breakfast would have to be a quick bowl of cereal if they didn't want to be late.

The mantel clock had long since chimed eight o'clock when Posey hopped on one foot, jamming her other one into a pump. She longed to try, just once, wearing Jack Rogers sandals to church, but knew better. The Curly Q had buzzed for a full week when Tina Anderson wore a spaghetti-strapped sundress to church shortly after moving to Spark. *Imagine not knowing to keep your shoulders covered in the Lord's house.* Posey could only imagine what they'd say about bare toes on display.

Callie Jane emerged from her bedroom, adjusting the sash on a beige dress Posey didn't recognize.

"Go change. That shade is unbecoming, and the dress is too big." She grimaced at the memory of her oversized Goodwill dresses. "Never wear clothes that don't fit properly."

"It's fine."

"Don't sass your mother. Honestly, Callie Jane, when did you become so insolent? People judge you by what you wear. That color makes you look sick. Put on the blue one that matches your eyes. Now scoot."

Cereal rattled into the bowls, sending the first stirrings of a headache shooting into Posey's temple. She grabbed the milk, folded back the paper mouth of the carton, and tipped it over the first bowl. Three drops plunked onto the flakes of cereal. She checked for a backup. Nothing. *Damn it.* With all the work on Cold Spring, she had neglected duties like grocery shopping. The mashed potatoes she planned to fix after church would be impossible to make without milk. The headache grew to a pounding in her temple. Heaving an exasperated sigh, she lined up the three bowls of cornflakes and poured orange juice over them in a continuous motion. She called her family into the kitchen with a crisp, "Breakfast is ready." Pulling the roast from the refrigerator, she slid it into the oven, set the dial with a flick of her wrist, grabbed her bowl, and headed for her bedroom.

She was smoothing her hand across the vanity's drawer front when Vern gently opened the door. "Ready?" he asked softly. "Callie Jane's already in the car."

With five minutes to spare, Vern swung the Cadillac into the gravel parking lot. Posey swallowed what was left of her mint and adjusted the collar of her silk blouse. As Callie Jane exited the car, Posey caught sight of the offending beige dress. She opened her mouth, glanced at her neighbors filling the sanctuary, then quickly shut it.

Posey began to move to their seats. Tina Anderson was chatting with a friend, blocking Posey's way to the Jarvises' coveted front-row pew that had taken Vern's family three generations to earn. Posey found Tina's presence grating, even though she didn't know Tina more than to acknowledge her existence if they encountered each other in an aisle of the grocery store or on Market Street's sidewalk. Maybe her irritation was because she owned clothes as fashionable as Posey's, or because Tina was always inappropriately friendly. Posey summoned her iciest voice. "Good morning. That's a greeting, not an opinion." Tina's face paled, and she scurried to her seat in an only-lived-here-two-years back pew.

As the Jarvis family settled in for the service, Posey scrutinized her daughter. She really did look wan. Was she sick? And when had she become so defiant? Callie Jane had always been her mouse, never saying a cross word or causing a minute of trouble. Posey squinted. What in the world was around her neck? A thin strip of leather held a metal symbol next to her heart. Was that a peace sign? She had seen one in *Look* magazine at the Curly Q just last week. Was Callie Jane becoming a communist?

The sermon focused on loving one another, a topic she thought had been exhausted after Valentine's Day. Plenty of other topics were available. She looked at her daughter. Like disobedience.

Brother Cleave was on a roll. "When we reach the heavenly gates, St. Peter will not inquire about our bank balances, or how many baskets we scored for the Spark High team, but how we showed love to those beloved to us."

She pondered how Brother Cleave knew St. Peter's line of questioning. Maybe it was written in the clergy handbook, or maybe Brother Cleave was telling the people what they wanted to hear.

The Jarvises were heading for the parking lot when Darlene approached. "How's the renovations comin'?" she asked anxiously. "I went over there to check on parking, and, my stars, it looks like there is a lot left to do. We only have a few weeks left before the reunion."

Posey blanched. She was way behind schedule. "The workers just have a couple of things to wrap up." Posey's shoulders tightened. "Everything's fine."

Darlene's brow was furrowed. "If you're sure. Because I'm the chairman and I can't mess this up."

"No worries," Posey said as she rushed her family out the church door. "Everything's under control."

Once safely in the confines of the car, Posey unclenched her jaw and turned to glare at her daughter in the back seat. "You look awful. I saw Tina Anderson staring. I am sure she was wondering why I let you out of the house looking such a fright." Massaging her throbbing temples, she turned to her husband. "Don't you think Tina Anderson was thinking how unattractively dressed Callie Jane was?"

His answer was unusually gruff. "No. I do not think that at all." He rubbed the back of his neck with his left hand as he steered the Cadillac toward their house with his right.

Once inside, Posey got to work on the food, banging pots and pans as she fumed over Vern's lack of support. She substituted rice for the mashed potatoes, and although Vern poked suspiciously at the replacement with his fork, he stayed silent. Callie Jane pushed her uneaten food around the plate, tears forming in her eyes.

After the dishes were done, instead of lying down for her customary Sunday afternoon nap, Posey followed her daughter into her bedroom.

"You look like death. You're pale, you're not eating, and you're emotional and defiant." She eyed her daughter's middle. "Are you pregnant?"

Callie Jane sank onto the bed. "Of course not."

Praise God. "Are you sure?"

"If I'm pregnant, there's gonna be three wise men marching down Poplar Avenue with gifts for the new savior." Callie Jane glared at her mother. "I've barely even kissed Trace."

"Then what is wrong with you?"

Callie Jane's voice shook. "I'm not marrying him."

"You most certainly are."

Callie Jane straightened her back. "I'm calling off the wedding. I mean it."

Her voice had an assured tone Posey had never heard from her daughter but remembered once coming from her own mouth when she told her mother she was leaving their tiny house and moving to Nashville the minute she graduated and was never coming back. She had broken that vow, of course, returning to Stadler Court, pregnant and scared, the day after CJ dumped her. She flinched as she recalled her emaciated mother's last words to her: *"Let me die in peace, Posey. Cancer is eating me up, and the last thing I need is the likes of you ruining my final days."* Before slamming the door on her daughter, she had added, *"You've made your bed, now lie in it."* Posey, stunned by her second rejection in as many days, had wandered aimlessly until she found herself at the church. The doors were locked, so Posey did her praying, and then her crying, in the wisteria-draped gazebo. Vern had heard her sobs, and the rest was history.

Posey never thought her daughter had a drop of her own gumption until now. She searched her heart for the right thing to say, but no wise words sprang to her lips. No kind words were available either. Unable to articulate even a sound, she waited until she could speak. "You are unwell. I will let you rest." She backed out of the room, closing the door softly as she left, intent on lying down.

After finishing the dishes, Vern slipped into the bedroom and tiptoed to his closet. As he shrugged into his khaki jacket, a small brass button dangling from the cuff caught her eye. First the debacle with Callie Jane and now Vern's jacket. A loose button was as bad as a baggy dress in an unflattering color. She thought for a moment about making him wait while she sewed it back on. No. She finally had a moment to herself, and it wasn't like the bodies in the graveyard would judge her for letting her husband leave the house unkempt, so she fell back into the pillows, making a mental note to fix the button after he got home.

"I hope you feel better," Vern whispered on his way to his weekly cemetery visit.

He returned home at his usual five o'clock. Posey was in the kitchen, jotting a grocery list into a spiral notepad. She sniffed. Was that the same chicken aroma? It *was*. What the hell was going on? As he raised his arm to rub his neck, her eyes latched onto the secure button on his right cuff. *It must have been the left one.* He removed his jacket, and Posey took it from him. "I'll hang this up for you."

Ignoring his raised eyebrows, she scurried to their bedroom. Closing the door, she sank onto the bed, examining the right cuff and then the left. Neither button was loose. She tugged at the brass discs to confirm with her fingers what her eyes could not accept. Taking hold of both sleeves, she waved them in a frenzy, the way a cat shook a mouse to break its neck. Nothing.

She sat motionless for a moment, numb, before she struggled to her feet and carefully hung the jacket in his closet. The puzzle pieces began to come together. Her first clue had been when Vern had stayed out all night after she announced they were moving to Cold Spring. And then there was the time he came home reeking of fried chicken while claiming to have been at the Emporium all day—the second clue. And now someone, certainly not Vern, had sewn his button back on, then fed him that same fried chicken. Someone, she realized, who was having an affair with her husband.

How long had the affair been going on? A month? Such intimate, domestic chores as sewing on a loose button or frying chicken together signaled that this affair had gone on long enough for the white-hot fires of passion to have burned down to the embers of a comfortable relationship. She lay on their bed, dizzy. At least a year.

Trying to keep the dual secrets of her silver flask and vinegar bottle in such a cramped house had been risky. With only two bedrooms and one bathroom, each Jarvis family member already had more information about the others than they cared to know. A nightmare, an upset stomach, it was all common knowledge. She'd come close to being found out only once in all these years, when Callie Jane had reached for vinegar to dissolve tablets of Easter egg dye, but Posey had swooped in just in time.

Now it was Vern's secret, not her own, that had been exposed.

· · · · · · · · · ·

The bedroom was dark. A quick glance at her nightstand revealed it was six o'clock, dinnertime. Everything was fine; there was a routine to adhere to. She roused herself and freshened her lipstick, which had begun to feather into the fine lines around her mouth, despite a decade of ritualistically slathering on wrinkle cream.

Somewhere between the leftover roast beef and the chess pie, she began to see the bright side. An affair would mean Vern would be more accepting of her divorce papers when she finally hopped from the Vern rock to the CJ rock.

As she served their coffee, she was overcome with an unexpected rush of pride. She gazed at her husband with new eyes.

He had always been a sad sack, lumpy and old, completely devoid of the Camelot charisma she longed for. She had married him, of course, but she had seen him as a solution to her problem, never as anything close to desirable. She must have overlooked something fundamentally attractive about Vern Jarvis. Hmm, she'd have to pay closer attention.

By the time the last wet saucer had been placed into the dish drainer, she had reconciled the whole situation. According to the tabloid rumors, Jackie Kennedy's husband had been a serial cheater, embroiled in numerous trysts. Jackie had tolerated the whispers with absolute silence, admirable grace, and noble dignity. Now it was her turn to do the same. Maybe she lived in more of a Camelot than she realized.

She studied her husband's florid face. Was he the strong silent type, like Gary Cooper in *High Noon*? Vern burped. "Good roast beef," he said, smiling. The image of Gary Cooper vanished from her mind. She watched his pudgy fingers struggle to loosen his belt as he lumbered to his recliner. John Wayne, maybe?

Chapter 12

Callie Jane

SUNLIGHT POURED THROUGH the window in the Emporium office. The day was warm for late March, and Callie Jane had tugged open the sash as soon as she and her father had arrived at the shop. She closed her eyes to allow a breeze to wash over her face. After months of misery, her heart was light. Other issues loomed, but at least one decision had been made.

When Trace had surprised her with a tour of the house they would share, the whole thing had become horrifyingly real. During that awkward ride back to Poplar Avenue from the building site, her thoughts were too scattered for her to speak, but she vowed to confess the truth. That resolution had opened the floodgates, and other choices that had been tormenting her quickly crystallized. It was high time she lived her own life as she saw fit.

Her stomach fluttered at the thought of the Curly Q patio lunch with Evangeline, a new Friday tradition that had started when the weather had become reliably pleasant. One of those other decisions involved Evangeline. Would she accept?

Callie Jane opened the alley door and entered the gravel parking lot, sunglasses and lunch bag in hand. A row of daffodils dipped in the breeze along the old stone wall that made up the far side of the alleyway. The maple that blessed her daddy's truck with shade in the scorching summer was sending out tentative celadon leaves. The forsythia had fully embraced the notion of spring and was showing off a riot of tiny lemon-yellow blossoms. She turned her face toward the sun. Earth's life was being renewed in Spark, and just maybe, so was hers.

"Are you planning on sunbathing or eating lunch?" Evangeline motioned her over to the small concrete slab behind the Curly Q and pulled out a chair from Queenie's patio set. She pointed to the *Gazette* lying on the table. "Two Creeper incidents the same week. Barbara Ricketts was in this morning and says her husband has questioned Tiny Hendricks twice. I do Mrs. Hendricks's hair, and she came in last week with her eyes all puffy and red, like she'd been crying." She grimaced. "Even following the sheriff's orders to keep windows closed and blinds drawn, I'm a little nervous to live alone."

"Maybe you don't have to live alone, if you like the plan I've come up with."

"Lay it on me."

Callie Jane popped the lid of her Tupperware bowl of salad. "I'm going to break my engagement. Trace is doing a great job as assistant manager, and if his daddy fires him because he's not engaged anymore, well, then that's got to be between the two of them." She paused for a moment, then nervously smiled as she spoke the next words, trying them on for size. "And I think I'm moving to California."

Evangeline nodded her approval. "I'm glad about calling off the wedding. His dad's not stupid. I've seen so many great improvements to the store. No way he'd fire Trace." She grinned. "And so cool about California."

"I've written to your brother for some advice."

"He'll be glad to help."

"I'm excited about doing it." She chewed a bite of lettuce. "Well, maybe doing it."

"What's stopping you?"

"My father. He's asking me to make decisions about stuff he's always handled. It's like he's working for me, instead of the other way around. Things must be worse with his health than he's letting on."

"I get that. But shouldn't you do what feels right for you?"

Callie Jane sighed. "I'll figure it out." She turned to Evangeline. "There's one more thing, and it involves you."

"Spill."

"First, I am going to buy a car. It'll have to be something really cheap, but I've looked in the Nashville classifieds and have found one I can afford. Then, instead of moving to Cold Spring—that's the ridiculous name my mother has dreamed up for the new house—I'll put *my* stuff in *my* new car and move to *my* new home, then start saving to move to California. Even if I don't go, it'll be good to have a little nest egg." She tucked her long hair behind her ears. "Here's where you come in. You said the rent on your place is high, and, well . . . so . . . I was wondering, could I be your roommate? I'd pay half the rent, of course, and whatever other bills."

Evangeline whooped. "Love it! We'll have a blast. I'm not making much yet at the Curly Q. Splitting the expenses will really take some pressure off me."

"Mind if I plant some flowers around the front door and by the back patio? I'm always happier when I've got my hands in the dirt."

"Sure thing."

Evangeline handed Callie Jane one of her cookies. "Good things come in threes. You're buying a car, calling off the engagement, and moving in with me. Care to add a fourth," she asked softly, "like telling your dad about not running the Emporium?"

"I haven't figured that out yet." Callie Jane glanced over at the brick building, her father's palace and her prison. "Telling him I'm moving away is the one thing that is gonna break my heart and his, but since I still have to iron out the details and get some money saved, I'm hoping to put it off for a bit." Callie Jane checked her watch. "I best be gettin' back."

Evangeline carefully folded her aluminum foil and tucked it inside her bag. "Call about the car when you have a chance, and if it's still available, we'll hop in Lady Liberty and go tomorrow afternoon. I get off work at three o'clock." Evangeline stood and hugged her. "I'm proud of you, Cal. Hey, are you okay with a nickname? I hate it when people call me Angie without asking."

"Sure. Callen is my real first name, supposedly given to the firstborn of every generation on my mother's side, but I've never heard of anyone else stuck with it. My parents always called me Callie Jane, but I like Cal too."

"All right, Cal it is, for a girl who's moving to *Cal*-ifornia. I hope you are proud of yourself."

Callie Jane realized with a jolt that she *was* proud of herself. She inhaled deeply, savoring the freshness of the air. Spring had sprung loose, and so had Callie Jane Jarvis.

Back at the shop, her father was at his desk, circling garage sales in the Nashville paper.

"Hey, Daddy, I need to talk with you about something. It's kinda important."

"Of course. Hang on a minute." He struggled to his feet and went to the sales counter. Reaching under the register, he extracted a "Back in a Few Minutes" sign and hung it on the door. He waddled back to his desk and pulled out Callie Jane's chair for her.

"I'm breaking my engagement to Trace."

"Why?" His voice was sharp. "If he's hurt you, he'll be answering to me."

She shook her head. "Nothing like that."

His brows were knitted. "But I thought this was the plan. You don't love him?"

She twisted the tiny gold ring still on her finger. "I *do* love him, but as a friend and nothing more. Everybody expected us to get married and I just went along with it, but I've realized marrying Trace would be a mistake."

"You and Trace have been buddies since you was both learning to ride tricycles. I can see where you've felt pushed into an engagement, and I'm sorry for any part I played in that. But are you sure? He's a good man."

Callie Jane blinked back tears as she saw the love and concern on her father's face.

"I think I just saw the answer," he said. "Trace isn't the one for you, so you're right to call things off. Never settle, Callie Jane. If you long for something with all your heart, then I'll be the first one cheering you on while you try your best to get it. But don't ever do something because you think it's what's expected of you, and not what you *want* to do." He ran his hands through his hair. "Being married is hard. Every life has its bitter with its sweet, but don't chain yourself to a lifetime of bitter, missing out on all the sweet the world has to offer." With a wistful look on his face, he looked down the aisle of the Emporium, its pin-straight inventory waiting for someone to come poking around for a pot holder or garden gnome. Regret tinged his words. "Trust me on that one."

"I dread telling him. He has a whole life planned for us."

"Better a broken engagement than a divorce. Just tell him the truth. Be honest and it will all be okay."

"Not marrying Trace is only half of it." She looked away, then back at her father. "I'm not moving to Mama's new house. I'm renting Evangeline's spare room instead."

"I'm not sure that's a good idea. Spark may be small, but there's still crime here. And the Creeper hasn't been caught yet." Her father paused. "Doesn't she live on Stadler Court?"

Callie Jane nodded. "Some of the kids in school called anyone who lived out there a Stadler. I overheard so many mean things being said about them in the lunchroom and on the playground. And now I'm one of them."

"It's wrong to call names, but I can't help but be worried about you living there."

"I'll be careful. I promise."

"Maybe you could find a room to rent from one of our neighbors. We could ask around at church." He took Callie Jane's hands. "That'd be safer."

"Probably so. But I've found a place I'm happy with that I can afford, and it's time I make my own decisions."

Her father sighed. "Okay, Callie Jane."

She could barely encircle her father's body to hug him. "I love you, Daddy," she said, even as she flinched over her lack of honesty about running the Emporium. Her final piece of news, that last bit of truth-telling, would have to wait. She couldn't break her fiancé's heart and her father's heart at the same time.

As she settled back into her chair, a breeze from the open window riffled pages of the *Nashville Banner* her father had discarded in the trash. A headline from the Entertainment page shouted at her.

BEATLES COMING TO TENNESSEE
The Beatles have announced the cities for their 1966
American tour. The Fab Four will be performing at
Mid-South Coliseum in Memphis for two shows on
August 19.

The Beatles. *Her* Beatles. All the way from England. On August 19, instead of enduring a rehearsal for her wedding the next day, she would be in the Memphis Coliseum, cheering as her favorite band performed. She tore the article from the paper and tucked it into her pocket, then counted out the days on her Beatles calendar until she would be in their presence.

· · · · · · · · · ·

The next afternoon Evangeline and Callie Jane followed the directions Callie Jane had scribbled on the back of an envelope to the location of her potential new car, about thirty minutes west of town. After a few miles of companionable silence, Callie Jane said, "Can I ask you something personal?" After Evangeline nodded, Callie Jane said, "How did you know you were a lesbian?"

Evangeline was quiet for a moment. "When I was younger, I wasn't like the other girls, giggling over some boy or dreaming of being a wife. It wasn't that I didn't like boys; it was just that I didn't see why my friends were making such a fuss. And then in high school, I got my first crush on a girl in my science class, Genevieve Calder. I was so confused, but also so happy at the same time. We had a couple of dates that summer, keeping it all a secret, of course. And then I met Becky and fell madly in love. I realized who I truly was for the very first time. I've never looked back."

"You're brave to think for yourself like that."

"And what would I be if I didn't think for myself?" Evangeline shook her head. "Don't get me wrong. It hasn't been easy. My parents kicked me out, which was awful. It was probably time for me to leave, but maybe don't tell me I'm no longer your daughter."

Evangeline glanced at her for a moment before returning her eyes to the road. "And now can I ask you something? How do you think Spark is going to deal with finding out I'm a lesbian?"

Callie Jane gazed out the window as they passed tobacco fields, handed down through families for generations. "Spark can be a wonderful place to live. If you get sick, or a family member dies, you can hardly get into your own kitchen for all the food people bring over." She tightened her ponytail. "But people around here like things that are predictable. When a person's different, some folks get scared. During my ninth-grade year at Spark High, we had a new math teacher who flunked one of her students. He skipped her class and never studied, so of course he failed, but he got revenge by starting a rumor she was a lesbian. I don't know everything that happened, but people were hateful. She ended up leaving town in the middle of the school year." Callie Jane glanced at Evangeline's expressionless face. "Maybe a big city would be a better choice for you and Becky."

Evangeline's voice was soft. "That's what we thought at first. One weekend last year Becky and I went to Chicago. Becky wanted to see the Field Museum of Natural History. She has a weird obsession with dinosaurs. Anyway, we were strolling down Michigan Avenue when I forgot for a minute we were in public and I kissed her cheek. Some guy stopped his car, jumped out, and yelled that he wanted to kill us both for being so disgusting.

Scared us both, badly. Turns out it's a *person* thing, not a *place* thing. When we were dreaming about being together one day, Becky suggested Spark. I was always talking about how I loved that visit to Aunt Arden's when I was a kid. Becky figured wherever we go we'll be judged, so why not go someplace that makes me happy? We decided to try it."

"I'll be honest, Evangeline. I'm nervous for y'all living in Spark."

Without turning her head, she answered, "I'm nervous about me and Becky living anywhere."

The friends rode silently for at least a mile. Callie Jane finally spoke. "Once people get to know you, I hope they'll see that you and Becky are just regular people." Callie Jane put on her sunglasses and added, "The dinosaur thing, though. I wouldn't mention that. Some folks around here say dinosaurs aren't real because they're not in the Bible." She grinned. "So that's what you're working with."

They arrived at the farm advertising the Volkswagen for sale. Evangeline turned off Lady Liberty's engine as they both stared at the faded white Beetle sitting in a field. Rust spots dappled the body like a metal Holstein cow, and a "See Rock City" bumper sticker covered most of a sizable ding. They approached the car cautiously. Callie Jane peered in the window, eyeing matted baby-blue shag carpeting covering the floor, dashboard, and part of the ceiling. Years of sunshine had faded the dashboard carpet in striated waves, from seafoam green to aqua to azure. A coordinating blue fur enrobed the steering wheel, and grass sprouted through a hole the size of one of her Beatles' singles in the floorboard.

Evangeline spoke first. "Whoo-boy. I can see why she's so cheap. You'll need to come up with a groovy name for this one."

She giggled. "And remember, it's supposed to make the car feel special, so no going with Piece of Shit or Rolling Repair Bill."

Callie Jane stood motionless, rooted to the patch of dirt beneath her feet. She had imagined something cute and sporty, maybe not in perfect condition but at least recognizable as a vehicle. Could a car droop?

Evangeline moved to her friend's side. "I've had to learn a lot about cars, and I can teach you. The basic stuff is pretty easy. As long as she's running, we can make this work."

A man approached, letting his screen door slam behind him. "Afternoon, ladies. Here she is." He snatched a faded "For Sale— Cheap" sign from underneath a windshield wiper and offered a test drive. To Callie Jane's surprise, the motor started right up. She pushed the bridge of her sunglasses closer to her face, gripped the fuzzy blue steering wheel, and took a quick spin, with the power of the engine matching the power surging through her veins. Freedom was loud and had a bit of a roar to it.

As she rolled down the window, the handle came off in her hand. She slowed enough to pop it back into place and kept driving. The car was more suited for the junkyard than the open road, but it ran well and the price was right, so she handed over the cash and drove back to Spark, straight to her parents' house, with Evangeline following closely behind to make sure she got there safely.

Callie Jane parked the car in her parents' driveway and gave herself a pep talk. She was a grown woman and needed to act like it. No more asking permission to live her own life, and no more making decisions based on how other people would react. As she looked at the simple house she had lived in since she was a baby, she hesitated. She knew moving out was the right decision, but she hadn't expected the wave of nostalgia that stopped her from getting out of the car. Images of celebrating birthdays, planting flowers in the garden, and making waffles with her daddy on Saturday mornings spun in her head. Opening presents on Christmas morning, losing her first tooth . . . it had all happened right there. She scowled. *Either you can grow up and run your own life, or you can stay an obedient little kid, doing whatever your mommy says.*

Tapping on the horn drew her mother to the window. She marched out to the driveway, hands on her hips. Callie Jane hopped out of the driver's side, hoping the confident smile she conjured up would distract her mother from her quivering knees.

"What in the world is this thing?" Her mother's arms were crossed against her body.

You can do this, Callie Jane. "Isn't it great?" Her voice shook only a little.

Her mother took a step toward Callie Jane. "Very funny. Now get it out of the driveway before the neighbors see it. They'll think this heap belongs to us."

Callie Jane squared her shoulders, bracing for the barrage that was bound to come. "It belongs to *me*. This is my new car."

"That is not a car. It's a shell of a car. Take it back to the junk-yard."

"No."

Shock crossed her mother's face. "What did you just say?"

Her voice was stronger now. "I said no."

"Why do you even need a car? You ride with your father in to work, and you can use Trace's truck."

Here it comes. Knowing this moment had been coming did not make forming the words any easier. "I'm moving out."

"Of course you are. We all are."

"No, Mama. I am moving to my own place."

Her mother cocked her head. "Is this because of that squabble we had when I told you to change out of that baggy beige dress before church? Whatever is going on, you are overreacting."

"This has nothing to do with my clothes, except that I am taking them with me. I'm moving out." Callie Jane pushed past her mother, marched to her old bedroom, and picked up the box marked *Callie Jane Yellow Bedroom*. "And I'm not marrying Trace."

"Are you having some kind of stroke?"

She faced her mother. "I'm fine. Actually, I'm better than I've ever been."

Her mother's voice was sharp. "What has gotten into you?"

"A backbone." Callie Jane gave the front door a swift kick and stepped onto the porch.

"You're confused." Her mother ran her hands through her hair, skewing her beehive. "You need to listen to me."

"What I *need* is to make my own decisions. You've been making them for me way too long." She opened the car's door and dropped the box on the passenger seat. "They may be bad decisions, even terrible, but they're mine to make. I know you love me, and I love you, but you've got to let me go."

Callie Jane loaded up the rest of her boxes, climbed into her car, and closed the Beetle's door, jiggling the door handle up and a little to the left to secure it. She pulled onto Poplar Avenue, leaving her mother standing in the driveway.

Laughing, she raised her fist in triumph, brushing the furry carpeting as she shouted, "We're out of here, Shelly!"

Chapter 13

Posey

FOR THREE DAYS, Posey had watched out the window, certain her daughter would come home, begging forgiveness for her defiance. And for three days, Posey had been disappointed. Time to take matters into her own hands. She got in the Cadillac and drove to Market Street.

Inside the Emporium her husband and daughter stood next to an enormous box with cookware all around them, acting like nothing was wrong. The tall pile marked *Frying Pans* teetered, threatening to tumble to the floor. Vern held a clipboard in his hand, while Callie Jane dutifully called out the prices.

Vern's eyebrows shot up when he spotted her. "What brings you down here on inventory day?"

She set her alligator handbag on the counter and, ignoring her husband's question, faced her daughter. "You and I are going to have a conversation, but first, I need to speak to your father."

Vern handed Callie Jane the clipboard. "Could you check the back for any more boxes? One might be hidin' under the shelves." Callie Jane shot her father a sympathetic look and headed for the storeroom.

Posey's words were clipped. "We've had a phone call from your cousin Phyllis. Seems her daughter, Joan, had a baby, and they're baptizing it in April, or maybe she said May. They've asked us to come."

Vern clapped his hands together. "Oh, how wonderful. Boy or girl?"

"I have no idea. And we're not going to Scranton. Those people mocked my accent, asking me to say *y'all* and *I reckon* like I was some kind of *Howdy Doody* puppet. I'm not giving them a second opportunity to humiliate me." She tugged the waist of her shirtdress. "Our excuse will be we're too busy with the wedding."

"The wedding?"

"Yes. Your daughter's wedding. August 20, remember?" Noting his puzzled look, she added, "She's getting the jitters, that's all. Cold feet are to be expected with someone as high-strung as Callie Jane."

"Callie Jane is not high-strung." His tone was sharp. "She's callin' off the wedding, and I say good for her. It's best for her and Trace both. Sure, they'll be upset for a little while, but they'll get over it."

She turned toward the storeroom and took a step. His voice deepened. "Leave her be."

"We're already on Brother Cleave's calendar, and I've told people the wedding's August 20, so it's too late to cancel. The dress is almost finished, and I've paid a deposit to the florist. There's going to be a wedding." She stomped to the curtain blocking off the storeroom. "Come out here, Callie Jane. We need to have a—"

"I said, leave her be."

"Callie Jane is my daughter, Vern Jarvis, and I will speak with her whenever I want to."

Vern raised his eyebrows. "*Your* daughter?"

She rolled her eyes. "Oh, all right. *Our* daughter."

Posey turned and called out, "Callie Jane!" Callie Jane parted the storeroom curtain and looked expectantly at her. "I need to speak to you privately. Come outside."

Vern's voice filled the room. "She's busy. We need to get back to this inven—"

"It's okay, Daddy. I've been expecting this."

Callie Jane stepped into the alley. Posey followed behind her, fuming.

Gesturing to the empty spot beside Vern's truck, she said, "At least you got rid of that hideous contraption you called a car." She drew a sharp breath and began. "I do not know what is going on, young lady, but you had better start talking." She pointed to the beauty shop next door. "Does Evangeline play a part in this? You've been spending a lot of time with her."

Posey saw the defiance flashing in Callie Jane's eyes. "I'm doing my own thinking."

"Have you told Trace yet?" When Callie Jane didn't immediately answer, she added, "Oh Lord, you have. Go find Trace right this minute, beg him to still marry you, and then come back home. We are moving *as a family* to Cold Spring, where you will live until your wedding."

Callie Jane straightened her shoulders. "No."

Posey sighed. Callie Jane was completely unmanageable, and she felt her tenuous grasp on her daughter slipping away. Time to change tactics. "Did he behave in an ungentlemanly manner? With it being this close to the wedding, just go ahead and give him what he wants and he'll forget you ever quarreled. You'll be walking down the aisle in no time."

A disgusted look crossed Callie Jane's face. She spoke quietly, with a steady voice. "No."

Posey sighed. "No to which part?"

"No to all of it! No, I haven't told him yet, and no, I'm not go-ing to manipulate Trace." Her voice grew louder. "And no, I'm not moving to Cold Spring. This must be hard for you to hear, but the wedding is off." She lifted her chin. "And I am renting a room from Evangeline on Stadler Court."

Posey froze. "Where?"

"You heard me. Stadler Court."

Posey felt a mix of shock and revulsion as her own childhood days on Stadler Court came rushing back to her. "I only want what's best for you. My whole life has been dedicated to raising you. Don't you see you can have so much more than I ever had?" She began to speak softly. "Being Mrs. Trace Humboldt means you'll be pro-vided for. People will respect you. You will have money, social status, and hopefully children. That's what every woman dreams of, Callie Jane, and it can all be yours if you play your cards right." She bit her lip. "And don't move to Stadler Court."

"I have told you the truth, and now I need to be honest. Those are the things you want for me, not what I want for myself. I get to decide what I'm doing with my life, not you." She took a step away from her mother. "I appreciate the sacrifices you have made for me. I know this is not what you want, but it's what *I* want, and that's what counts." Posey stiffened as her daughter hugged her. "You may not believe me, but I love you." Posey felt Callie Jane's arms release her. "I need to go, Mama." Callie Jane turned and walked toward the Emporium door.

Posey watched her daughter disappear from view and then whispered, "I love you too."

Her purse. She had left her stupid purse that held her car keys and flask on the sales counter. She crossed to the Emporium's back door, needing two shoves to get it open. She snatched up her bag and was halfway down the center aisle when Vern said,

"I called cousin Phyllis and accepted the invitation for the baptism. It's May 8. You can come or not, but I will be there. And it's a girl, just like Joanie wanted. Seven pounds, six ounces. Her name's Emily."

Posey slammed the door on her way out.

. . . .

The gravel sprayed as she hit the brakes in front of her new home. She surveyed the wide porch of her sanctuary, Cold Spring, as she threw the Cadillac into Park. Her mouth curled into a smile, recalling how Vern had scolded her about the name, reminding her that cold springs could be found all over Spark. Cold Spring referred to a season, not a water source. Her affair with CJ during the cold spring of 1947 was the happiest time of her life, when Posey Burch had the world by the tail, living the life she was meant for.

She slid from the car, twisting her ankle as she stepped on the tiny stones. A paved driveway would be better, but that would cost a fortune. For now, she'd have to get by with Aunt Milbrey's pea gravel.

Her first stop was the kitchen for ice, retrieved from the freezer compartment of the tiny refrigerator whose motor was humming as reliably as a baritone in a barbershop quartet. She hadn't given up on that Foodarama, but it would have to wait until she wasn't paying so many repair bills.

Her next stop was the library. Mercifully, gin never went bad, so she could enjoy the hoard of Gordon's her aunt had so kindly left behind.

She studied the intricately carved antique secretary as she drank. It reminded her of something, but what was it? A memory of a long-ago trip to Nashville with Vern tiptoed into her brain, when they had stopped by an antique shop on Harding Road to see what a fancy junk store looked like. As Vern dug through the landscape paintings in the front, she had wandered to the back, drawn to an enormous slant-top secretary. The price tag had made her eyes pop, but she pretended to be interested to learn more about it.

"And, of course, there are secret compartments," the saleslady had explained. *"Every secretary has hidden drawers and false fronts to hide valuables. This one has eight. Here, let me show you."* The woman had deftly pulled away what had appeared to be solid columns. *"Document drawers to hide your valuable papers."* She opened a door and slid what Posey had thought to be the solid back to reveal a space large enough for even a millionaire's cache of jewels. *"And the big things go here."* Posey had been mesmerized, making a mental note to check any secretary she encountered.

Now, soaring at least eight feet tall right in front of her was such a piece.

After resting the drop-down top on its slats, she surveyed the dozen or so potential hiding places. She grasped the twin fluted columns flanking the center of the desk, holding her breath in anticipation as they slid forward. Peering inside, she cursed. Nothing. She pulled out every drawer. Empty. She slid the false-back privacy panel away from its delicately carved walnut frame to reveal a cavernous, empty hole. *Damn it.*

Grabbing her bottle, she went through the butler's pantry on her way to the secret office. Silver bowls rested on the glass shelves above the soapstone counter, while a regiment of silver trays, black with tarnish, stood in a dozen or so vertical compartments. Aunt Milbrey may have been as crazy as a bag of squirrels, but she'd been a rich bag of squirrels and hadn't minded spending her husband's fortune on luxuries.

After popping the door, she changed into her work clothes, then entered the conservatory, grimacing at the lingering smell.

Raising her glass, she toasted, "To Milbrey, my beloved, eccentric aunt or cousin or whatever. You *were* a silly goose, and there's still no such thing as a catio." The heat flushed her cheeks as she recalled being corrected. *"She who owns the house names the rooms."*

"Now it's a conservatory."

The room stood empty, as she had long since hauled the cat paraphernalia to the trash. She had a lengthy list of needs to transform it into the conservatory of her dreams—bamboo furniture with tropical-patterned cushions, a baker's rack crammed full of exotic orchids, and one of those palm frond ceiling fans. Garage sale season would soon be in full swing, and she'd keep a sharp eye open for sunroom furniture advertisements. If that didn't pan out, maybe Nashville Patio would have an end-of-season sale. That wouldn't be until after Labor Day, though, and the reunion was in May. She'd have to watch the classifieds.

Posey had left the kitchen pantry as the last area to clean. The idea of pitching out ancient canisters of oatmeal and sleeves of petrified gingersnaps repulsed her. Rodents could be nesting in paper towels, or roaches might swarm out of pasta boxes. She shuddered, tossed back the last of her drink, and headed into the kitchen. Grabbing a garbage bag and a pair of gloves from under the sink, she began removing items from the shelves. A bug scuttled from under a rusty can of tuna, sending gooseflesh up her arms.

A large gold tin, about the size of a toaster, caught her eye. Oddly placed, it sat at the back of the otherwise empty top shelf. She pulled down the box and was greeted by the face of a young lady wearing a crown, looking very much like the young Victoria of the bedtime stories she'd told to Callie Jane. *Empress Shortbread Cookies*, the label proclaimed. She turned the tin to read the slogan—*Fit for Royalty*—and heard the unmistakable sound of sliding coins. Ripping off her gloves, she tore open the lid.

Gasping, she took a half step back. Inside lay stacks of hundred-dollar bills, each neatly secured with a yellow rubber band. One bundle was loose. Most were hundreds, although a few smaller bills lay on top. Some loose change rested on the bottom of the tin. Swaying, she closed her eyes and willed herself not to faint. With weak knees, she barely made it to the kitchen table before collapsing into the chair.

She counted the stacks four times before getting the same number twice. Forty-three thousand, one hundred thirty-two dollars, along with the thirteen cents that had saved her from throwing away a fortune. She looked to her right, then to her left. Was she certain she was alone? Rising from the table, she steadied herself with trembling hands and rushed to the front door, tripping on a rug in her haste. She peered through the sidelights and twisted the deadbolt, then bumped the wall of the hallway as she hurried to check the back door. Locked. *Thank God.* She returned to the kitchen, closed the curtains above the sink, and counted the stacks one more time. *Is this mob money?* She sat back in the chair and took a few careful breaths to calm her nerves. *Who cares? It's mine now.*

She willed her pounding heart to slow down. It took both of her shaking hands to hold the Gordon's bottle steady enough to pour. *Well, well, well. Aunt Milbrey was the silly goose that laid the golden egg.*

She stumbled to the freezer for more ice. As she shut the door, she decided to order a Foodarama the first minute she could get to a phone, and to make sure Barbara Ricketts heard about it the second minute. Her hand shook, splashing gin as she topped off her glass, holding it aloft to watch the clear liquid swirl down its ice cube obstacle course.

The ramifications of her find soaked into her body like the gin coursing through her bloodstream. *Finally I can quit being my mother and live like my father. I can shed the last stench of Stadler Court still clinging to me and embrace the patrician world of my father.*

Her shoulders tightened as she flashed back to the only time she had spoken with her father. After a thunderous fight with her mother, a thirteen-year-old Posey had packed a bag, taken her mother's car, and driven to the Belle Meade address she had copied from one of the sporadic checks sent to her mother.

A man had opened the door and stared at the teen on his doorstep. To Posey, it was like looking in a mirror. The same dark hair and the prominent jawline that looked so rugged on a man and so determined on a girl were unmistakable. He was her father.

"I've come to live with you."

"Look, miss, I have no idea who you are."

"I'm Posey." When he did not respond, she added, "Don't you recognize me from the picture Mama sends you every year? I'm your daughter."

He moved onto the slate landing and shut the door quietly behind him. Glancing back toward his house, he hissed, "My wife is inside, and she's not going to know anything about this." He reached into his pocket and pulled out his wallet. "How much?"

Posey stared at his wallet and then at him. "This isn't about money. It's about loving me." She stepped forward. "Mama says you love me, that you always wished we could be a family. I've always loved you too." She gestured to her suitcase. "I've come to live with you."

His response was branded onto her heart. "Your mother has told you a fairy tale. She has never sent me any photograph of you. You are not my daughter, not in any way that matters. I do not love you. We are not a family, and you are never going to live with me. The money I pay that woman was my insurance that you'd stay out of my life forever. Now leave before someone sees you."

She shook the seminal memory of her childhood from her head and returned her attention to the matter at hand—her newly found fortune. That money could get her a whole suite of conservatory furniture, with custom fabric and finishes. She could hire a fleet of workmen to finish the repairs. And a gardener. She looked at the towering stacks of cash. Several gardeners. She toasted her good fortune with another slug of gin. CJ would be in awe of the oasis of elegance she had created in a desert of mediocrity. She could practically feel the weight of the heavy diamond on her left-hand ring finger.

She checked her watch. *Damn it. Almost time to get home.* After all her celebrating, driving would be tricky. The last thing she needed was that idiot Sheriff Ricketts or his power-hungry son, Billy, pulling her over.

She poured tap water into her glass. *Very responsible, Posey.* She gazed at the bills as she sipped her water. Could it all really be hers? The lawyers had completed the paperwork that included the house and contents, with no mention of a cookie tin filled with cash, so they didn't know. *No one knows.*

She knew exactly where to hide it. Carrying the box like a regent's crown being ushered through Westminster Abbey on coronation day, she approached the secretary and slid open the largest hidden compartment, which perfectly accommodated the tin and its bundles of cash. She placed the thirteen cents into her pocket.

Chapter 14

Callie Jane

THE KITCHEN WAS bathed in sunlight. She still couldn't get used to the peaceful mornings, so different from the hectic start to her days at her parents' house. She stretched as she stumbled toward the alluring aroma of coffee, tucking her long hair behind her ears. Evangeline was already dressed for work, finishing the last bite of her breakfast.

"Did you sleep well?" Evangeline asked as she fanned herself.

"I thought I would be up all night, between it being so hot and worrying about what I'll say to Trace, but I slept great." She poured herself a cup of coffee. "Better than I have in months."

"I'm glad. You've been stewing about this way too long." Evangeline poured Muse's kibble into her bowl and deposited it on the floor. Grabbing the latest *Gazette* off the counter, she examined the front page. "The Creeper struck again. This time on Clover Road. Everybody knows about the sheriff's order, but it says here the victim couldn't sleep in the heat and decided to take her chances and open the window." Evangeline's voice was tense. "The sheriff needs to find that guy and arrest him."

"My mother says Mike Ricketts couldn't catch a tadpole in a mud puddle."

"That's pretty harsh."

"There's some kind of history between the two of them, but I don't know the story." She drained her cup. "And I don't want to know it."

"I don't blame you. So what's your plan for the day?"

"I'm talking to Trace after he finishes work this afternoon. Daddy gave me the day off so I could plan out what I'm gonna say."

"You nervous?"

"I am." Callie Jane dropped two pieces of bread into the toaster. "I babble when I get anxious, so I'm gonna practice and just hope it goes well."

"It will, Cal. Just be honest."

Callie Jane pushed her hair from her face. "This hair is making me bonkers. Maybe I should let you cut it."

Evangeline grinned. "I've been dying to take my scissors to that mane. No offense, but it makes you look about twelve. Whatcha got in mind?"

"I'd love some bangs, like Jane Asher."

"Who?"

"I forget not everyone is as obsessed as I am. Paul McCartney's girlfriend."

"Oh, got it. Although your roommate is not a Beatles fan, she is a hairdresser who can copy any style. Do you have a photo of her?"

"You're the best. Let me grab a picture," she said, heading for her room. She dug through a box of Beatles fan club newsletters and then triumphantly waved a photo of Jane Asher. "Found one!"

"Cool. Let's get those bangs happening."

Evangeline pursed her lips as she studied the picture, then combed Callie Jane's hair and began to cut. As a foot-long lock of hair fell to the tiled floor of the tiny bathroom, Callie Jane felt lighter and turned her head to peep in the mirror. Could a haircut make someone look British?

"Hey, hold still. You don't want crooked bangs."

"Sorry. Did you know in England they call bangs *fringe?*"

Evangeline grinned. "You really are obsessed. Just a couple more snips."

After Evangeline finished, Callie Jane swept the long strands of her hair from the bathroom floor, pausing every few swipes to admire her reflection.

After helping Muse down the three concrete steps to their patio for a quick potty, Evangeline headed off to work.

Callie Jane walked down the narrow hall to her bedroom. A chamber in Princess Victoria's palace could not have pleased her more. She'd had her own room at her parents' house, but this space was fully hers. She grinned. Living on the wrong side of the tracks wasn't so bad.

On her first day in her new room, she had pulled the Botticelli postcard of Venus from her flea market box and the Empress card from her tarot book and tucked them into the frame of the mirror hanging over her bureau. Now she studied herself in the mirror, flanked by two feminine ideals. Could it be that she was prettier with bangs? Or maybe it was the glow of freedom. *Good things come in threes is what Evangeline says.* She shook her head at her silliness, counting herself as a trio with Venus and the Empress. She stole another look in the mirror. *But still, I'm looking pretty good.* She reached into the drawer of her dresser and pulled out her Venus pendant and slipped it over her head. *Pretty darn good.*

She sat in silence at their kitchen table as she collected her thoughts. Muse limped over and nuzzled her hand as if offering

support. Trace got off work at four. She would be waiting for
him in the parking lot.

....

Seeing Trace's beat-up red truck made her heart race, and any
confidence she'd felt earlier evaporated like August dew in the
hot sun.

She nosed Shelly next to the truck and lay her head on the
steering wheel but immediately jerked back up. The blue fuzzy
material had a stench—a mixture of mold and glue—she hadn't
noticed before. *Great, I should have named her Smelly, not Shelly.*
"Sorry, Shell." She patted the dash. "We'll be okay. I've just got
to get through this."

She grabbed a bag of Cat Chow from the floorboard. She had
to be careful with her words. She tended to blurt things out without thinking when she was nervous or scared, and at that
moment she was both. Maybe more practice would help. "Trace,
we both know this isn't the right thing." She shook her head.
"You deserve someone who can love you completely." Food
rattled into two cat bowls as she scanned the woods for the feral
cats she called Gray Boy and Pearl, and Trace called Trouble and
Nuisance. "Trace, I can't marry you." None of it sounded right.
She sat at the employee picnic table outside the BuyMore, fear
drumming her spine as she picked at a crack in the wood.

She gulped at the sight of Trace walking out to his truck.
Sweat broke out in her armpits, and she briefly felt she might
vomit.

"Hey, Trace," she called, giving a half-hearted wave.

"Hey. What are you doing here?" He cocked his head, studying
her bangs. "You cut your hair. It's, uh, quite a change." Pointing

to her car, he said, "Someone abandoned this clunker right next to my truck. I'll have to call Harold at the filling station to haul it off."

"Um, that's my new car."

He looked at the rusted Volkswagen and then back at her. "That's yours? How much did they pay you to take it off their hands?"

"I bought it."

He shook his head. "It doesn't look safe. What if you're driving home one night and break down? We've got a maniac out there."

"Uh, can you sit down for a minute? I need to talk to you."

He plopped down on the bench across from her and frowned. "Uh-oh. This can't be good. Is Mama bugging you about a china pattern? She went to Castner-Knott the other day and wants to show you what she liked." Trace frowned. "I know she can be a lot to deal with sometimes, but she's just so excited."

"Um, no. Trace, I don't want any china. I mean, I don't want a wedding at all." She blinked as tears began to form.

"Really?" His smile stretched across his face. "I'm so glad."

"Huh?"

"We'll elope." He ran his hands through his hair. "Honestly, I'd prefer just running off, but I didn't want to spoil your dream of a fancy ceremony."

She shook her head. "No, Trace. It's not just the type of wedding. I don't want a wedding at all." She took a deep breath and continued. "You are my dear friend, but I am not in love with you."

He blinked at her. "Say what, now?"

"I am breaking our engagement. I'm so sorry." She wrestled the tiny diamond ring off her finger and set it on the splintered picnic table.

"I don't understand."

"We've been friends since we were born, and I hope I don't ever lose your friendship." She brushed her fingers across her unfamiliar bangs. "People always said we'd get married one day. I just assumed they were right and that it was meant to happen. When your mama was so excited and thought I'd said yes, I didn't want to embarrass you so I didn't say anything." She lowered her eyes. "That was a mistake. I led you on, and I regret that." Reluctantly, she returned her gaze to Trace. "You have your whole life figured out, and I have *nothing* figured out. I want to believe in my own dreams, not someone else's. I'm not exactly sure what those dreams are yet, but I'm going to find out." Tears stung her eyes. "I don't want that house. I don't want to stand behind you as you build your BuyMore empire, and please don't hate me, but I don't want to be your wife."

"You're calling off the wedding?"

"Yes."

Trace stared at her, stunned. Then a smile broke across his broad face. "Praise the Lord."

"Wait, what?"

"I don't want to marry you either."

Chapter 15

Posey

POSEY SPRANG FROM the bed. "It's moving day," she sang. The April 17 calendar square had been saturated with periwinkle stars for weeks, with a few vermilion ones filling in the blank spaces. Leaving the cap closed on the family fuschia pen had pinched her heart, but her stubborn daughter had some hard lessons coming up, and Posey had done her best.

Posey threw open the curtains. "It's finally here. Can you believe it?"

Lifting his tousled head from his pillow, Vern struggled to his elbows. "It's the only thing you've talked about for weeks, so yes, I can believe it."

"I barely remember Aunt Milbrey, and here I am, her sole heir, about to move into her mansion." She gave a Julie-Andrews-on-the-Austrian-mountaintop spin. "It's just like when Brother Cleave read from Romans last Sunday about the righteous being rewarded on earth. God 'will render to every man according to his deeds.'"

She didn't acknowledge her husband whispering, "Exactly," as she left the room, but she rolled her eyes as she pirouetted to the kitchen. As the coffee brewed, she gazed at the tiny window overlooking the carefully mulched area of their yard where Vern's tomatoes flourished every summer, twining through his father's rusty wire cages, bending with the weight of their fruit. He'd planted as usual two days prior, despite having resigned himself to moving.

"*This garden's had tomatoes put in every April 15 of its life, and I'm not breaking that tradition.*"

"*You can't pack a garden, so it's the Neals who'll benefit from your work, not you.*"

She hated that plot of soil. He and Callie Jane would spend hours out there, shutting her out completely. If Vern insisted on planting one at Cold Spring, she'd make sure she couldn't see it from the house.

She poured herself a cup of coffee, adding a splash from the vinegar bottle before tucking it inside the small *Kitchen* box sitting on the counter, containing only the family calendar, her set of Teflon pans, and some tea towels she thought looked French.

As soon as Vern emerged from the bathroom, she began barking instructions. "Put your razor and toothbrush in the box marked *Vern White—First Night Home*. With everything in a jumble during the move, we'll each have one box of essentials 'til we can get our things unpacked. It's genius." She sat on the foot of their bed. "I'll drive straight over to the house to make sure everything is in order." Truth be told, everything was already in order, but she wanted a few minutes alone at Cold Spring to admire all her hard work and celebrate her good fortune, but that was something Vern didn't need to know. "The movers will be here about eight, so you have to supervise them loading up, and I'll direct them where to put the boxes in the new house. Make sure they don't forget my vanity."

"No one could forget your vanity."

She shot her husband a look. "Some of us take pride in our appearance and do not let ourselves go. And I need you at the house by ten at the latest."

Vern threaded his belt through his pant loops. "I'm gonna wait 'til Hannah and Grady get here so I can remind them how to jiggle the front door key just right and where the fuse box—"

"Good Lord, Vern. They can figure all that out themselves." She snapped the clasp of her watch. "What time are they arriving?"

"Any second. They've been so excited, and when Hannah asked could they come this morning, I said yes. She 'bout squealed when I told her the tomatoes was already in and growing." His tired face lit up. "Callie Jane was so smart to suggest the Neals as tenants. A young couple, so in love and happy, with a little one on the way is just what this house needs."

"I just hope you're charging them enough."

"The rent's my business."

Her cheeks tightened. "I need to get going. Ten o'clock sharp."

Vern clipped on his tie. "After I get the Neals settled."

As she climbed into her Cadillac, she surveyed the tiny cottage she had lived in for almost twenty years. "I will never set foot into that run-down dump ever again." As she passed the mailbox with the hand-painted address, 4513 Poplar Avenue, she added, "Goodbye and good riddance to all the bad luck that stupid thirteen brought me."

Creekside Road was shaded with oaks and sycamores, dappling the sunlight as she drove to her new home. A bend in the road offered a panoramic view of a valley and Flat Rock Creek. Paradise.

She guided her car down the winding driveway and into the parking area, bordered by a long row of overgrown boxwoods. Stepping from the car, she said, "My house," out loud, still needing a bit of reassurance that it was, indeed, hers. "The grandest in Cooke County."

She licked her lips as she approached the massive door, smiling at the white impatiens cascading from glazed ceramic pots. An American flag affixed with a shiny brass bracket to a fluted column snapped smartly in the breeze, seeming to salute her as she approached the wood and glass front door. She stepped onto the sisal mat and twisted the key. "Welcome home, Posey Jarvis," she whispered.

Each of Cold Spring's rooms glowed with elegance, illuminated by the sun streaming through the dozens of freshly washed windows. She began her tour in the dining room, made resplendent by the newly polished mahogany double pedestal claw-foot table and matching breakfront. She frowned at the portrait of the breathtakingly beautiful woman over the sideboard. Was that really Milbrey? She waved her hand. It was her dearly departed aunt from now on. The only person who could correct her was busy sobbing in Alabama, still devastated by her sister's revenge.

She spun from room to room, twirling like a ballerina into the kitchen for a glass. Continuing her tour, she paused at the slant-top secretary for gin, then toasted the antique that held her most precious secret, the Empress tin of cash.

Could this day get any better? she wondered as she moved to the conservatory to check on her orchids. The nursery owner had called her showy cattleyas "the queen of orchids," but Posey had promoted them. She'd bought a dozen, to the delight of the shopkeeper, and nestled them onto a baker's rack *just so* to catch the sun. Posey nodded in satisfaction. A conservatory filled with the empress of orchids for the empress of Cooke County.

The conservatory was appointed with the most luxurious furnishings the patio store had to offer. She was particularly proud of procuring an intricate bamboo screen that looked exactly like one she had admired in a movie. Outrageous up-charges for custom fabrics and finishes had been a point of contention, but forking over the extra money had been worth it. Posey finished her drink and went to the front porch to await the movers, bending to pinch the price tag from the fern cradled in an elaborate wrought iron plant stand by the door. She settled into a wicker chair, her heart drumming with excitement.

The catch of grinding gears echoed down the driveway, and she clapped her hands as the truck trundled down the long drive. Finally.

Two men dressed in blue coveralls hopped out of the cab. "Miz Jarvis?" one of them drawled.

"That's correct. Come this way."

"Yes, ma'am." The men unhooked the latch and wrestled open the metal doors, each grabbing a box.

"Every box is marked with the paint color of the room it belongs in. She glanced at the boxes the men held. "The *Vern White* ones go in the bedroom on the left, and the *Posey Pink* ones belong in the bedroom on the right."

The vanity was the last item off the truck. She had chosen a spot for it under the window to take advantage of the natural light when applying her makeup, but once the movers had placed it there, she shook her head. "Could you just scooch it over about three feet to the left?" The second location also proved unacceptable, so she instructed the men to try the opposite wall. "You know what? Under the window was the perfect place after all. I should have trusted my instincts." Satisfied after the vanity was returned to its spot under the window, she said with a lilt in her voice, "There we go." Posey thought she detected a hint of sarcasm when the younger man asked, "Is this perfect? Because we want it to be exactly where you want it, right under the window like you said in the first place."

One of the movers handed her a clipboard and she scribbled her name at the bottom, then ran her hand that had held their germy pen down her skirt. The two folded dollar bills she was going to give the men as tips stayed in her pocket. *That was definitely sarcasm.*

Vern lumbered through the doorway, looking at the men making their hasty retreat, and whistled. "Whoo-boy. Those guys was sure sour."

She scowled. "Maybe they were counting on some help from the man of the house." He struggled out of his khaki jacket and hung it on the hall tree. "Where were you?"

He rubbed the back of his neck. "I told you where I'd be. At the house, getting the Neals settled."

He was probably with Miss Brass Button. She hated the idea of Vern believing he was getting away with something, but she also felt a prick of pride about her silence regarding her inside information. Knowledge was power, and she had plenty of both. The unevenness of it was delicious, knowing her husband's secret while he remained completely oblivious to hers.

He gripped the wooden stair rail as he ascended the steps. "Which room is ours?" He paused on the landing, struggling to catch his breath.

"I'll show you once we get up there."

As she stood by the room on the left, she gestured for Vern to enter. She watched as he slowly took in the boxes marked *Vern*, the handsome canopy bed, and a pair of Victorian chairs huddled on either side of a lone window like two biddies settled in for a good gossip. Vern turned to his wife. "I thought the moving guys was finished."

"They are."

"Then where's your stuff?"

"In my room, down the hall. It's only natural that I have the one with the bigger closet."

He shuffled to one of the chairs and sank into the brocade cushion. "What do you mean, *your* room?"

She had been dreading this moment. "You snore loud enough to wake the dead. And you complain about how I kick you during my nightmares. This way we'll both finally get a good night's sleep."

"You want separate bedrooms?"

"No, I don't *want* separate bedrooms. We *have* separate bedrooms. We lived in your parents' matchbox for almost twenty years, with me having no say about any of it. It's my turn now, and we have our own rooms." She tucked an errant strand of hair behind her ear. "It's really quite civilized. Jackie and John Kennedy had separate bedrooms."

"Look how it turned out for him. Not so good."

She clenched her jaw. "He didn't get assassinated because he and his wife slept in different beds."

He struggled to his feet, his face turning a blotchy red. "I never wanted this house. But I came because I made you a promise when I proposed that I'd make your dreams come true, and I'm a man of my word. But this is too much." He grappled with his *Vern White—First Night Home* box, staggering a little as he headed for the stairs. "If you're okay with separate rooms, then I figure you'll be okay with separate houses."

"You're leaving our home?"

"I'm leaving *your* home and going to *mine*. Somewhere I'm loved and wanted."

"What the hell does that mean?" She flinched as Vern gave her a sharp look and left without answering.

She watched from a window as Vern loaded his box into the truck, which would be parked at his mistress's house that night, a place he now called home.

Chapter 16

Callie Jane

EVANGELINE WAS POURING two cups of coffee into mismatched mugs. "I would have given anything to be an ant on that picnic table, listening to you break up with Trace." She snorted. "I still can't believe he said 'praise the Lord.' You must have just died." She giggled as she adjusted her Mary Quant–inspired miniskirt, a hand-sewn gift from Becky.

Callie Jane's eyes crinkled. "I know, right? There I was, thinking I was breaking his heart, and the whole time *he* was thinking marrying me was something he had to do. Right before I got to their house the night he proposed, his mama told him that *my* mother had told *her* that I had been sobbing for weeks about him not asking me to marry him yet. He was so upset about me crying that he just blurted out the proposal without really thinking it through." Two pieces of bread sprang from the toaster. "A complete and total lie, of course, but what else should I expect from my mother?"

Grabbing the tub of margarine from the fridge, she carried their breakfast to the table and glanced out their tiny kitchen window. "It says a lot about him that he was willing to honor his commitment, even though he felt it wasn't right either. He talked to Mr. Humboldt about calling it off, but his daddy told him he had to go through with it." She lowered her voice to a baritone. "'Humboldts keep their word, son.' Trace had made up his mind to be happy, to make *me* happy. And he really wants a wife and children, and he *does* love me, so he had been trying to look on the bright side. That's why he went a little nuts with the house and everything." She chewed thoughtfully. "Once we both realized the truth, we cracked up."

"So how did you leave it with him?"

"We hugged and said we'd always be friends, and then he kissed my cheek and I left."

Evangeline poured them each a second cup of coffee. "So what's next for you, Cal?"

The trill of the phone made them both jump. Evangeline grabbed the receiver, then frowned as she listened. "Oh, honey. I'm so sorry." She paused, shaking her head at whatever was being said on the other end of the line. "No, of course I'm coming. I know you can handle it yourself, but that's the whole point, isn't it? I'll be there this afternoon." She paused again, this time smiling. "I love you too."

"What's happened?" Callie Jane asked after Evangeline hung up the phone.

Tears sparkled in Evangeline's eyes. "Becky's mom has taken a turn for the worse. I need to go to Ohio." She rose from her chair and crouched beside Muse stretched out on the floor. Stroking her graying muzzle, she asked, "Could I leave her here with you?"

"Of course."

Evangeline gave her a grateful smile. "Her kibble is on the shelf. Put her bowl in its regular spot so she can find it. Remember, she's blind as a bat, but she'll do okay as long as you talk to her so she knows where you are."

"Don't worry, Mama. I'll take good care of her."

Watching Evangeline sail out of the driveway gave Callie Jane a rush of excitement. She was alone, in charge of the house and everything in it. *This independence thing may work out.*

She walked over to her record collection and thumbed through her Beatles singles. She selected the one with "She's a Woman" on one side and "I Feel Fine" on the other. Which side to choose? She smiled and put on "I Feel Fine" and danced across the den. She was an adult, living on her own. Patting Muse as she napped in a sunbeam, Callie Jane spoke in a soft tone, telling Muse she had to go to work. "I'll be back at lunchtime to let you out."

· · · · · · · · · ·

As she stepped inside the shop, she knocked her shin against a cardboard box in the doorway. "Hey, Daddy." No response. A pot of coffee was always on when he was there, but the stained carafe sat empty. Sweat prickled her armpits. Something was wrong. "Daddy?"

"Hey, hon," he croaked. Her father was hunched over in the tweed recliner. His hair was plastered to his forehead, his shirt-front darkened with sweat. "Just needed a minute, that's all."

She ran her hand across her father's damp face. "I'll call Doc Grisham."

He struggled to a sitting position. "Just lost my breath. Could you bring me some water?"

She rushed to her father with a tall glass. "Don't drink too fast. Take your time." She watched anxiously as he sipped the water. "How about some aspirin?"

"No thanks, sweetie." He ran one hand through his hair. "I tried to carry in a heavy box, and it took the wind right outta me. I just need to sit here a minute." Glancing up, he smiled.

"You've got on my favorite dress. I love those little red flowers sprinkled all over the white cotton."

"Please don't change the subject. You need to go back to the doctor."

She was expecting her father to argue, but instead he answered, "I did. Grisham says whatever's going on with me is beyond what he can diagnose in Spark. He referred me to some fancy cardiologist in Nashville, Dr. Ryan. Grisham said he's the best heart specialist in Tennessee."

Callie Jane's voice was full of concern. "Why didn't you tell me? And when do you see this doctor?"

"No sense in worrying you until I knew what was going on. I see him May 11. Doc Grisham had to pull some strings to get me an appointment. They went to med school together."

"I'm going with you."

"There's no need for that. Besides, I need you here running the shop."

"We're going together to that appointment. The Emporium can be closed for a few hours."

"All right, then." His shoulders sagged, and a shaft of morning sunlight highlighted his deeply etched forehead. "To tell you the truth, I'll be glad for your company." He sat a little straighter. "But I've got two rules. One, I'm not agreeing to any surgery, and you can't argue against me on that."

"Let's wait to see what this Dr. Ryan says before we decide anything. What's the second rule?"

He looked her in the eye. "Not one word to your mama about this. You know how she loves to awfulize."

She grinned. "Now *that* I can agree to."

"Thank you for keeping my secrets," he said, studying her for a moment. "I like your bangs. They make you look older."

"I was trying to look like Jane Asher."

"I'm not sure who that is, but she'd be the lucky one to look like *you*." He wiped his neck with his handkerchief. "Could you help me with that box in the doorway? There's a Dutch oven in there I want to put in the window."

She got the message. No talk of doctors or heart attacks. At least for now.

. . . .

They worked silently at their two desks, with only a couple of customers to break up the morning. When lunchtime rolled around, she explained she needed to let Muse out. "Do you want to eat early so I can keep you company? I'd hate for you to have your lunch alone." She noticed the empty spot on his desk that for every morning as far back as she could remember housed the plaid lunch box brought from home. "Did you forget your sandwich?" She smiled. "Or was Mama too busy to buy tuna, with all the commotion of moving?"

"Uh, no. She didn't . . . I wasn't . . . I mean, I thought I'd eat at the Blue Plate today."

Something was up. Her father hadn't eaten lunch at the diner in years. *"Can't. Savin' for retirement,"* he'd say if she ever suggested it.

Callie Jane pondered what was going on with her father as she walked home. Unlocking the door, she called, "Muse, it's me." The ancient Lab came lumbering out of Evangeline's bedroom. Her tail wagged in greeting, and Callie Jane bent to caress her gray snout. "I thought we'd eat together on the patio."

Two rusted screws were all that held the handle of the sliding glass door in place. The landlord had promised to fix it, but for now, a chipped blue broom handle was the only way to keep it secure. She removed the stick and tugged the door open, then walked Muse down the concrete steps to the bistro table. "Just one more step and you've got it."

As she devoured her grilled cheese sandwich, she glanced around the twenty feet or so of the fenced-in backyard, her eyes lingering on the new bed of daisies, transplanted from her father's garden. Having something growing in the earth, planted by her own hand, made the run-down house a home.

Was that a wasp nest in the corner of the window? It was. She'd have to knock it down so a wasp wouldn't get in the house. With all the Creeper trouble, she was grateful the slope of the backyard meant her window stood about ten feet from the ground. Even Tiny Hendricks wasn't that tall.

She refilled Muse's water dish in the kitchen, carefully returning the bowl to its exact spot. She splashed her fingers in the water. "It's right here, girl," she said before giving the dog an extra pat and heading out the door.

Phil Brody's truck pulled into the Emporium's parking lot just as she arrived back at the shop. He hopped out of the truck with a shopping bag in his hand. "Hey, Callie Jane. I was just picking up some crocheted afghans from one of my best suppliers. People are crazy for anything handmade these days. Anyway, she asked if I knew anyone who could use some yarn. Her husband bought it for her, but it's too thin for what she needs. I remembered your daddy saying y'all are always looking for yarn. It was free. Want it?"

"Absolutely!" She took the bag from Mr. Brody's outstretched hand. "Thank you."

"Glad it found a good home." He jumped back in his Chevy. "Headed out to Dixon King's for some more of his honey. Can't keep it in stock."

Pushing open the Emporium door, she lifted the bag to show her father. "Phil Brody just gave us some free yarn. Okay if I run it out to Hannah? She said she needs some."

"Sure."

Callie Jane jotted a few numbers in the sales book. "I'm selling myself that Moses basket to give her as a baby gift."

"Nope. You can't buy it."

"Oh, does someone else want it?"

"It's a gift from both of us. Just write down 'For Hannah' and take it."

She grinned. "Thanks, Daddy."

When Callie Jane pulled into the gravel driveway, Hannah came to the window and gave Callie Jane a hearty wave and a big smile. Callie Jane sat in Shelly for a moment, grappling with her emotions. She loved that house and missed living there, but was so proud of herself for moving out.

"Glad to see you again," Hannah called from the porch. "Everything okay?"

Callie Jane grabbed the Moses basket and yarn. "Daddy and I have a gift for you." She walked through the door Hannah held open and set the Moses basket on the kitchen table. "I remember you admired it in the shop when you first told me you were expecting. And the yarn is from someone who couldn't use it."

Hannah peeped in the bag. "There's so much, and it's cotton! I don't have the cash to buy it all, but maybe I could get one skein now and get some more later after I've saved up."

Callie Jane shook her head. "No charge. A lady gave it to Phil Brody, he gave it to me, and now I'm giving it to you." She smiled. "Good things come in threes."

"Thank you," she said. "I already know what I'll make with it." She touched the basket. "And this is beautiful. I have the perfect place for it in the nursery." She stopped. "I mean, in your room."

"You were right the first time. It's a nursery now."

She smiled shyly. "Would you like to see?"

Callie Jane picked up the basket. "I would."

The single bed she had slept in almost every night of her life had been replaced with a crib, and the patterned curtains her mother had hung had been exchanged for white ones, but the rest of the room looked the same. The last time she'd been in that room, she had been a bundle of nerves, telling her mother she was moving out. So much had happened since then—she had rented a room from Evangeline, broken her engagement, and planned a new life, or at least the beginnings of one, in California. As soon as she thought of California, guilt flooded her mind. What about her father? His health was failing, and he was counting on her more and more these days, even before she started running the shop.

On top of the dresser were several neat stacks of knitted baby blankets, booties, and sweaters. Callie Jane picked up a tiny sweater. "How gorgeous!"

Hannah smiled ruefully. "I know I've made too many, but with being off from the bank, I have plenty of time on my hands, and I like to stay busy. If I'm not out in your daddy's garden, I'm knitting."

"Have you ever considered selling these? Phil Brody was just telling me how people love buying handmade things. I bet he could get a lot for them and pay you a commission."

"I've never thought of my knitting as more than a hobby. Do you really think people would want to buy them?"

"I do. Why don't you pick out some things for me to take to him, and I'll see what he says."

Hannah grabbed a few blankets and several sweaters, then added a pair of booties. "Let's try these. I'll find something to put them in."

After Hannah filled a bag, she handed it to Callie Jane. "It would be such a blessing if Mr. Brody could sell a few. I could use the money to buy some things for the baby."

Taking one last look around the house, Callie Jane said, "I should probably get back to the Emporium."

"Before you go, can I cut a few daisies to send back to your father?"

"He'd like that. I'll come with you."

Being back in her father's garden was both wonderful and heartbreaking. Every plant was a sign of her father's love, but knowing he wasn't there to tend each bloom and sprout was almost too much to bear. She couldn't imagine a scenario that would bring her father back to his beloved garden, but the next best thing was having someone as devoted as Hannah lovingly care for it.

As Hannah snipped the stems, she said, "Grady and I never could have dreamed of having a place as fine as this, and we are both beholden to you for thinking of renting it to us."

"I'm just grateful this house has a family to love it." Callie Jane took the daisies from Hannah's hands. "Daddy and I both are glad you're here."

....

The Emporium had been busy that day. Her father was in his element, chatting with customers as he rang up their purchases, with the daisies proudly displayed on the front counter. During the first quiet moment they had all day, Callie Jane turned to her father. "Are you going to start a garden at the new house?"

"Maybe next year."

"Have you put up bird feeders yet?"

"Nope."

Her father without his plants and birds was unimaginable. "Why don't I put in a garden for you? You can supervise to make sure I'm doin' it right." She smiled. "I'm pretty good, though. I've learned from the best." She added, "And it'll just take a minute to hang some feeders."

"I love you for offerin', but my heart's just not in it this year." He smiled sadly. "Next year, okay?"

"Sure, Daddy. Next year."

"Things have quieted down, so why don't you head on out? I bet Muse would love having you home early." He handed her purse to her and opened the door to the alley. "Love you, hon."

She marked through the day's calendar square, her countdown to the Beatles concert, then started for home. *I forgot to tell him Evangeline is looking for a clock radio.* She turned to go back into the shop but stopped. The tiny office window framed the face of her father smiling broadly as he held the phone's receiver in one hand and patted his hair into place with the other. Hmm. Her mother was full of secrets, but maybe her father had a few of his own. She cocked her head as he adjusted his tie, even as she rolled her eyes at her overactive imagination.

Once back at home, her book from the banker's box about California engrossed her for the next few hours. Drinking a glass of red wine, she studied temperature charts and public parks, famous vineyards and the rugged coastline. She yawned and checked the clock. Eight thirty. *Too early for bed.* She stopped herself. *Says who? If I want to go to sleep, I can.* Brushing her teeth, she studied herself in the mirror. Her daddy was right; she *did* look older with bangs. Old enough to be on her own, an independent woman who could make her own decisions and live her own life as she saw fit, not only surviving but thriving.

Muse seemed delighted with the early bedtime and happily trundled off to her bed in Evangeline's room. Callie Jane switched off the lights, except for the one in the den so the house wouldn't be totally dark. She'd never spent a night alone in her entire life. *And this is how you're going to celebrate, with a night-light?* She toggled the lamp off, went to her bedroom, and crawled beneath the covers.

Low growling invaded her dream. A red wolf with glowing amber eyes chased her as she dashed across a frozen field. She tripped over the ice-covered ground, pitted with ruts and holes, slicing her hand on a sharp stone. A river of blood cascaded down her white dress. As the wolf grew closer, she struggled to her feet, frantically casting about for sanctuary. Frigid air pierced her lungs. And then claws and fangs sank into her body, tearing her exposed skin.

Another growl, louder this time, entered her brain, waking her. She bolted up, her heart pounding, as Muse bounded past the bed. The dog lunged at the window with a terrifying snarl, her teeth snapping. Callie Jane jumped from her bed and rushed to the window. A face met hers, and then she heard the crash of the outdoor bistro table mixed with a sickening yell. A figure was running across the patio toward the open gate, hitching up his pants.

With adrenaline rushing, she raced to the patio door. She grabbed the broomstick from the track, jerked open the door, and dashed dow—n the steps, raising the broomstick like a spear. "You'd better run, coward!"

He tripped as the neighbor's floodlight snapped on. For an instant, the figure's face was illuminated as he scrambled to his feet, a shock of red hair revealing his identity.

Chapter 17

Posey

COLD SPRING WAS quiet and lonely, with a humid heaviness filling the rooms. Posey had paid more than she wanted to for newfangled central air-conditioning, which the slick Nashville salesman had assured her would kick on automatically with the turn of a dial, but the unit in the basement was still, despite being set on sixty-seven. *Vern would know what to do.* Posey took a long pull from her glass. Calling a professional would require yet another withdrawal from Golden Goose Bank.

She had assumed Vern would come slinking back after one night away, but she had been mistaken. When dusk arrived for the second night without his return, she curled into a newly upholstered chair in her library, consoled by a cold glass of gin, and cried. She recoiled from the notion that she might actually need Vern for more than doing chores and providing her the comfortable title of *wife*. She'd always viewed Vern as a useful necessity in her life, like a doorstop or wristwatch, but as she sat alone in her massive house, she was shocked to realize his steadfast presence was a solace to her. She bit her lip. Her behavior had driven him into the arms of Miss Brass Button. Now she had no CJ *or* Vern, with only herself to blame. She downed the rest of her drink, ice clinking against her teeth as the last drops filtered down her throat.

She sat at the head of her mahogany dining room table to eat her TV dinner, resisting the need to accept this new truth dawning on her. She had fancied herself an independent woman who could run the universe single-handedly from the day she had graduated high school, but she was realizing the truth. She could not survive on her own.

As she prepared for bed, she thought of her idol. Jackie Kennedy had managed to keep her husband despite his wandering eye, but as Posey lay awake in her sweltering bedroom, she wondered if she could do the same. She drifted off into a fitful sleep as she listened for the crunch of Vern's tires.

When she woke the next morning, her room was dark, announcing a cloudy day. She made her way down the hall and peered anxiously into Vern's room. Boxes lay where the movers had left them, and the bed coverings were pristine. She twisted her wedding ring. He had not been home. After adding two extra splashes of gin to her morning coffee, she began her day. A distant rumble of thunder rolled across the leaden sky. *Great. Rain.*

The Spark High reunion committee was due shortly at Cold Spring for a breakfast meeting, and she had to finish preparing the house for its social debut. She vacuumed and dusted, straightened and fluffed. A glance at the clock sent her buzzing into the kitchen. She swung open the massive Foodarama door and removed a tray of pastries. Though she'd never admit it, the new refrigerator kept everything in a near-frozen condition, requiring at least twenty minutes for the food to thaw before it could be eaten, despite three trips from the repairman.

As she laid the tray on the sideboard, she saw a jagged bolt of lightning crash to the ground right outside the window, prickling the delicate hairs on her arms. Pulsing thunder rattled the windowpanes. *Oh Lord, what happens if it rains on reunion night?* She needed these oafs safely contained on the terrace, not unsupervised in her house. Everyone was invited to gawp at the outside, not scurry about the inside like a pack of inquisitive country mice. She wanted them to feel like hungry peasants, staring wide-eyed through a bakery window at treats they could never afford, with Barbara Ricketts being the most tattered, ravenous urchin of all. The only solution was a tent.

The doorbell chimed its Westminster notes as Posey was setting a pitcher of cream onto a tray. Who would be tacky enough to be early?

Peeping through the sidelights, she spotted Darlene fumbling with a drenched umbrella, holding some letters. As Posey swung open the massive front door, Darlene said, "The mailman and I pulled up to your driveway at the same time. Here you go." Handing the stack to Posey, she tilted her head toward the plaque by the door and asked, "What's that fancy sign say? I don't speak French."

Posey had no idea, but she knew Darlene didn't either. She placed the mail on a table and answered, "To the victor go the spoils."

Darlene's head swiveled as she took in her surroundings. Her eyes were as large as the plates on the sideboard, and her open mouth mimicked the round spout of the silver urn.

"It looks like everything is finished. Thank goodness." She craned her neck to see down the hall. "This place is like a palace."

Posey took Darlene's arm and guided her from the entryway. "Let's chat in the library while we wait for the others. You can give me the latest on the Creeper."

After she settled Darlene into a wing chair, she asked, "What's the news from Dewey? Is Mike any closer to finding this maniac?"

Darlene shook her head. "The trail's gone cold." She shrugged. "Or Dewey's clammed up." She tugged at her too-tight jacket. "He may be a little bit put out with me that I told some stuff I shouldn't have." She leaned in to whisper, even though they were alone. "I *did* overhear Barbara Ricketts tellin' Queenie somethin' yesterday at the Curly Q that is too perverted to put in the paper." Pursing her lips, she added, "It's not ladylike to repeat."

Perversion made it that much more interesting, and Posey had to know. "We women have been helpless against this monster. The only way to protect ourselves is with knowledge." She leaned in closer. "What is it?"

"Nancy Tisdale bought her daughter, Cheryl Ann, some days-of-the-week panties for her eighteenth birthday. Nancy did her wash last week and hung it out on her clothesline. When she went to bring it all in, Tuesday was missing!" Darlene made a face. "I hate to think of the Creeper havin' a hold of Cheryl Ann's panties."

Posey was unimpressed. "Nancy probably left them in the washing machine, or the wind blew them off the line."

"Nope. There was two empty pegs between Monday and Wednesday. Someone took them."

Now we're getting somewhere. "Sounds like the Creeper is stalking his next victim. Have the Tisdales seen anyone at their window?"

"Not that I've heard. Maybe—"

Darlene was interrupted by the booming doorbell, announcing the arrival of the other committee members. After ushering them in, they stood in the foyer, gaping. A flush of pride covered Posey as she observed their astonishment. She delighted in her next thought. *What will CJ's first reaction be?* She had come to accept that he probably didn't even remember her after all these years, but that bow tie *did* give her hope. Even if it was a coincidence he had worn their secret signal, having him see her reign over the social event of the decade would change everything. All those old feelings would come rushing back and she would be in his arms, and his bed, once again.

The committee moved through their agenda quickly. Darlene might be scatterbrained, but she was uncharacteristically organized when it came to making sure the reunion went smoothly. As they were wrapping up their meeting, Posey made a play for the tent. "We need to consider what to do in case of inclement weather." Facing a sofa full of blank stares, she rephrased her concern. "What if it rains? We need to tent the whole terrace."

Darlene frowned. "I don't know, Posey. Our costs is already as high as a cat's back." Her eyes swept over the room. "Couldn't we just move it all inside?" Gesturing, she said, "Looks like you got the space."

Posey silently berated herself. She should have thought of a valid objection to having the party inside before bringing up the idea. "Let's all pray for good weather. Maybe we can get Brother Cleave on it."

After the committee left, Posey poured herself a generous glass of gin. Downing it, she reveled in the warm burn, then helped herself to a second glass to celebrate how well her plan was coming together.

Thumbing through the mail Darlene had given her, she spotted the latest Nashville Garden Club newsletter. Tearing it open, she began to read, then sank into a chair, her legs weak. Under a photograph of a house she did not recognize, the headline read, "President Hosts Club Members at Her New Home." Blood pounded in her temples as she read the first line of the article. "Frances Vanderbilt's new home and garden delighted those attending her housewarming fête." Her mind reeled back to the largest silver bowl in Frances's orchid-filled conservatory. *Awarded to Frances Vanderbilt, Senior Class Golf Champion.*

CJ had divorced Frances and kicked her out of Eden Hall, stripping her of her married name. Was this another sign? Posey briefly told herself it was just a coincidence, but the evidence was overwhelming. A bow tie could be chosen without thought, but a divorce was another matter altogether. She clasped her hands together. CJ divorced Frances because the title of wife was going to be bestowed upon someone else. Her.

Chapter 18

Callie Jane

AROUND 11:00 A.M., Callie Jane woke and sat upright. Her rigid spine was sharp against the unyielding slat of the oak headboard. She drew her knees to her chin and smoothed the cotton nightgown tented over her legs, puzzling out exactly what had happened. Earlier that morning she had woken with a start, thinking for a moment the Creeper was still nearby. Once her pulse had stopped racing, she had phoned her father to say she had a terrible headache and would be in late, then had gone back to bed. Muse lay on the floor beside her, ears pricked, as she fitfully slept.

The night before came back to her in shards. The Creeper and Callie Jane had locked eyes, but it wasn't until the neighbor's outside lights flipped on that she had recognized his face. She brushed the bangs from her eyes. Had she really seen Wasp Fentress? The moonless night had made it hard to see, and the adrenaline and fear coursing through her body had kept her from thinking clearly. She shook her head. She had to be wrong. Wasp was only a kid, maybe fifteen years old. She rubbed her forehead. Was one glass of wine enough to cloud her thinking? She couldn't be right. The Creeper was a man, not a child.

A low growl snapped her eyes wide open. Her gaze flew to the window. Only a dark sky promising rain. Muse settled back onto the wooden floor and a rush of love flooded Callie Jane's heart. Muse had saved her. Without her warning, Callie Jane would have been completely unaware she was being spied on. Arthritic to the point of hobbling, how had she managed to leap to the window? Maybe Muse's adrenaline had fueled her body the same way it had her own. "Thank you, sweet girl," she whispered.

Cautiously slipping out of bed, she wrapped herself tightly in her robe and crept to the kitchen, shivering at the sight of the sliding glass door with its broken lock. "Come on, Muse. Potty time," she called. The tiny patio and postage stamp yard were empty, and her mind understood the Creeper was long gone, but a new prick of fear demanded that she scan every inch before venturing from the relative safety of the house. The dog limped to the door, allowing Callie Jane to help her down to the concrete slab, past the bed of now-crushed daisies, and to the small strip of grass beyond. The knocked-over bistro table jangled her already-taut nerves. She bent to set it aright but froze. It was evidence. She backed away, noticing the now-fallen wasp nest, angry residents stalking across its papery cells. Had Wasp knocked loose the wasp nest? She rubbed her aching temple. Nothing made sense.

Callie Jane helped Muse up the steps, supporting her hips when she struggled to step over the threshold. She gave the broomstick an extra shove in the metal track and went to the kitchen.

Searching her mind for what she knew of the Creeper, she scooped coffee into the pot. He had targeted only houses that had young women in them and had been chased from more than one Spark yard. Had anyone hinted that a boy, not a man, was the Peeping Tom? She stared at the grounds. Had she already added the second spoonful? *No idea.* She added more. According to the *Gazette* articles she'd read, no one had ever reported him breaking in, or had even gotten a good look at him. She grimaced. Until last night.

She filled Muse's bowl with a hero's extra scoop of kibble, then changed her water. She poured a cup of coffee and inhaled deeply, comforted by the familiar smell. Should she call the sheriff? The encounter needed to be reported, but was she willing to give a statement that included Wasp Fentress's name? What if she was wrong? But what if she was right? The red hair was so vivid in her memory. It wasn't her nightmare or the wine. The person had red hair. Didn't he? Or was she confusing the Creeper with the red wolf in her dream? A sob choked her. She rubbed her bleary eyes, exhausted from a sleepless, tension-filled night.

In the bathroom, she twisted the shower knob on, then immediately off again. As much as she longed for the warm water to wash away the terror of the night, she could not allow herself to be so vulnerable, alone and naked. She snatched a washcloth from the towel bar. A sponge bath would have to do.

Chilled through despite the already-hot day, she added a third layer of clothing, a *Beatles Forever* sweatshirt she had scored in a Nashville Goodwill. As she ate a piece of toast, she mulled over her next steps. Did she have the nerve to call Sheriff Ricketts? He'd press her for every detail, no matter how small. What if he asked whether she could identify the Creeper? The toast turned to cotton in her throat and she spat it onto her plate. She resisted the urge to run to her father, a little girl who needed someone else to fix her problems. He had his own issues, and she wasn't going to make things worse.

She needed to get her thoughts together before she saw him. Weighing truth and honesty on a balance scale, she landed on truth. A watered-down account of the night's events would convey what happened without stressing his already weakened heart.

Although she always walked to work, her knees were too shaky to carry her even that short distance. Thank goodness she had Shelly.

She opened the Emporium door. "Hey, Daddy." She gulped. "I've got some news. The Creeper paid me a visit last night."

The whites showed all around the irises of her father's eyes. "The Creeper was at your window?"

His sudden pallor slowed her words. "Yes. I'm okay, though."

"Dear Lord." He rubbed his face. "Did you get a good look at him?"

She couldn't tell him she thought she saw Wasp Fentress. Her father would tell the sheriff, who would take the boy in for questioning. The rumors would cover every inch of Cooke County faster than a freak snowstorm in March. If she was wrong, the whole town would hate her for ruining an innocent child's life. People were still clucking about the time Linda Fentress accused Rennie King of stealing five dollars from her till at the BuyMore. The bill was discovered the next week amid the dust bunnies and desiccated grapes under Linda's station when Mr. Humboldt waxed the floor, but the damage had been done to both Rennie's reputation and Linda's. No, if she wasn't sure about seeing Wasp Fentress, she couldn't say a word. She had to lie. "No."

He stumbled to his office chair, steadying himself with his hands. "The Creeper," he said, his voice cracking. "At my baby's house." He ran his still-shaking hands through his black hair. "Start from the beginning. Tell me everything."

She edited as she spoke. "It happened really fast. I'm okay. Really."

He rose from his chair and hurried to the sales counter. Winded, he knelt by the shelf under the register and began digging behind the stack of spiral notebooks chronicling decades of Emporium sales. "Here it is," he said as he withdrew an item from the depths. *Sweet baby Jesus. A gun.* Her father had never displayed a moment of violence, and she could not reconcile the image of him holding a weapon. The black steel of the muzzle sent a chill chasing across her heart.

"I didn't know you had that."

"For if I ever got robbed." He sank into his chair. "I'm calling the sheriff, and you're going to tell him everything you told me. Then I'm going to show you how to defend yourself. You're going to keep this gun by your bed until the Creeper is caught." He shook his head. "I'm so sorry, Callie Jane. All this time I thought I'd need to keep my store safe, but it was my own child I should have been protecting."

The image of Wasp, just a kid really, flashed in her mind. "He didn't try to hurt me. I don't need a gun."

"Yes, you do. We don't know what he's capable of. What if he comes back?" His voice was tense. "Or what if he decides peepin' ain't enough?" He reached for the phone and dialed. "Sheriff Ricketts, it's Vern Jarvis. Callie Jane was the Creeper's target last night." He nodded. "'Bout five minutes. 210 Stadler Court."

Her father plucked a grimy scrap of paper off his bulletin board and dialed the number written in pencil. "Vern Jarvis here. I'll make that swap you've been after. Come by the Emporium later today and we'll settle up. The dining room set for the rifle."

Her cotton mouth returned. "Rifle?" she whispered.

"A customer came in wanting to trade a rifle for the dining set we have up front. I said I didn't sell firearms and didn't have any need for one." His laugh was more of a choke. "Turns out I did after all." He rummaged in his drawer, extracting a box of cartridges from underneath a sheaf of papers. "The sheriff'll be anxious to talk with you." He lumbered to the front door, flipped the sign to "Sorry, We're Closed," and turned the lock. Returning to her side, he said, "We'd better get going." He paused. "Have you told your mama?"

She pulled her macrame purse from her desk. "No, but I guess I have to. Could you imagine how scared she'd be if the Creeper went after *her*? I'm glad you're there at Cold Spring to protect her."

He didn't meet her gaze. Instead, his face paled, and he inched from the door back to his desk, steadying his body with his hand along the wall. He dropped into the chair, then cradled his head in his hands. She watched anxiously, licking her dry lips. Sweat dotted his brow. Was he having a heart attack?

"Daddy," she whispered.

"I need to be there to protect my wife. It's a husband's duty."

He wasn't making sense. She looked at her father with new eyes. Was he not staying at Cold Spring either?

When they reached her car, Callie Jane opened Shelly's passenger door. "Why don't I drive?"

He looked dubious. "She's been checked over, right? Harold said it was safe to drive?"

"A coupla things needed fixing, but she's all squared away now."

Her father worked to maneuver his body into the Volkswagen. She glanced at him, unnerved by the revolver in his hand. "Who taught you to fire a gun?"

"Ever' boy learns to shoot from his pap. And now you'll learn it from me. I guess the world ain't like it used to be, even in Spark. You and your mama both are gettin' lessons."

"I don't want to know how to shoot. Guns scare me."

He frowned. "I don't insist on much, but this is one of those times. You need to know how to protect yourself."

Callie Jane knew she'd lose this argument. She would learn how to use the gun to appease her father, but she could never shoot Wasp, or anyone else.

"Okay," she sighed.

The patrol car was already in the driveway. Mike Ricketts approached the Volkswagen. "Vern, Callie Jane." He nodded. "Show me which is your bedroom window."

Before approaching the unlatched gate, she closed her eyes, pushing away the images of the previous night, and led her father and the sheriff into the small fenced enclosure. She crossed to the far side of the patio and pointed up. "It's that one. He must've stood on this to reach," she said, gesturing to the metal table. "I guess he lost his balance, 'cause I heard a yell and then a thud when he hit the concrete." She bit her lip. "I had meant to pull the shade down, but I forgot."

"How much of his face did you see?"

"It all happened so fast." Time for another lie. "I didn't see his face at all. He fell as soon as I looked at the window."

Eyeing the window and the table, Mike said, "'Bout six feet from the top of the table to the sill. I'll bring a tape out here and measure it up." He made a note in a spiral book. "I need your statement. Can we go inside?"

Mike sank onto the sofa and clicked his pen as he gazed at Callie Jane. "Start from the beginning and tell me everything you remember." The sheriff scribbled his notes as she recounted most of what had happened. She turned bright red when she got to the part about his pants being down, but Mike didn't even pause when he wrote that detail in his notebook. "What time was this?"

"I went to bed early, so maybe a little before ten?"

"And you're sure you didn't get a good look at his face?" Callie Jane shook her head. "Hair color? Eyes?"

She studied the floor. "No, sir."

Mike stood. "Show me your bedroom."

As she passed through the den, her eyes darted to the bookshelf. Their marijuana was concealed in a box, but it wouldn't be hard to find. Surely he wouldn't search the whole house. She nibbled her fingernail.

Mike walked to the window and studied the patio below. "That fall was bound to smart. I'll check with Doc Grisham about any broken bones."

Her father walked Mike to his car, then returned to the house with the revolver and cartridges from Callie Jane's car. "Fixin' to rain. I was hopin' to take you out to your mama's house to teach you how to shoot. Guess we'll have to do a dry fire for now, practicing with no bullets. Once it clears off, I'll teach you to shoot for real. It's been a long time, but I reckon it'll come back to me."

He picked up the revolver. "This is a .38 Special. It holds five bullets." He pushed open the cylinder, revealing empty chambers. "Put you a bullet in each of these and then close it." She shuddered. The empty chambers looked like the cells of the wasp nest that the Creeper had knocked from her window as he fell. After showing her how to aim and shoot, he placed the weapon in her shaking hand. "You try it."

The gun was heavy and cold. She forced herself to take it and follow her father's instructions, even as she promised herself she'd never use it to harm anyone.

After a couple of practice shots, he announced, "You've got it. Of course, we'll need to try it with ammo."

"I can get Trace to show me. He's always shooting tin cans at his gran's house. We're having dinner tomorrow at the Blue Plate. I'll ask him then."

He nodded his approval. "He knows his way around a gun and has steadier hands 'n mine too." He patted her arm. "I'm glad y'all is still friends. I've always liked that boy."

She grinned. "Me too."

"I'll load it for you in case the Creeper shows up again, but promise me you'll get Trace to shoot with you right away. This can't wait."

"I promise." She told herself that wasn't a lie. Learning *how* to shoot someone wasn't the same as actually shooting someone.

"Good. Any more questions?"

"No. I've got it."

"Any chance I could talk you into coming to Cold Spring, just 'til they catch the guy? I understand you wantin' to be on your own, but if I had both you and your mama under one roof, I could protect you better."

"No, but I love you for asking. We'd better get back to work." She gave him a weak smile. "Wouldn't want my boss mad at me."

··········

Business at the Emporium was mercifully slow, and her muscles were beginning to unkink when the insistent honks of a horn and yelling voices interrupted her thoughts. "Watch where you're going, ya damn fool!" A door slammed.

Her father sighed. "That'd be Fentress." He stood, straightening his tie.

"Fentress?" she whispered, steadying herself on the chair's wooden frame. *Please, no. Not Wasp.*

"The customer making that swap. Hatch Fentress. I'd rather not do business with the likes of him, but I need a rifle quick." The door's brass bell jingled.

She sprang from her chair. Wasp's father was in the shop. *Sweet baby Jesus.* What if his son came to help hoist the heavy table? She grabbed the first thing her hand lit on, a doll. "I . . . I need to see if we have any more of these." She rushed into the alcove that served as their storeroom, the curtain flapping behind her like a flag in a tornado.

"Hey there, Fentress," she heard her father say. "I see you've brought a helper."

Chapter 19

Posey

AT 9:58 A.M., the lecture hall at the hospital was almost filled. Posey approached the now-abandoned check-in desk and perused her choice of unclaimed name tags. A paucity of female doctors meant she usually had to hunt for a name that could be taken as a woman's, like Leslie or Pat. A few times she had to settle for a Robert or Joseph, ready to be Roberta or Josephine if need be, aided by a well-placed scarf obscuring the name. She affixed Dr. Lee Hamilton's name tag to her blouse and slipped into a seat just as the doors closed.

She considered CJ's divorce, now doubting that it had anything to do with her. *If he really wanted me, he'd have made the hour-long drive to Spark long ago*, she chided herself. Still, she could enjoy being in his presence and settled in for her annual fill of his handsome face.

When she had stayed at Eden Hall as a nineteen-year-old, one of her sorties into his office had revealed a handwritten note, thanking CJ for speaking at an upcoming cardiologist conference in Nashville. "We eagerly anticipate hearing your thoughts on the newest developments in cardiology every spring. See you in April!"

A few phone calls had been necessary to nail down the time and place that first year, but once she had the details—third Thursday in April, Carpenter Hall—she was a faithful attendee. Staring at her beloved for a full forty-five minutes allowed her to drink in enough of him to sustain her until the next lecture series. One year she arrived only to find that CJ would not be speaking that year, so she learned to always call ahead and confirm his presence.

Once, posing as Dr. Kelly Jackson, she had brazenly risked joining the doctors for a coffee break that immediately followed the lecture. Dizzy at the thought of being so close to CJ, she had been debating approaching him when a voice called, "Kelly? Is that you?" She'd hightailed it for the door, vowing to stay in the relative safety of the auditorium seats from then on.

....

Sheets of rain had pounded Spark since midmorning, but the skies had cleared in time for a spectacular sunset. Streaks of deep red and pink intersected a golden light above the tree line. Settling back into one of her brand-new wrought iron chairs, she took a pull of her gin, reveling in the joy of having seen CJ that morning. He seemed to grow handsomer every year, and listening to his commanding tone and watching him walk about the stage as he pushed the buttons on his carousel of slides was thrilling.

As the entire sky washed with a purple tint, she turned to study the now-immaculate beds of foliage bordering the terrace, wrinkling her nose at the rain-soaked, tangy mulch the landscapers had spread. Beauty came at a price.

The terrace would be perfect for the reunion, which was three weeks away. The rest of the house was a work in progress, but her plan to keep everyone outside would curtail any snooping. If questioned about any unfinished projects, she had a speech ready about historical integrity and finding just the right craftsmen to do the work properly.

One of the dozen hydrangeas framing the terrace swelled with spherical buds promising white flowers. *Thank the Lord.* Bushes groaning under cascading blue sprays screamed low-class tacky, although most of Spark favored the cerulean mopheads so omnipresent in the South. Hydrangeas surrounded their old house on Poplar Avenue, bursting with enormous blooms the color of a summer sky. Vern had insisted on keeping them, despite her demand that they be replaced with creamy Annabelles. His mother had planted them, and Vern adored each old-fashioned leaf, branch, and petal. It was rare he put his foot down about something, but it happened every once in a while.

Vern. She hadn't counted on him moving out over separate bedrooms. The image of her husband walking out the door gnawed at her. Living with his floozy mistress and calling her place *home* wounded her more than she would admit. After a few deep breaths, she reassured herself, *He'll come back.* As she took the last sip of her drink, she flashed back to the image of his truck disappearing from view as she watched from an upstairs window. She refused to acknowledge the needling jabs of fear that he had left for good. *He's got to come back. This divorce will be on my schedule, not his.*

Just as she tilted her glass against her lips, she heard the crunch of tires in the pea gravel driveway announcing a visitor. When Vern's battered truck rolled into view, relief washed over her, drenching her in gratitude. She stood, smoothing her crisp cotton skirt, and thanked her lucky stars Vern was home.

When the truck's door slammed, she turned to greet her husband, a smile plastered on her face. She narrowed her eyes. Was he gripping a baseball bat? Vern caught sight of her on the terrace and strode toward her. And that wasn't a bat—it was a rifle. Her heart stuttered. Was he going to shoot her? She considered running for the conservatory, the closest shelter. With wobbly knees, she took two hesitant steps toward the house. Maybe a dash to the kitchen.

Vern reached out to her and stilled her thin arm before sinking into a chair. He leaned the gun against the wrought iron coffee table, and her heart rate slowly returned to normal. She wasn't being murdered.

"I've got some news," he said.

He's leaving me. She dropped into a chair opposite his and gripped the armrest, the metal edge digging into her palm.

He licked his lips. "It's Callie Jane."

She bolted upright. "What?"

"The Creeper paid her a visit last night."

Posey gasped. "Is she all right? What happened?"

"She's okay, just shook up."

"Have you called the sheriff? She needs to come home right this minute." She rubbed her temple. "It's got to stay out of the papers. Promise me, Vern, nothing in the *Gazette.*"

"I spoke to Mike after he was done talkin' to Callie Jane. He said he'd keep it quiet." He pulled at his sweat-stained collar. "I asked her to come here, but she won't. She wants to be on her own, and I can't say as I blame her. That's why I gave her a gun and taught her how to fire it, since she's got no man living there." He pulled the rifle to his side. "And I'm gonna do the same for you."

Posey eyed the weapon. "You're off living God-knows-where and you're going to leave me in charge of protecting myself, with only a rifle I don't even know how to shoot? Shame on you, Vern Jarvis. Your parents would roll over in their graves if they knew how you were treating me."

He rubbed his fingers against his forehead. "I was talkin' about the *shooting* part, not the *no man* part. And I will thank you to leave my parents out of this." He cleared his throat. "I'm stayin' at your Cold Spring so's I can do my best to keep you safe." He dabbed at his sweaty brow with his handkerchief. "But if I'm at work and you scream, who's gonna hear you?" He cocked his head toward the fields and trees she had been admiring moments earlier. "Them squirrels? Maybe the orchids in the *conservatory* can save you."

"There's no need to be ugly." She stood, willing her legs to support her. "I'm going inside to call my daughter." She started toward the door but turned back to her husband. "You may teach me to shoot the gun."

Posey gripped the phone's receiver as she waited for her daughter to answer. Upon hearing Callie Jane's soft voice, Posey started in. "Come home now. I insist."

Callie Jane sighed. "No. I can take care of myself."

Posey's nostrils flared. "I think this incident proves the opposite. You have a lovely room here, and you need to be in it, safe."

"I'll be all right."

Tears of frustration formed in Posey's eyes. "I don't know that. *You* don't know that. Stop trying to prove you're so independent and come home."

"No." There was a pause, then Callie Jane added, "I'm hanging up now."

Posey stared at the receiver now buzzing with a dial tone, then slowly returned the phone to its cradle and turned to climb the stairs to her bedroom, where her flask awaited.

Later, when Posey peeked in Vern's bedroom on her way to the kitchen to make dinner, she spied him lifting his shirts from a *Vern White* box and hanging them in the closet. *Praise Jesus.* Had he broken things off with his floozy? Who knew, but he was under her roof tonight and would stay there, at least until the Creeper was caught. Her plan was back on track.

·· · · · · · · ·

After a sleepless night of churning thunderstorms, Posey's eyes were scratchy and her mood was foul as she made her morning coffee. Relentless rain pounded the windows, and her head throbbed at the thought of yet another roof leak. She tapped her foot, studying the family calendar as she waited for the carafe to fill. An addition in black to the May 8 square of the calendar caught her eye, formed in her husband's neat, schoolboy print: "Vern—Baptism in Scranton." A line tracing through the following two squares made it clear Vern would be gone for three days, returning just before the party. She rubbed her stiff neck.

When Vern entered the kitchen, she chose to ignore the calendar entry and asked, "Is Callie Jane minding the store while I get my lesson?"

Vern's eyes crinkled as he smiled. "Yep. She's doing so well. I feel good about her running the Emporium after I give myself that gold watch."

"You bought yourself a gold watch?"

"It's a joke." Her blank stare stopped his chuckle. "When people retire, the boss gives them a gold watch as a token of appreciation for years of loyal service."

"So you think you've been loyal?"

He cut his eyes to hers, and his words slowed. "I was kidding. I'd have to present it to myself, because I'm my own boss." He pushed his coffee cup away. "At least at the Emporium." He stood. "Let's get started with your lesson. With this frog strangler, we'll have to settle for being inside. There'll be plenty of room in the entry hall for now, and we can practice shooting outside when it clears off."

He retrieved the gun and walked with her to the foyer. "This here's what they call a manstopper, a Savage 340 .30-30 rifle."

She had never seen this side of her mild-mannered husband. His demeanor was positively rugged. Her heart fluttered. This may have been Vern's most Camelot-like moment, and for an instant, she could appreciate what his mistress saw in her husband.

"Here's how you load it."

"Just show me how to aim and pull the trigger."

"Okay. I'll load it for you after we're done. First, slide the safety off, then pull this knob up and toward you. Now push it forward and down." Vern held the rifle in the joint of his right arm. "Keep the butt end against your body like this and lay your cheek against the stock. Get a bead on your target and take a full breath. Let out half, hold it, then squeeze the trigger, real gentle-like." He handed her the rifle. "Now you try." She rested the rifle butt against her shoulder. Vern shook his head. "It'll kick back on you like that, and you'll give yourself a helluva bruise. Lower it down near your armpit."

Posey tried again.

"That's better," he said.

His eyes searched the hall. "We need a place to store it, close enough where you can get at it quick, but safe enough that nobody disturbs it by accident." He moved to the heavily paneled door of the coat closet. "Maybe in there." He opened the door and studied the shelf. "Come in here and see how easy you can reach."

She did as she was told, thrilled with her husband's commanding tone. On her tiptoes, she said in her best breathless Jackie voice, "Yes, I can reach it fine."

"All right, then. That's where we're keepin' it." He loaded the magazine and set the rifle on the back of the closet shelf. "It's loaded. Don't touch it unless you need it." He shrugged on the rain jacket hanging on the coatrack. "I gotta get back to work."

She watched her husband's rattletrap pickup wind its way down the undulating drive, then crossed the floor to the closet, opened the door, and stroked the smooth wooden stock of the loaded rifle with her red-tipped index finger. *No one is ever going to hurt me and live to tell the tale.* She gently closed the door, patting one of the heavy panels as the latch softly clicked into the strike plate.

Chapter 20

Callie Jane

HER FATHER LOOKED up from the front window display as Callie Jane entered the Emporium. "How's your lessons comin'? Should I call you Annie Oakley?"

She had confessed to Trace that she would never be able to shoot anyone. He said he understood but urged her to learn, just in case. *"That way you can be honest with your father and still know how."*

"They're great, Daddy. Trace is a good teacher. And I've invited him to go with me to the Beatles concert as a thank-you for teaching me."

"It makes my heart easy to know you can protect yourself," he said as he moved a picture frame. "You missed a call from Phil Brody. He sold out of all the little sweaters and things, and he wants you to give him as much as you can next time."

"I can't wait to tell Hannah."

He smoothed the tape on a hand-lettered sign reminding his customers to "Remember Mama on Her Special Day—May 8th." "This thing fell again. Masking tape won't hold worth a durn in this heat wave."

"Air we can wear." She fanned her hands in the already-warm room and took the sign from her father, propping it against a hobnail glass vase in the window. "That should do it." She smoothed the quilt folded on the headboard of the oak bed that had taken the place of the dining table her father had traded to Hatch Fentress for a rifle. "I'm glad Grady could help you set this up. I think having him work in the shop is a good idea." Touching her father on the shoulder, she softly added, "Grady is going to start taking Fridays and Saturdays for you so you can rest." Her father shot her a look of gratitude. "You take it easy and try to get your strength up, especially before we see that Nashville doctor. Don't lift anything heavy."

"I couldn't even if I wanted to. I'm glad you hired Grady. That was smart." He shook his head. "It was embarrassing having you and Linda Fentress wrestle that table out the door. I don't know why Hatch couldn't'a had his boy come help. Having two girls and an old man doin' my work for me just ain't right."

Callie Jane wiped her suddenly clammy hands across her dress. She had been so relieved when Wasp's sister had entered the shop instead of Wasp, but then her brain had conjured the idea that Wasp was avoiding her because she could identify him as the Creeper.

Her father mopped the back of his thick neck with his handkerchief. "I'm as weak as a rat-chewed hay string."

She laughed. "I haven't heard that one before."

"That's 'cause I just made it up a coupla days ago."

"Promise me you'll take it easy."

"I will."

The etched lines around her father's eyes deepened as he offered a sad smile. "Let's talk about you takin' over the Emporium full-time. I was hopin' to have some more cash in the bank before I retire, but I'm thinkin' it needs to be sooner instead of later."

"Don't say that. You just need to get stronger."

He shook his head. "A body knows. God gives us that, telling us when time is short. I need to be wrapping things up."

Her heart sank. "Let's wait 'til we hear what that doctor says. I bet he gives you a pill that'll make you feel like a young buck again."

Callie Jane was desperate to change the topic of conversation. "Are you looking forward to the baptism in Scranton? You almost never get to see your cousins."

"I'm not going. With the Creeper and all, I don't feel right about leaving. I said yes right away because I was so mad at your mama, but once I cooled down, I realized I had to stay home."

"Don't cancel. You never do anything for yourself."

A look she didn't recognize crossed his face. "I'm no saint, Callie Jane. And what if you all need me?"

"We'll be okay. I promise." She took his hands. "For once in your life, do what you want to, not what you think you need to."

"Maybe you're right." He paused. "I would like to see ever'body once more before . . . Well, I'd like to see everyone." He stared out the window, then turned to face her. "Okay, I'll go."

The Emporium had a steady stream of customers, but as soon as the clock read five, her father shooed her out the door. "I still have some work to do, but you head on home," he explained as Callie Jane x'd through the date on her calendar. "You need a good night's sleep before driving to Memphis to get those Beatles tickets." As she fetched her purse, he added, "And do your old man a favor and stop by the filling station on the way outta town and have Harold check the fluids." He grabbed a Tennessee road map from the shelf under the register. "I've marked out your route. With the new interstate in, you should be there in four hours, four and a half, tops."

Reaching for the map, she said, "You always take such good care of me," then pecked him on the cheek.

"Be careful," he said, his voice splintering.

The Emporium door banged behind her as she approached the now-familiar wooded path leading to her house. Evangeline was due home that night, and she wanted to make a special dinner for her return. Spinach lasagna? Maybe their favorite—a chef salad.

A voice called out, "Hey." Trace jumped to his feet from where he'd been seated on the rock wall bordering the parking lot. "Can I talk to you for a minute?"

"Sure. What's up?"

Trace bowed his head, avoiding her eyes. "It's about going to the Beatles concert with you."

"You're not thinking about the money for the ticket, are you?" She smiled. "It's my treat, remember?"

"I can't go."

"What?" She sat heavily in the spot on the wall Trace had vacated. "Why not? You said you would."

"I, well, here's the thing." He examined the dust on his boots. "There's, um, someone who doesn't want me to go."

"Who? Your mother?"

"It's not her." He cleared his throat. "I have a girlfriend, and she says I can't go anywhere with another female, especially one I was engaged to."

"A girlfriend?" Her bangs ruffled in the breeze. "You haven't mentioned her."

"I didn't want . . . I mean, upsetting you is the last thing I wanted to do, so I didn't tell you. I met her a few weeks ago at the state 4-H Jamboree. She's from Bell Buckle."

A smile spread across her face. "I'm happy for you, for you both." She touched his forearm, already tanned from the spring sun. "I hope she's good enough for you."

"She is." His face lit up. "I'm wild about Laurie Anne. Being with her doesn't mean I've stopped loving *you*, though. Remember that night when I asked to speak to your daddy about marrying you? I was so nervous my knees were shaking. I hadn't asked his permission ahead of time, since I didn't even know I was going to propose until right before you came over. I thought he'd be mad, but instead, he asked me the one thing I could answer with complete honesty. He asked me if I loved you, and I said I always had and always will." He smiled at Callie Jane. "That's not changing, ever."

She stood. "And I will always love you, Trace. Laurie Anne's a lucky girl, and I wish you the best." She hugged him before turning for home.

. . . .

The sun was bright the next morning as Evangeline and Muse stood together on the driveway. "Be careful, Cal. Don't pick up any hitchhikers and don't go too fast. Shelly's a good car, but she's an old lady, and it's best not to push her."

Callie Jane laughed. "I'll be okay. And I know you'll be safe with Muse here, the bravest guard dog in the world. I still can't get over the way she lunged at the Creeper." She opened the car door. "I've got my lunch, my map, and the car repair book you gave me. Your tire-changing lesson was very thorough. I am prepared for anything."

"A pretty girl on a mission on the open road? Don't be so sure." Evangeline winked. "Leave some room for the unexpected, a little magic. That's half the fun of a trip."

After Harold pronounced the car roadworthy "on the inside, not so much on the outside," she navigated Shelly toward Memphis. As the familiar sights of Spark dropped away, her thoughts turned to her future.

She had come up with an idea that felt right in her soul—to move to California and work with plants. But having only an inkling of a plan was not the same as having an actual plan. She needed to save a lot more money before she could go, and she had to figure out what to do about telling her father, but her heart was peaceful when she imagined herself under a golden California sky. And that was a start.

As the heat of the day grew, she rolled down her window. She drove past farm after farm, all greening up after a long winter, and thought of the year-round growing season and verdant fields of Southern California. Coaxing avocados, grapes, or even flowers from the rich earth, with dirty hands and a happy heart, could be her everyday life, so far from the tobacco and soybeans she knew.

Four hours into her drive, the skyline of Memphis came into view, and her pulse quickened. Could she find her way to the Coliseum? With only one wrong turn, she successfully guided Shelly into a lot next to the massive domed building that looked like a spacecraft ready to rocket her to a new world. The sun reflected off the white roof, dazzling her eyes. She tightened her ponytail and joined a long line of people along the sidewalk. Mostly her age, they were dressed in blue jeans or shorts and T-shirts, in contrast to her yellow sundress.

Two teens were talking in line ahead of her about an upcoming protest in downtown Memphis. She listened in awe as they discussed the struggle for racial equality. She'd read reports in the *Nashville Banner* about civil unrest, but hearing about it firsthand made it seem so much more real. Her admiration for the teens' bravery as they discussed facing fire hoses, snarling dogs, and even bullets was eclipsed only by the sadness of knowing that such protests had to happen at all. She silently sent the two a prayer of safekeeping as they reviewed their plans.

Pride surged through her body as she bought her single ticket. She alone was enough. She didn't need Trace or anyone else to make this experience whole. *Main floor, section FF, row 12, seat 3.* Her heart skipped. She was going to see the Beatles! She carefully tucked the ticket into her purse, zipping it securely into the side pocket.

As she walked to her car, she frowned. Was a tire low? A closer inspection revealed a bolt deeply embedded in the rear driver's side tire.

The tall young man with shoulder-length brown hair she'd spotted in line was approaching the car next to her, a station wagon bearing a California license plate. "Hello, Sunshine." A dimple dipped into his cheek. "Looks like you might need some help."

She gave one shoulder a shrug. "Just a flat tire. I can fix it."

"A sexy, self-sufficient woman. Cool." He nodded to the spare. "At least let me be a gentleman and lift that out for you, or would you prefer to do that on your own?"

"I wouldn't say no to some muscle."

The man gave her a level look before maneuvering the tire to the ground. "Has anybody ever told you that you look like Jane Asher?"

She swept the bangs from her eyes and smiled. "Didn't I see you buying tickets for the concert?"

"Just one, but yeah. No way I'd miss the chance to see the Beatles before I head back home to California." He leaned against his car, his well-developed arms folded, observing Callie Jane as she expertly began removing the deflated tire.

"Me too. The one ticket part, I mean. And the California part too. I'm moving there." She spoke the words from her soul, startling herself with their certainty. But were they true? Her stomach fluttered with excitement. Maybe.

"Cool."

He bent to retrieve the lug nut she was reaching for and placed the tiny metal piece in her outstretched palm. "I'm in section JJ, main floor. How about you?"

"I'm main floor too." She gave a final twist to the wrench. "Section FF. Maybe I'll see you at the concert."

"Sure thing, Sunshine. I'd dig that." He grinned. "Remember, JJ."

"I'd better get going, JJ." She tossed her blonde ponytail. "We self-sufficient women have places to be."

He raised his hand to smooth an errant strand of her hair and ran a finger along her jawline. As he moved closer, she shivered, smelling icy wintergreen on his breath.

"I've wanted to kiss you since you said you could change your own tire." With a smile, he asked, "Would that be okay?"

She nodded, hoping she wouldn't dissolve into a pool of nerves and flesh on the asphalt. He cupped her face in his hands and bent to gently touch his lips to hers. Warm and soft, with urgent yet gentle exploring, the kiss buckled her knees. Callie Jane encircled her arms around his back, returning the kiss with a passion she didn't know she was capable of. Trace's pecks had been sweet and mildly intriguing but had never affected her like this kiss did.

"Perfect," he said before releasing her. He winked, then got into his car with the "Make Love, Not War" bumper sticker.

"Bye, JJ," she whispered. She stumbled to her car. With her heart thrumming in her chest, she watched as her mystery man disappeared from view. She didn't take a normal breath until she had passed Jackson, eighty miles out of Memphis.

· · · · · · · · · ·

When Callie Jane floated through the carport door into her kitchen, Evangeline was fixing Muse her dinner.

Callie Jane dug her ticket out of her purse to show Evangeline. "I got two things I really needed in Memphis: a ticket to the concert and a kiss from a gorgeous stranger." Saying it out loud sent a thrill through her body.

Evangeline's eyebrows shot up. "I need to hear about that kiss."

"It's quite a story. And here's a third thing I brought back from Memphis: self-confidence." She held up three fingers as she said, "I am a confident, sexy, capable woman. How about that?"

Evangeline nodded. "What do I always say? Good things come in threes."

Callie Jane danced around the kitchen, waving her ticket in the air. "August 19 is going to change my life."

Evangeline filled Muse's water bowl from the faucet. "I think the change has already been set in motion, Cal." Setting the bowl on the floor, she added, "That confidence was always there, waiting for the right time to come out. I'm glad to finally see it."

"Thanks." Callie Jane spun, her yellow dress belling as she twirled. "I'm as happy as a pig in mud."

Evangeline laughed. "I swear, being from Ohio means I miss about half of what people say. Just when I think I've learned all the Southern expressions, I hear another one. Like this morning at the Curly Q. Queenie was giving Tina Anderson a hard time about going to the Poconos with her boyfriend. She told Tina she could sleep in a heart-shaped bed but had better not come back with a baby-shaped belly. Tina said it wasn't like that. Her boyfriend was sick. Said he was . . ." Evangeline knitted her brows. "Damn it. What did she say? Something about wheat or straw." She snapped her fingers. "Oh yeah, she said he was as weak as a rat-chewed hay string."

Callie Jane froze as she realized the implication of Evangeline's statement, then sank onto a chrome chair. "Tell me everything you know about Tina Anderson."

"I stay out of my clients' business, but Queenie thinks she's having an affair with a married man. She doesn't know who, though."

"I do." She looked up at Evangeline. "My father."

Chapter 21

Posey

THE CURLY Q'S basin was digging into Posey's neck, but what was hurting her most that morning was the discovery she had made the previous afternoon while snooping in Vern's bedroom. Nestled beneath the socks and undershirts packed so neatly in his father's valise was a small velvet box. When she had lifted the hinged lid, a delicate, crystal-encrusted heart on a silver chain sparkled at her. She never should have told Vern about that phone call from his cousin. *The truth is overrated.* If she had kept her mouth shut, Vern wouldn't have known about the invitation to the baptism and would be home with her, where she could keep an eye on him. Surely to God he wouldn't introduce his mistress to his cousins, but the necklace proved he had finagled a way to be with her. She scrutinized the piece of costume jewelry, destined for Miss Brass Button's adulterous neck. *Something cheap for someone cheap.* After closing the lid, she tucked it back into the valise and soothed herself with a full glass of gin.

··········

Their fight about his going to the baptism had started shortly after she discovered the necklace. "I don't see why you would accept the hospitality of people who mocked your wife."

"They invited me, and I'm going. They invited you too, which was very kind after what all you said to them during our honeymoon visit. I don't have much family, and I cherish what little I've got." He kept his back to her, stirring another spoonful of sugar into his already-sweetened coffee.

"How about cherishing *me* and refusing to accept the hospitality of people who were unkind to me. I'm your family too." She slumped at the kitchen table, rubbing her temples, then looked up to add, "At least for now." She bit her lip, instantly regretting her words.

He turned to her, his face blank. "At least for now? Are you saying you're going to divorce me? Because that might not be a bad idea. You could sue for abandonment, with me going clear off to Pennsylvania for a few days to celebrate the commitment of my cousin's baby to Jesus Christ, our Lord and Savior, at the Scranton All Saints' eleven o'clock service." He snorted. "That there's a scandal. Any judge would see it your way."

Shut up, Posey. If he learned his secret was out, he could decide the damage was done, and might go ahead and divorce her and marry that woman before she had CJ's engagement ring on her finger. There'd be a divorce all right. Not because some tawdry woman had lured Vern away but because by then she'd have a rich doctor chomping at the bit to make her his own.

Instead of snapping any of the caustic remarks that cascaded to her tongue, she changed tactics and softened her tone. "I'm sorry, honey." Ignoring his surprised look, she stood and pecked him on the cheek. "I'm just cross that I'll have to do without you for a few days." She handed him the coffee mug. "Drive safely, and give my love to cousin Joan and baby Evelyn."

He strode to the entryway of Cold Spring. As the solid mahogany door swung open, he said, "Emily. The baby's name is Emily, not Evelyn."

"Right, whatever." Vern was likely unable to hear her remark, as he had already slammed the door. She peered through the sidelight, observing her husband staring down at his key ring, with his oafishly large feet frozen on the mat incongruously scripted with the message *Welcome*. A total of four keys dangled from the chain. How hard could it be to find the right one? She fumed. Was he pausing to make his departure more dramatic?

....

"Mrs. Jarvis?" Evangeline called, interrupting Posey's torrent of thoughts. "May I shampoo you now? Queenie should be finishing up with Mrs. Kitchner here in a bit."

She nodded, sliding her head into the bowl. The warm water and suds washed the argument from her aching brain, and by the time Evangeline had massaged the crème rinse through her hair, she had convinced herself that all was well with the world. At least well enough.

The towel turban Evangeline was tucking behind Posey's ears was warm from the dryer, offering a moment of lilac-scented relief from her stress.

"Looks like she's running a little behind. Why don't you sit at my station while you wait?" Evangeline gestured to the chair beside Queenie's and then headed for the back.

Lurelle, the owner of Honeybelle's dress shop, handed Queenie another pin from the box on her lap as Queenie secured a roller onto her head. "Something's going on, for sure."

Queenie wagged her finger. "That gal's got herself a boyfriend she don't want any of us to know about. He's bound to be married, 'cause she's not sayin' hardly anything about him."

"It's hard to keep a secret around here, but she's done a good job."

Posey strained to hear, yanking the terry cloth turban away from her ears. *Who are they talking about?*

"She said she can't see him very often." Queenie shrugged. "How does someone like her meet a man who's living somewhere else? She can't exactly afford to travel the globe, and it's not like handsome strangers are flocking to Spark in search of true love."

Lurelle rubbed her hands together. "Maybe he doesn't live somewhere else. Maybe he's right here in Spark. She was in the shop a coupla days ago and bought a lovely dress. It was black, with a scalloped hem. But then she added something to her order." Lurelle shook her head, clucking her disapproval. "A lacy negligee meant for my married customers. Why would she need that?"

Queenie grinned. "She's going to the Poconos. She let it slip she was headed there this weekend, and got all flustered when I asked her about it."

Lurelle frowned. "Where is the Poconos?"

Queenie answered, "Not rightly sure, but I hear it's quite a fleshpot. They got sunken bathtubs and heart-shaped beds." Queenie raised her eyebrows and gave her friend a naughty wink. "And mirrors on the ceiling."

Lurelle cocked her head. "Well, that's dumb. Why would you want to see— Oh, I get it." She playfully swatted Queenie's arm. "You rascal."

Queenie pinned the last curler into place. "There, hon, you're ready for the dryer."

Posey's gut and brain figured out at the same moment who they were discussing. She jumped from the chair and dashed to the bathroom. Turning on both faucets full blast, she sank to her knees, hoping Evangeline was far enough away to miss the sound of retching. After heaving up her toast and black coffee, she dabbed at her lips with a paper towel torn from the roll hanging above the sink, straightened her dress, popped a mint in her mouth, and opened the door.

Lurelle was raking through the magazines. "Hey, Posey, you're smart," she called. "Do you know where the Poconos are at? Near Gatlinburg, maybe?"

Before settling on Niagara Falls for their wedding trip, Posey and Vern had considered honeymooning at the Away in a Manger Motel in the foothills of the Poconos, thirty miles south of Scranton, Pennsylvania.

She pasted on a hasty smile. "You're exactly right. The Poconos are part of the Smoky Mountains in East Tennessee." *Good God, could this day get any worse?* Back to her mission. "You and Queenie were having an interesting conversation." She looked at Lurelle's curler-encrusted head expectantly.

"Just a little beauty shop gossip." Lurelle cast her eyes toward the awaiting dome. "I'd better get under the dryer before Queenie fusses. You know how she is."

Her knees were shaking, and the bile still burned her throat. She was desperate to learn that hussy's identity, and both Queenie and Lurelle knew who she was.

Undaunted, she turned toward Queenie's awaiting chair. Queenie could pry the unvarnished truth from victim or perpetrator, and never went to print until she had a corroborating source. If Queenie said it, it was true.

She slid into the chair. "So," she began, "I hear we have a Spark resident headed to the Poconos." She studied Queenie's reflection in the oval mirror opposite her chair. Had pity crossed her face? *Does Queenie suspect something? Could she possibly know it will be Vern who'll be sleeping in the other half of that heart-shaped bed?*

"Yes, we do, and it's a scandal." Queenie reached for a brush on her table, sending the glass Barbicide cylinder soaking the combs and scissors crashing to the floor. "Oh my goodness! What a mess!"

As Queenie mopped up the liquid, Posey whispered, "Accidents happen." A tiny red bubble of blood was forming on her ankle. She needed a bandage but was so close to the truth that she'd bleed out before dropping the subject. "So what was that about the Poconos?"

"It seems we have a secret rendezvous happening this weekend. A few days ago—"

Queenie gasped in horror as she stared at the drop of blood blooming on Posey's leg. "You're bleeding!" She rushed toward the back of the shop and returned with a first-aid kit.

As Queenie bent down to tend Posey's wound, Posey debated the wisdom of one last effort. "So you were saying . . ."

"There. Your leg's all fixed up. Just need to wash my hands and then finish this hair."

After Queenie returned from the bathroom, she took a comb from Evangeline's station and began working. "Did you see that article about how one of those Beatles said his band was more popular than Jesus Christ? And he said something ugly about the disciples too." Queenie frowned. "We are the role models for our Spark youth, and we need to make sure they have nothing to do with that type. I'll suggest Brother Cleave preach on it Sunday." She slicked a strand of hair with Dippity-Do, then peered into Posey's pale face. "Callie Jane's goin' to a concert in Memphis. She's not going to see the Beatles, is she?" Queenie had a furious look on her face. "No child of mine would be paying good money to be in the presence of somebody claimin' they're better than Jesus. Shameful."

When Callie Jane first discovered the Beatles, almost every conversation somehow included them. Posey had tuned out as much as possible, but even she knew who John Lennon was after she had casually commented around the dinner table one night that she hadn't known the Lennon Sisters had a brother. Callie Jane had gently corrected her mother, and Vern had sat stone-faced, but she had caught the look between her husband and her daughter, who once again had excluded her as they shared in one of their little jokes.

Queenie peered at Posey. "So is she going to a Beatles concert?"

Posey squirmed in the beauty shop chair and croaked, "The Monkees. It's a Monkees concert she's going to." She turned to Evangeline, who was setting a new Barbicide jar on Queenie's station. "Isn't that right?"

Evangeline nodded. "Yes, ma'am. She loves the Monkees."

Chapter 22

Callie Jane

AFTER SETTING KIBBLE out for the feral cats, Callie Jane settled onto the picnic table seat behind the BuyMore to wait for Trace. When he arrived a moment later, she handed him one of the Blue Plate's breakfast sandwiches. "Thanks for meeting me. I really need some advice."

"I'm always glad to help." He took a bite of his sandwich. "What's goin' on?"

"For starters, my mother is furious I broke things off with you."

Trace grinned. "Well, I *am* a good catch."

Callie Jane snorted. "True." She looked toward the woods, searching for Gray Boy and Pearl. "Her drinking is getting worse. The other day I watched from the Emporium window as she tripped over the doorway of the Curly Q. When I went to help her up, I realized she wasn't hurt, she was drunk. I had to drive her home." Callie Jane shook her head. "I used to think if I was quiet enough and didn't cause her any trouble, she wouldn't drink or yell at me or Daddy." With a shrug, she added, "Never worked, though. The older I got, the more I realized how horrible she was. When I was little, I thought all mothers were that way, and then later I thought she was just shallow, but now I realize she's empty. There's a body there, but no soul."

Trace's face was somber. "I know my mama made sure you were at our house as much as possible, and it took me a long time to figure out it wasn't just because you were my best friend."

"I'll always be grateful to her for that." She sighed. "There's more. I'm pretty sure my dad's having an affair with Tina Anderson."

Trace's eyebrows shot up. "Really?"

"This sounds terrible to say, but for the last year or so, he's been happier than I've ever seen him. And when he hurried me out of the Emporium one day, he was fixing his hair and adjusting his tie while he was on the phone. No one needs to spruce up for junk store business." She paused. "And Evangeline repeated something Tina told her that was exactly what Daddy had said to me a few days earlier."

Trace balled up the waxed paper. "So how do you feel about all this?"

"I just want to get away—from my mother, the Emporium, Spark, everything, and start over where nobody knows me, where everything I do is to suit myself, not someone else."

Trace's voice was quiet. "Then do it."

"Just like that? Say goodbye and leave?"

"Yep. I love Spark and plan on living out my days right here. That's what I want, so that's what I'm doing. You want to leave, so that's what you should be doing." He looked toward the employee entrance of the BuyMore, the door Callie Jane knew he had happily entered and exited for over a decade, helping his father the way she helped hers. "Any idea where you want to go or what you want to do?"

She had spent most of her life feeling as directionless as a leaf twirling in the eddies of Flat Rock Creek. Now, though, things were different. *She* was different.

"I think I want to go to California and work with plants or flowers."

"And why wouldn't you do that?"

"My dad—"

Trace gently laid his hand on her arm. "I asked about *you*, not your dad. Is your father doing what he wants?"

Callie Jane nodded. "Yes."

"Is your mother doing what she wants?"

"Yes."

"Are you doing what you want?"

Callie Jane sat silently.

"Exactly." Trace tapped the faded picnic table. "Remember the last time we sat here? You and I were both a mess, trying to make everybody else happy, even though it'd mean we were miserable." He blushed. "No offense. But think about that lesson. Are you going to spend your life trying to suit someone else, or are you going to do what you want and take a chance on being happy?" His face clouded over. "I'd miss you every day, sweet Callie Jane, and I say this with nothing but love, but get the hell out of here."

· · · · · · · · · ·

Callie Jane stepped through the back door of the Emporium and walked to the truck, still thinking about Trace's advice. *"Get the hell out of here."* When he had said it, she was ready to hop in Shelly and take off, like some romantic heroine in a movie. But reality beat down on her with the intensity of the blazing

May sun. She had no money, and her Emporium salary, while fair, wasn't exactly enough to finance a move across the country. And there was her father's failing health. She didn't believe her own cheerful chatter about this doctor prescribing a miracle pill that could undo years of damage. She sighed. The only place she was going was to Nashville, to meet with the man who could change both their lives with a few words.

The sun had heated the truck's chrome door handle, searing Callie Jane's hand. Using her shirt hem, she opened first her door and then her father's before hopping in. A bouquet of daisies lay on the floorboard, wilting in the heat. Their first stop would be the cemetery, and then Dr. Ryan's.

Watching her father secure the Emporium's back entry, she wondered what they both would know the next time they crossed the familiar threshold. His health had always been a concern as his massive frame grew with the passing years, but lately her worry had changed from a nagging watchfulness to constant monitoring. She had slowly taken over all Emporium business, except for the chatting and visiting with her father's customers. He claimed he felt fine, but his clammy skin and frequent breaks to catch his breath told a different story.

He pulled the driver's door closed. "I appreciate you comin' with me." He smiled weakly. "I'm a little nervous to hear what this Dr. Ryan's got to say."

"I bet we get good news." She had always been a terrible liar.

"Hope you're right, but as long as he don't say surgery, I'll be okay."

"If you need an operation, then maybe we should do it."

He didn't answer her and instead drove in silence through Spark, passing Strickland's Drugstore, the BuyMore, a few residential streets, and then field after field of tobacco plants, their broad leaves shimmering in the sun. Once they were on Nashville Highway, he finally responded. "No knives. It's my life, and I'm the one in charge of it." He shook his head. "I don't have control over much, but I *can* say I'm not getting cut open." He turned off the smooth paved highway and guided the truck onto the rutted gravel of Cedar Hill cemetery's main drive. They passed through Heaven's Promise and Grove of the Gospel as they wended their way to the Garden of Eternal Life. Dull, lichen-covered headstones spoke of eras gone by, but others gleamed with the newness of a recent death.

He put the truck into Park, grabbed the flowers, and hoisted himself out of the driver's seat. "The cemetery people want us to buy plastic ones." He gestured to the garish bouquets standing pin-straight in urns bolted to grave markers. "They say it looks more uniform. But Mama loved fresh flowers, so I bring these." He stroked the white petals and whispered, "Daisies was her favorite."

As they walked across the carefully tended plots, he said softly, "I wanted to be with my parents before I hear what this fancy doctor has to say. I appreciate you indulging me."

"I'm glad to, Daddy." Callie Jane took a seat on a concrete bench. "This day is all about you."

A granite heart spanned the two graves. He brushed grass clippings from his mother's name and then gently touched the chiseled date of his father's death. Laying the bouquet just below the point of the heart's base, he adjusted it so the flowers could be equally shared between the graves.

He lumbered to the stone bench and sank onto the narrow seat beside her. "He was two months younger 'n me when he passed. Guess that makes me runnin' on borrowed time."

"Just because your father died early doesn't mean you will."

"The headstone place calls what I bought for them a companion marker. And that's what they were, companions, all through life. Mama didn't hardly last six months without him. I had 'em carve 'Beloved' on there. *Beloved* is an odd word. It means someone loved you, but it's also an instruction, to be loved. It's hard to figure out what that really means, but I know it's important."

He wiped his hand across his mouth. "Next to them is where I'll be layin', with room for your mama beside me." He paused for a moment, then added, "I imagine we'll be gettin' separate headstones to match our separate bedrooms." His face darkened. "I apologize. You don't need to hear something like that."

They sat in silence, and she ached for her father. The whole town adored him, but the one woman who did not was his wife. "Daddy, I know about Tina."

A robin hopped from one branch to another on the weeping willow that shaded the graves beside them. He spoke softly. "I'm so sorry. I'm a failure as a husband."

"No, you're not. Mama is impossible to live with. She belittles you every chance she gets and doesn't appreciate what a wonderful man you are. If you've found someone you love, who loves you back, then I say good for you. You deserve to be happy. Everyone does."

"I'm not sure I do. A good man would honor his wedding vows."

Tears pricked her eyes. Her father had been the one who filled her Christmas stocking and made sure she had an Easter basket every year. Her second-grade drawing of a bluebird had been tacked to the wall by his Emporium desk since the day she proudly gave it to him. He'd eaten Crispy Critters cereal every morning for six months straight to help Callie Jane get enough box tops to send in for a Linus Lion mascot. They had both cried when she lost the state spelling bee by one letter, and he had wrenched his knee dancing a jig when she was named Spark High valedictorian.

She put her hand on her father's sweat-dampened back. "You are a good man and the best father. Never think differently."

He continued to study the robin, now gliding effortlessly through the sky. "I went in to see Raddy Tisdale the other day. He handles all my legal matters, such as they are. I transferred the Emporium to you." His smile was wan. "I hope you'll let your old man stay on as an employee for a little while. I have a few things to finish up."

"No one could imagine the Emporium without you, me included."

He took her hand. "I did something else at Raddy's. I made some changes to my will. The house on Poplar Avenue is yours too. Your mama never cared for it, and she's got enough house already."

"Please don't talk about being gone. This doctor will fix you up."

He didn't answer and instead returned to his truck, with Callie Jane following. Before cranking the engine, he said, "Maybe so." He looked out the window for a moment before adding, "Being able to call you my daughter is my biggest blessing."

They rode in silence to Church Street in Nashville, with its endless row of shops, offices, and looming, nameless structures. He scanned the buildings. "I can't find 472."

Pointing to a parking lot, she said, "Pull in there. I'll hop out and find it, then come back and get you."

"I'll come too."

She shook her head, watching the sidewalks rippling with heat. "No. There's no sense in you getting all worn out. It'll just take me a sec."

He gently put his hand on her arm. "About Tina. I know you think less of me, and I think less of myself. But here's the thing. When I stood outside your mama's house before I left for the baptism, I happened to look down. I was standin' on her 'Welcome' mat in a way that blocked out all but the 'me.' I took it as a sign that I deserved to do something just for me. My cousin thought I was a nut, crying all through the service, but in that church in Scranton I finally felt okay about doing something for myself. Your mama loves two people: you and herself. But Tina loves *me*." He heaved out of the seat. "And that's worth something."

"It's worth a lot."

She guided her father to the glass door, its brass hardware glinting in the sunlight. *What are we about to hear?* She pushed the thoughts of bad news away and studied the seemingly endless list of names on the felt-board directory. "Here it is, Daddy," she croaked. "C. James Ryan, Cardiology. 229."

The pair sat in silence on the small sofa in the sumptuously appointed waiting room. She grasped her father's hand. "Everything's gonna be all right," she said. "Dr. Ryan will get you squared away." *You are such a liar, Callie Jane Jarvis.* Her throat burned, as dry as Flat Rock Creek in a drought.

She struggled to her feet and paced across the room. The watercooler cups were flimsy white cones, reminiscent of the county fair Italian ices she looked forward to every August. She downed the water in one gulp. A nurse opened a heavy oak door. "Mr. Jarvis?" Callie Jane helped her father to his feet, and they both followed the woman down the hall. "Have a seat," she said, opening the door to Exam Room 3. "The doctor will be with you shortly."

A tall, ruggedly handsome man of about fifty entered. "Mr. Jarvis? I'm Dr. Ryan. How are you today?"

"Tolerable," he replied. Callie Jane wouldn't have recognized her father's thready voice if she hadn't seen his lips moving. She examined his face, noting beads of sweat dotting his brow. "And this here is my daughter, Callie Jane. She thinks I could use a second set of ears."

Dr. Ryan nodded. "It's always a good idea for a patient to have a family member with them." He shuffled the papers on his clipboard. "I see you're from Spark." His face tensed. "I once, uh, knew someone from there." He frowned, and his blue eyes darkened. Turning his attention back to his papers, he said, "I've gotten your test results back."

Callie Jane sat up straighter. "What tests?"

The doctor glanced at her father, who answered, "I had tests done at a lab a while back."

"I wish you'd told me. I would have gone with you."

"Didn't want to worry you." He faced the doctor. "Before we get into those results, you need to know something. I will not be operated on."

"Let's not get ahead of ourselves."

He straightened his spine. "Listen, Doc. My father died in surgery, and I don't want to follow."

Dr. Ryan pushed his horn-rimmed glasses farther up the bridge of his nose, which drew Callie Jane's attention to his deep blue eyes. "I can't force you to do anything, Mr. Jarvis, but I will tell you this. If you refuse surgery, you will need to get your body healthier. You're at least a hundred pounds overweight. Your heart is weak and is working too hard to support all your extra weight. Do you exercise?"

"I bowl ever' Tuesday."

"Find some kind of exercise you will do every day. Maybe walking would be a good place to start. We can discuss it later." The doctor cleared his throat. "Now, let's have a look at these findings."

The room was hot and her heart pounded in her ears. Dr. Ryan seemed to be speaking through cotton batting, forcing her to strain to make out his words as he discussed arteries and blockages. "It appears you have some fairly significant heart disease. You are a good candidate for surgery, but as you have made clear, that is not something you are willing to do. I'd like to examine you before we discuss options beyond exercise." He turned to Callie Jane. "Would you mind stepping out for a few moments?" Flipping the papers on his clipboard, he added, "Actually, I'll walk you to the lobby. I need something from the front desk."

Was there news he wanted to tell her out of her father's hearing? She gulped, her throat burning. *I'm so nervous.*

As Dr. Ryan led Callie Jane through the halls, he said, "I don't suppose you can talk him into heart surgery. It's his best hope for a normal life." He frowned. "I apologize, but could you remind me of your name?"

"Callen, but everybody calls me Callie Jane." She cringed. She hated her real name.

The doctor's eyebrows shot up. "Callen's my name too. How about that?" He opened a door marked *Waiting Room.* "I'll have my nurse come back for you when we're finished with the exam."

Odd coincidence they were both Callen. She guzzled another cone of water, a fruitless attempt to soothe her throat.

She absentmindedly picked up a *National Geographic*, looking at, but not seeing, the pages of photographs. As she dropped the magazine back onto the table, the word *Coventry* on the address label caught her eye. She picked it back up. "Dr. Callen James Ryan 229 Coventry Circle" had been scribbled over with a black marker but was still visible. Why was that address so familiar? She looked at the label again. *229 Coventry Circle.* She gasped. The address her mother had used on her falsified Nashville Fine Arts application form. *"Oh, I made it up."* She sat there stunned. The fact that her mother had lied to her was no surprise, but the existence of her made-up street was. Coventry Circle was very real, and was Dr. Callen James Ryan's home.

"I see you're from Spark. I once knew someone from there."

Memories flipped like images in a slideshow carousel. With a sickening jolt, she thought of a possible answer to so many of her childhood questions. Why she didn't have the dark hair of both her parents. In a playground full of Susies and Sallies, why her name was so unusual. Callen Jane. Callen James. *"It's a family name, given to the firstborn."* Why her beautiful young mother had married such a meek older man. She sank back onto the cushion, nauseated. Could it be? The thought was so far-fetched, but also felt so right.

"Miss Jarvis?" The nurse stood in the doorway. "Dr. Ryan asked me to bring you back to your father's room." With shaking legs, she followed the nurse down the maze of hallways. Opening the door, the nurse smiled and said, "Here's your daughter."

Vern Jarvis was sitting on the exam table, his fingers fumbling with a button of his short-sleeve white shirt, identical to every other one hanging in his bedroom closet. Callen James Ryan was standing at the window, studying a medical chart, with a shaft of afternoon sunlight illuminating the blond hair so like her own.

Chapter 23

Posey

POSEY WATCHED, ARMS crossed, as Vern scooped cottage cheese onto his shredded iceberg lettuce. "You've really taken this diet thing to heart."

"I'm gonna eat salads and walk to the shop every day." Vern burped the Tupperware bowl. "I'm drivin' in this morning, though. I'd never make it in this heat." Vern faced her. "Hope it cools off before the reunion starts." He shrugged. "It's a shame your air-conditioner's too fancy for me to figure out. Hot as hell in here."

She pouted. "It's the second time the damn thing has broken, and they can't come fix it 'til next week."

Vern dropped his salad into his lunch box. "Remember, I'll be home late. It'll take me a while to sort out that bookkeeping mess."

Posey had been puzzling out a way to disinvite Vern from the reunion ever since she had confirmed CJ's band would be providing the music for the party, but she hadn't dreamed up a plausible plan that would get rid of her husband for the night without raising eyebrows. Vern himself had solved the problem by announcing he needed to work late. She figured he'd be with Miss Brass Button but let it drop—she had other fish to fry.

Her pulse raced as she watched Vern climb into his truck. Less than ten hours until she saw CJ. Would he speak to her before the band even started? Or would he wait until after the last song, then seek her out?

She fanned herself with her to-do list. The May heat was oppressive, even by Spark standards. She made a mental note to get more bags of ice from the grocery store as she headed to the terrace for her final walkthrough. *Paying the landscapers overtime was worth it,* she mused as she inspected the pristine flower beds. And ordering the tent was a smart move. *Not that these clucks would know a party tent from a circus tent.* It offered shade, but more importantly, it radiated significance. Something a socialite would do.

Throughout the morning and into the afternoon, a succession of delivery trucks came and went, and by three o'clock, everything was in place. Tables with crisp white cloths and hydrangea centerpieces awaited the guests.

The conservatory was command central, with a desk displaying name tags made from yearbook pictures. Darlene had laid them out in neat alphabetical rows, but as soon as Posey cranked on the fans to help abate the lingering catio smell, all the name tags had blown off in a whirlwind of faces. Cursing, Posey had changed the angle of the fans, picked up the name tags from the floor, and dumped them on the check-in table in a jumbled heap.

As she was about to begin the tedious chore of re-alphabetizing, she checked her watch and jumped. Her Curly Q appointment was in ten minutes. She had chosen a dramatic updo for the evening, forgoing her usual beehive. Could Queenie pull this off? The two of them had studied an old *Life* magazine picture Posey had saved, depicting Jackie Kennedy reigning over a 1963 state dinner for Charlotte, Grand Duchess of Luxembourg, and Queenie promised she could re-create the look.

··········

The Curly Q was abuzz with excitement about two events: that night's reunion and a new *Gazette* article about the Creeper. Darlene read aloud.

> ### CREEPER FOILED! SPARK UNDER SIEGE!
> Sheriff Mike Ricketts received a call late Monday night about a shadowy figure at a local resident's home. A couple was preparing for bed when the man heard a sound and slipped out a side door to check his yard. A man, described only as tall, ran from the flower bed beneath their bedroom window. "My son, Deputy Sheriff Billy Ricketts, and I have increased our patrols, and we urge all residents to be vigilant and to continue to keep windows locked and curtains drawn, even during this unprecedented heat wave."

"As hot as it is, who can stand to have their windows closed?" Darlene fanned herself with the *Gazette*. "I wish Mike could figure out who this man is before we all expire in our own homes from the heat."

"I don't ever remember a May this hot," said Queenie as she combed through Posey's hair. "Lucky us, going to the one house in Spark with central air-conditioning."

It had been a grueling session in the chair. They were both close to tears as Queenie had pinned and teased, parted and combed, until Posey was satisfied. Exhausted, she returned home and was greeted by the Swinging Sawbones warming up to "Moonlight Serenade." Her heart beat so fast she thought she might faint. As much as she wanted to see CJ, she slipped upstairs. She would reveal herself to him at the height of her triumph, as a successful hostess reigning over the party of the decade. The white shift dress she had chosen from Rich Schwartz in Nashville for the occasion was simple but elegant and would ensure all eyes were on her. The night had finally arrived when she would see CJ. And he would see her. Then their love story could finally resume.

The grandfather clock chimed five as she made her way to the secretary. *You are one lucky lady.* The reunion would be dry, with no libation stronger than the lime sherbet punch Darlene had insisted on, but that didn't mean the hostess couldn't spike the contents of her cup. But how to make sure no snoopy classmate spotted her? She searched her brain for where to hide her bottle. After settling on the perfect hiding place, she set one of the bottles on the shelf beside Vern's rifle and gently closed the door.

She climbed the stairs and strode to her bedroom window. A second-floor vantage point was the perfect place to see without being seen. CJ was setting up a music stand. A lump formed in her throat and she felt dizzy. Holding on to the windowsill, she studied her old lover, whom she had last seen at his cardiology conference. Her eyes lingered over his lips, anticipating his kiss. "Soon, CJ," she whispered.

Checking herself in the mirror, she squinted as she examined every pore. Did her lips need another swath of color? No, her makeup was perfect. *Picture perfect.* She smiled to herself. Dewey would be arriving in a few moments, capturing the images that would be on the front page of the next issue of the *Gazette*.

· · · · · · · · · ·

Dewey had just snapped a photo of Posey next to her secretary when the doorbell rang, announcing the first guests. Posey greeted them and, in one fluid movement, ushered them through the sweltering house and into the conservatory for their name tags. Between trips to the coat closet, she mingled and smiled, nodded and laughed, as the guests congratulated her on such a lovely event.

She glanced toward the stage, her eyes tarrying on CJ. Was he looking at her? She narrowed her eyes, desperate to see. Yes, he was definitely glancing her way. Her heart thumped. He leaned over to a bandmate to whisper something, and then the unforgettable first notes of "Green Eyes" enveloped her. *Our song.* The divorce announcement *could* have had nothing to do with her, and the green tie *might* have been a coincidence, but this third sign cinched it. She swayed, faint from excitement.

· · · · · · · · · ·

Strains of Glenn Miller's "In the Mood," mixed with excited chatter, swirled through the air as the after-dinner coffee and desserts were being enjoyed. Darlene stepped to the band's microphone to wrap up the evening. Posey's pulse was racing. Right after she accepted Darlene's thanks for hosting the reunion, she would find CJ.

"Class of 1946, what a joy it is to be together again on this beautiful night, even if it is hotter 'n a June bride in a feather bed." Darlene pulled a damp piece of paper from her bosom. "I've written a poem to commemorate this evening." She cleared her throat and began in a solemn tone, "'We were once lads and lasses. Now we're old and wear glasses. Some of us are bald, while others to heaven have been called. Some have seen success, and others are just a mess. As the clock of life slowly ticks, we love you, Spark High class of '46.'"

When the clapping subsided, Darlene continued. "We are so lucky to have Posey Jarvis as our hostess." She shielded her eyes against the band's lights. "Posey, where are you? The class would like to say thank you." The gin had wobbled Posey's walk, so she used a deliberate, measured gait, like a bride slowly approaching her groom, as all eyes followed her to the stage.

Darlene ad-libbed as Posey picked her way to the front. "Ladies and gentlemen, let's have a round of applause for Posey Jarvis, our own queen of Spark High and, really, all of Cooke County." As she ascended the stairs, Posey stumbled over one of the band's cables. With quick reflexes, Darlene steadied her, then set her back on her feet. Posey grabbed the microphone. "Empress," she slurred. "I'm the empress of Cooke County, not the queen."

The crowd was silent. Darlene took the microphone back. "Thank you again, Posey, from the bottom of our hearts for this unforgettable night." The smattering of applause echoed in her brain as she descended from the stage, looking for CJ.

Her heart squeezed. She'd know that silhouette anywhere. He stood on the lawn near the carport, smoking a cigarette. Knees shaking, she approached. "I've gotten your messages, CJ."

He looked blankly into her face. "Huh?"

Posey peeped at him through three layers of Parisian Midnight mascara. "I want you too."

CJ dropped the cigarette butt and ground it into the dirt with his shoe. "I think you've got me confused with someone else."

"You wore the green bow tie I gave you for a St. Patrick's Day party. I saw the picture."

"Everybody wears green that day. And my wife, my *ex*-wife, always picked out my clothes if there was press coverage."

"But you played 'Green Eyes' a little while ago." Posey's voice quavered. "That's our song."

"I don't know that many songs. 'Green Eyes' is one of 'em." CJ shook his head. "Look, lady, I have no idea who you are."

Posey stepped closer. "I'd think you'd remember the person you made love to in every room of Eden Hall."

Squinting, he said, "The girl from Vassar?"

Her voice was sharp. "No. I'm Posey. Posey Burch."

Recognition flooded his face. "The bitch who cost me my marriage? I hoped to hell I'd see you again one day so I could tell you how you've ruined my life."

She stepped back, stunned. "But, CJ, you love me. We can be together now. And Callie Jane, she's your daughter. We can be a family, the three of us."

"I do not love you. We are not a family, and we are never going to be together." His eyes narrowed. "Frances found your damn earring. I cooked up some story about finding it in the grass and assuming it belonged to Patsy Bremerton, one of her garden club pals, who, lucky for me, died in a car crash right after Frances got home from New Zealand. She had no way to check the story, so I was in the clear."

A couple strolled by, plates of cake in hand, laughing loudly.

He lowered his voice to a hiss. "I learned to be more careful, and we were fine for years, but a few months ago she nearly ran into you with her car in our driveway. She got suspicious, wrote down your license plate, and hired a private investigator."

His voice was flinty and hard, not at all the smooth, honeyed tone she remembered when he was whispering into her neck how beautiful she was. "The guy tailed me and found me with a nurse from the hospital. Frances kicked me out that morning, filed for divorce that afternoon, then listed Eden Hall for sale and bought herself a new house the next day."

Posey was thirteen again, hearing how she was worthless and unloved. CJ's voice, so much like her father's, pounded in her ears.

"But it's *your* hou—".

"The house was *hers*, given to her by Daddy Vanderbilt as a wedding gift."

"But how does screwing some nurse have anything to do with me?"

"Because the PI didn't run the license plate until a few days ago. Since he'd already caught me with the nurse, his work was done, but I guess he figured there might be other women and could get more money out of Frances if he could find one." He jabbed his finger in Posey's face. "Do you know who the car in our driveway belonged to? Vern Jarvis. Whose wife was Posey Burch Jarvis. *PB* from the earring. She called me screeching about how I'd been a cheater all along, which blew my story that the nurse was my one mistake and that I would spend the rest of my life making it up to her if she would only take me back."

Stars swam around Posey's head, and she briefly felt she would faint. "This isn't my fault."

"It is *completely* your fault. No Cadillac halfway up my driveway, no suspicious wife hiring a PI. No PI, no finding me with the nurse. No nurse, no divorce. And thanks to that stupid earring, no chance for a reconciliation."

Posey took a step back.

"I lost a hospital board position I was up for, and I will never be allowed to darken the door of the country club again."

He gestured toward the band now packing up their equipment. "Those guys stuck by me, but they're the only friends I've got left."

"Hey, CJ," a band member called. "Let's head out."

"You destroyed my life." He turned away but added one parting shot. "That's what I get for slumming."

Darlene rushed up. "There you are, Posey. Everyone is starting to leave." She took Posey's limp arm and dragged her toward a gaggle of classmates.

After numbly saying good night to the last of her guests, Posey made a final trip to the closet. She drank a glass of gin without slowing for a breath. Her life was over. She staggered outside. Plopping herself on the low rock wall, she kicked off her painful shoes and dropped her head in her hands.

Lurelle's voice startled her. "Looks like we've got enough leftover desserts for all of us to take some home." The cleanup committee. She'd forgotten Darlene, Lurelle, and Queenie had signed up to gather the trash and empty plates. "So what do y'all think of the famous Cold Spring?"

Darlene's unmistakable voice filtered through a gap in the tent flap. "When I went looking for the powder room, I found an office that had a bunch of Dutch Boy cans piled in a corner, next to a stack of ladies' work clothes covered in paint. A half-empty bottle of gin was on a bookshelf, and a nasty mold was growing at least a foot up the walls. Seems Posey has more than a few secrets in this rickety old mansion."

Lurelle chuckled. "A mansion that smells like cat pee. When I was getting my name tag from her *conservatory*, the odor about knocked me over. We all did our best to forget about her being a Stadler when she married Vern, figuring she had to be something special if sweet Vern, of all people, picked her as his wife, but her behavior tonight was too much."

"And did you see the way she nearly fell into the drums? I almost didn't catch her." Darlene giggled. "If I didn't know better, I'd think somebody spiked the punch."

Queenie said, "She drinks, all right, but a lot more than just some spiked punch. The other day she was as drunk as a skunk at her appointment. As she was leaving, she fell flat on her face, sprawled out on the sidewalk." She paused. "Who could blame her, though? I'd sure be drinking if my husband was running around." Queenie clucked disapprovingly.

Dear God in heaven.

Gasps from all the ladies reverberated in Posey's eardrums. *No, no, no.*

Darlene was the first to speak. "What are you saying, Queenie?"

"I'm saying Vern is cheating on Posey," Queenie answered. "Vern seems so nice, but it's always the angels that turn out to be the devils."

Lurelle sounded puzzled. "What in the world are you talking about?"

"Vern offered me a brownie a couple months back, and I noticed they tasted unusual. I asked where he'd gotten them, and he said, 'My beloved made them for me.' I never figured Posey for the Betty Crocker type, but I said, 'How nice,' and forgot all about it until last week at the church social when I was talking to . . ."

Someone was dragging a table across the flagstone terrace, drowning out the next bit of conversation. *Damn it. Stop that racket.*

"So at the social I took a bite of the brownie and asked about her recipe because it tasted so different from a regular brownie, and she said her secret ingredient was cardamom. Something about those brownies has been bugging me all week. I finally figured it out when I tasted Lurelle's tonight."

Lurelle's voice was dubious. "What do my brownies have to do with Vern cheating?"

Queenie spoke slowly. "Yours are completely normal. I had tasted the flavor of *her* brownies, the ones with cardamom, only once before—in the brownie Vern had given me, saying the woman he loved made them." As the women gasped, Queenie dramatically added, "*One* of us was talking about his wife that day, but the *other* one was talking about his mistress."

Silence descended on the cleanup committee. *Who, damn it?* Every nerve was stretched, every cell screaming, *Who made those brownies? Who is Miss Brass Button?*

Lurelle chimed in, "This solves the mystery of the whole Poconos thing."

Who went to the Poconos with my husband?

The van carrying the band equipment started up, and as Posey tried to make out what they were saying over the engine, she could catch only a few words. Words that would decimate her world, like *shocking, stunning,* and worst of all, *humiliating.*

As the truck roared away, Queenie's voice was as clear as the bell on the Emporium door. "When you think about it, though, can you really blame Vern? He's such a kind, gentle man, and he's stuck with the likes of her. He probably gets frostbite every time he kisses her."

Darlene snickered. "*If* he kisses her. She should change the name of the house from Cold Spring to Cold Fish."

After the laughter died down, Lurelle spoke. "Poor Posey, or no, what did she call herself? The empress of Cooke County. Poor empress. And to think we used to have her up on a pedestal."

Posey silently cursed the reunion and her classmates, then wished straight to hell CJ and Frances Vanderbilt Ryan.

Lurelle's voice softened. "I feel kinda sorry for her."

Queenie was next. "Vern's the one I feel bad for." The sound of a metal pan being scraped filtered from the tent flap. "All right, we've got things pretty clean. Let's head on home, ladies. It's already past eleven."

Posey stumbled to her feet, abandoning her pumps, and lurched toward her house. Steadying herself on the massive banister, she struggled to remain upright as she climbed the steps. Passing Vern's empty bedroom, she weaved toward her own. She threw herself on the bed, the racking sobs she had fought to keep at bay finally overtaking her body.

After she couldn't cry another tear, she began plotting. There must be some way to fix this. Right now, there was only Queenie's speculation about a plate of brownies standing between her and the recovery of her reputation. Sleep claimed her as her brain whirred with possibilities.

....

The shrill ring of the phone woke her. She squinted at the clock. After midnight. Who would be calling at this hour? "Hello?"

"Posey, it's Mike Ricketts. Sorry to disturb you, but I'm calling with official sheriff business. Is Vern home?"

The gin lay across her brain like a fog. Had Vern returned while she was passed out? "Can you hold on for just a moment?" She dashed down the hall, confirmed that Vern's bed was empty, and ran back. She would never admit her husband was unaccounted for. Hadn't she been embarrassed enough that night? "Of course my husband is home. Why?"

"A call came in about a suspicious vehicle hidden behind some scrub out on Nashville Highway. Someone saw a man skulking around the perimeter of a house and thought it might be the Creeper. It's Vern's truck that's up in the bushes."

So his mistress lives on Nashville Highway. "My husband is certainly not the Creeper," she shot back. "His truck must have been stolen."

"Could be, but I need to talk to Vern about it. Can you put him on the phone?"

She couldn't let the sheriff know the truth. If he said anything to his cow of a wife, Barbara would delight in making sure every soul in Spark knew about the affair. Word would probably get out regardless, thanks to Queenie, but she'd be damned if she let Barbara Ricketts have the scoop that confirmed it. No, Barbara couldn't know Vern was spending his evening elsewhere, which meant Mike couldn't know either. She needed to buy some time. "I'd rather not disturb him, Sheriff," she purred. "He worked late and is exhausted."

An idea popped into her head. *I can teach Vern a lesson and use stupid Mike Ricketts to do it.* "Tell you what. There's a spare key hidden in one of those magnetic box thingies under the bumper. Can you drive the truck back over here and then talk to Vern in the morning?" *Vern will be stranded miles from home. That'll show him.*

"I don't know, Posey. How'd I get back to my squad car?"

"Couldn't your son come pick you up?"

A pause hung in the air before the sheriff answered. "He's on assignment."

"I can drive you back to your house. It would just take a minute. You could get the squad car in the morning."

"Naw. It's best I come home in my own car."

"Okay, then I can run you back to your car on Nashville Highway."

"Seems like a lot of trouble."

She needed a reason to bring that truck home. *Think, Posey.* "Vern is picking up leftovers from a garage sale early tomorrow morning. He needs his truck first thing. A favor between old friends doesn't seem too much to ask."

"Is that what I am, an old friend?" Mike chuckled. "I never could say no to you. Okay, Posey. I'll do it."

"Thank you, Sheriff." She rubbed her aching temples. "And could you put the truck in the carport? I have service vans coming to pick up the rental items from the reunion and don't want to block their way. Just park it beside my Cadillac." *That way Vern won't see the truck when Miss Brass Button drops him off.*

After hanging up the phone, she flinched at the splintered memory of what had transpired with CJ and what she had overheard by the tent. Pushing the sharp words from her mind, she focused on the job at hand: fooling Sheriff Ricketts. *That shouldn't be too hard.* She tore off her party dress and scrambled into her most daring peignoir set, rose pink with black silk threads woven into a lattice pattern at the collarbone. She brushed her teeth and gargled with Lavoris, then blew a cinnamony breath into her palm and sniffed. Once downstairs, she curled up in a wing chair to await the sheriff's arrival.

Mike Ricketts gave a firm knock on the carport door. She adjusted her gown to more fully show her breasts and wobbled to the door. "Thank you, Sheriff," she said as his eyes took in the tableau she had so carefully set. "You were certainly clever, realizing Vern's truck was stolen before we even knew it was gone."

"Just doin' my job, serving the fine citizenry of Spark."

She placed her hand on the doorknob. "Let's go get your car, shall we?"

He glanced toward the top of the massive staircase. "You sure Vern isn't up?"

"Heavens, Mike, would I lie to the law? Isn't that a felony?" She gestured to her silk gown, as delicate and intricately constructed as a spider's web. "What would your wife say, hauling me into jail barely decent?" She pushed a fallen curl off her face. "I wasn't too surprised Barbara skipped the reunion. She never did like me, but what's a little smooch in the cloakroom between old friends? Engaged isn't the same as being married."

Mike grinned. "Barb likes you fine. It's just most of her friends were in my class, so she'd rather go to my twentieth next year. And I remember a lot more than a kiss, but that's a secret between—what'd you call us?—*old friends*."

"Sure, Mike," she said with only a bit of a drunken slur.

"Best be on our way. It's already after one o'clock."

She giggled. "Let me grab a jacket to cover up and my purse. It wouldn't do to operate a motor vehicle without my license." *Will he tell me I'm in no condition to drive back home?*

Without a word, Mike got behind the wheel of the Cadillac. Posey slid in beside him. *Too stupid to see I'm drunk.*

They were both silent during the long drive to Mike's squad car on Nashville Highway. If she could figure out who owned the adjacent property, she'd know Miss Brass Button's identity. *Do I dare ask who lives there?* Mike parked the Cadillac.

"How frightening for the woman in that house to have been visited by the Creeper. I hope she's okay." She looked expectantly at Mike.

"Can't discuss official business, you know." He took one long, last look at Posey. "Such a pretty gown." Winking as he got into his car, he added, "See you in church."

As she waved at the sheriff and pulled away, she cruised by the small white house, studying it the way she scrutinized the mansion on Coventry Circle. The simple structure and scrabbly yard were typical of the modest houses on the outskirts of town. *If I knocked on the door, would he answer it? Or would she?* She glanced down at her peignoir. *Better not. It's enough to know the address.* She navigated back to Creekside Road, being careful not to speed. She didn't know where Billy Ricketts's assignment was, but she couldn't be pulled over, drunk and in a negligee. *The father may be stupid, but the son isn't.*

After she was safely back at home, she allowed the events of the evening to flood her brain. She swayed to the living room and poured herself another drink, replaying all the stinging words she'd heard that night in her mind as she sank into a chair. CJ blamed her for wrecking his marriage, and, knowing Queenie's love of gossip, Vern's affair would be common knowledge before the sun had fully dried the dew from Spark's grassy yards. Thinking she could concoct some kind of story to mitigate the brownie debacle was pure foolishness.

She held her aching head in her hands, then rose from her chair and staggered into her dining room, where twin chandeliers hung like earrings, throwing fragmented light about the room. The news of Vern's affair would be cascading through every home and business in a few hours. The Saturday morning crowd at the Blue Plate, ladies browsing for a new dress at Honeybelle's, shoppers at the BuyMore stocking up for the weekend—they'd all be gossiping about her. She was about to lose everything. "Hell, it was probably all gone already!" she yelled to Milbrey's portrait. CJ. Her husband. Her standing in the community. Her reputation. "You'd know something about that, wouldn't you, Creekside Crone?" She drained her glass and heaved it at the portrait. Splinters of Waterford crystal rained down at her feet.

The scratch of the front door key was amplified in the still room. Vern had returned. Posey lurched toward him, dressed in the gown he had bought for her back when he was still trying to save their marriage. He cleared his throat. "I've got some bad news."

Supporting her weight with one hand on the back of a heavily carved dining chair, she brayed, "Oh, do you?"

"After I finished my bookkeeping, I went out back, and my truck was gone. Somebody stole it. I had to walk home."

"So your truck was taken from behind the Emporium?"

Vern nodded. "I'll take it up with Mike in the morning. It's not worth much, but I guess somebody wanted it."

"Somebody wanted *something*, all right." Her voice was quavering. "Why don't you have a look-see in the carport and then come tell me about how someone made off with your truck while you did your bookkeeping."

He wordlessly walked to the back of the house. When he returned, he said, "We need to talk."

"Damn straight we do. The whole town knows about Miss Brass Button."

He looked blankly at her. "Who?"

"Your mistress, Vern Jarvis." She sank into the soft cushion of a chair. "Why did you do this to me?"

"You're not going to believe me, no matter what I say."

"Try me." Her whole body was shaking.

"It's about me, not you. I fell in love with a woman who thinks I am smart, and kind, and generous."

"Oh, I bet you've been generous. What's her name? Who is she?"

"Someone who makes me feel like a good man." He hung his head. "That's all I ever wanted, to be good enough for someone, just as I am."

"And what about your wife?"

"You don't need me. You never have, not after you got that ring on your finger. Remember the night by the church, when I found you bawling in the gazebo? You looked so beautiful, so fragile, wailing about being pregnant and getting dumped by the father, some hotshot doctor." He grimaced. "The smell of wisteria still makes me sick."

Facing her, he continued, "I remember you sobbing, barely able to get out the words about how he said you weren't good enough to be his wife. I felt so sorry for you." He looked into her eyes. "I often wonder what woulda happened if I hadn't decided to go for a walk that night, or if I hadn't heard you crying and gone to help." He paused. "Or if I didn't have the kind of heart that made me feel like I could be your knight in shining armor and rescue you." Looking down the long hall toward the carport housing his truck, he said, "When you said yes, I thought I was the luckiest man alive, getting a beautiful wife who already had what I wanted most in the world, a child I could call my own." He shook his head. "I'd say it was the biggest mistake of my life, except I got my Callie Jane."

Posey glared at her husband. "I tried, hard. Those first few weeks, I made a real effort to fall in love with you." She burped. "I was grateful and wanted things to work out."

"Guess it didn't take."

"So you feel justified having a mistress."

"No," he answered softly, "but I do feel *loved* having a mistress."

Blood pounded in her temples, and Vern's voice sounded as if it were floating from underneath Niagara Falls, like on their honeymoon when they gave up trying to make themselves heard over the roar of the water.

"Maybe you should go back to the piece of trash who loves you."

Vern's voice was sharp. "That's a good idea. I'll tell her we're divorcing, and I'll propose to her right then and there. Feel free to offer your congratulations." He headed for the carport door, then turned to face her. "But you're wrong about one thing. She's not trash. She's the finest woman I know." He gave her a look of pity. "Your fancy doctor was right. You *weren't* good enough for him. And you're not good enough for me either." He slammed the carport door.

She staggered to the hall closet. Pushing aside the half-empty bottle of gin, she extracted the loaded Savage 340 .30-30 from the spot Vern had chosen on the shelf. She followed her husband out the door and leveled the gun at him, lining up her target just the way he had taught her. She didn't see that well, and really should have gone to an eye doctor by now, but it didn't matter, as Vern was still quite large, despite being on a diet in an effort to save his heart.

Tears streamed down her face as she called his name.

Vern turned. "Posey, no! Drop the rifle!"

She lowered it, shaking with sobs. "Why did you humiliate me? Couldn't you see that all I wanted was to be loved?"

"Put the gun down. It's loaded." Vern took cautious steps toward her. "I never meant to hurt you."

Posey raised the gun to her shoulder, her hands trembling. "You *did* hurt me. Men *always* hurt me. And now you'll know what it's like to be hurt too."

"You don't want to do this, Posey. We can divorce, and I'll take all the blame. Just put the gun down. You can start a new life and finally be happy. That's the truth."

Posey shook her head like a petulant child, repeating the only advice her mother had ever given her. "The truth is overrated." Her finger crept to the trigger.

Vern lunged for the rifle, and Posey jerked it away from his grasp. The weapon discharged with a report that startled them both.

As Vern crumpled to the ground, the rifle recoiled against her shoulder, knocking her down. Blood dripped from the wall of the carport, falling in fat drops to the cement slab floor. After a stunned moment, with her ears ringing, she crawled to her husband and cradled what was left of his head in her lap, his blood soaking the pink silk of her peignoir.

Chapter 24

Callie Jane

AS CALLIE JANE tried to sleep in her sweltering bedroom, Trace's advice kept playing in her head. *"Are you going to spend your life trying to suit someone else, or are you going to do what you want and take a chance on being happy?"* She flipped her pillow, recalling Evangeline's explanation of why she moved to Spark: *"Why not go someplace that makes me happy?"* The voice of her father echoed in her head as she kicked off her sheet. *"A bluebird does what its heart wants and flies to where it's happiest."* The final voice that churned through her head was her own, a declaration she had made to her father as they discussed whether he should go to Scranton for the baptism. *"You deserve to be happy. Everyone does."* She had spoken the truth that day, and it was time to listen, even if—no, especially since—that voice of reason belonged to her.

She gave up on sleep and padded to the tiny kitchen and poured herself a drink from the faucet. As she gratefully downed the water, she tried to settle her overly tired brain. After pouring a second glass, she quietly opened the sliding glass door and descended the steps onto the patio. A slight breeze ruffled her hair, and she turned her face to take advantage of the moment of respite from the record-breaking heat.

Under the soft light of the moon, with the rhythmic whirring of the cicadas providing the background music as she thought, Callie Jane made a decision. Trace was right, Evangeline was right, and her father was right. Most importantly, *she* was right when she gave advice to her daddy she had been afraid to take for herself. *You deserve to be happy. Everyone does.* She was going to California. Returning to her bed, she fell into a deep sleep.

· · · · · · · · · ·

The insistent ringing of the phone woke her. *What in the world?* She stumbled to the phone, fumbling in the dark for the receiver.

"Callie Jane? This is Sheriff Ricketts. I need you to come to your mama's house right away."

Her throat was suddenly parched, and she could barely get the words out. "What's happened?"

"I'd rather not get into it over the phone. Can you just get over here as soon as you can?"

She swallowed hard and managed to articulate, "I'll be right there."

When she opened the unlocked door of Cold Spring, her mother was seated on a sofa in the library wearing a white shirt and a navy skirt, with the sheriff writing earnestly in a notebook. They both looked up when she walked in.

Her mother, who was dabbing her eyes, spoke first. "There's been a tragedy." She glanced at the sheriff and dabbed again. "Your father has been shot."

Callie Jane stared at her mother, seeing her mouth move but not fully comprehending her words.

"He's dead." Her mother choked out the words between sobs.

Callie Jane managed to guide her body into a chair before her knees gave out. Her throat burned and the throbbing in her temples became a pounding inside her skull.

"Last night while your father and I were sleeping, I heard a sound outside. I thought it might be the Creeper, so I reached over to your father and woke him up." She blew her nose softly into a handkerchief. "You know how protective he is . . . I mean, was. He went downstairs to investigate."

A roaring sound filled her ears. *No, no, no, no.*

"He took a rifle with him. I heard a yell and then a loud bang. I ran to the bedroom window and caught a glimpse of someone." She glanced at the sheriff, who was listening intently. "Someone racing across our driveway toward the woods."

The room spun like some out-of-control fair ride. She grabbed the edge of her chair to prevent herself from being thrown to the floor. Closing her eyes, she willed the image of her ghostly white mother to dissipate. She tried to speak, but what emerged from her mouth was a guttural croak.

"Oh, honey, it's awful, I know." Her mother's Peter Pan collar rested on her delicate clavicle, resembling the misshapen angel wings of the salt dough Christmas ornament Callie Jane had fashioned in kindergarten.

A thin voice she assumed must be her own said from off in the distance, "I don't understand what you're saying."

"That Peeping Tom has been tormenting our community, and the sheriff said the danger was escalating. It was only a matter of time before something dreadful happened."

"Are you saying the Creeper killed Daddy?"

She nodded solemnly. "I am."

Callie Jane turned to the sheriff, fully expecting him to say this was why he had called her to come to Cold Spring, that her mother was having some kind of break with reality. Instead, he stood and said, "I'm so sorry. I thought it best that you be here with her."

Callie Jane's voice shook as she faced the sheriff. "Is this right? The Creeper killed my father?"

"We don't know that for sure yet." He closed his notebook. "I'm glad you're here, Callie Jane. I've called the coroner in Nashville to come get the body—I mean, Vern. The carport is a crime scene, so neither of you go out there." He gestured to a paper sack. "Posey, I'm taking the clothes you had on. They're evidence. Gotta get a few more photographs and bag up the gun, then I'll wait in the carport for the coroner. Billy's comin' too. Posey, I'll need to interview you more thoroughly, but that can wait." He walked to the carport door. "I'll see myself out when we're done." Turning to face the women, he added, "My deepest condolences to you both."

Callie Jane sat numbly in the chair, trying to absorb the news that her father was gone.

Her mother went to the kitchen and returned with a glass of water. "Try to drink something."

After a few sips, Callie Jane dropped the glass on the side table and lurched from her chair, knocking the table to the floor. Shards of glass sprayed skyward. She stumbled to the bathroom, frantically pulling the door closed behind her before she vomited twice, then curled into a ball on the floor.

Rhythmic knocking on the door pounded her brain. *This isn't real. This isn't real.* Squeezing her eyes closed, she willed herself to wake up from the worst nightmare of her life.

Her mother tapped insistently on the door. "Please come out of the bathroom. I want to tell you something that may help."

She struggled to her feet and yanked open the door. "What could you possibly tell me to make this better?"

"Come sit down," her mother said, patting the empty spot on the sofa. "Here, beside me." She took Callie Jane's hands in her own. "Everyone makes mistakes, myself included. When I was young, I made a foolish decision about a handsome, powerful man and ended up pregnant. I was devastated and returned home to Spark brokenhearted, trying to figure out what to do." She stroked Callie Jane's cheek. "Having a baby as an unwed mother was not in my life plan, even if that baby was you."

Callie Jane had put most of this story together on the drive back from Dr. Ryan's office, but it was surreal hearing it from her mother's lips.

"Vern found me crying, and I confessed why." The tone of her mother's voice became softer. "He said he wasn't able to have children of his own and had planned to never marry, because he'd be denying his wife a chance at a family. He offered to marry me and raise you as his own." She pushed the hair from her eyes. "He said his most fervent wish was to have a family, a wife and a child to take care of, and that if I married him, his dream would come true."

Tears of frustration pooled in Callie Jane's eyes. "How does any of this help?"

Her thin lips formed a smile. "Vern Jarvis is not your father."

"Yes, he is."

The irritation in her mother's voice was palpable. "Were you not listening? Telling you this is very difficult for me. The least you could do is be attentive."

Callie Jane's swollen eyes bored through her mother. "Oh, I've been attentive, all right. Callen James Ryan may have gotten you pregnant, but Vern Jarvis is my father."

Her mother's eyes widened, and her words pulsed with anger. "How do you know his name?"

Callie Jane rose to her feet, hatred for her mother surging through her body. "I know a lot of things, like how you manipulated Daddy into marrying you so you wouldn't have the shame of being pregnant and unwed. I know how you thanked him for that by making his life a living hell. I know how you never looked around—even once—to see that you had a beautiful life, one that people would sell their souls for. I know that Daddy escaped to his garden, his sanctuary, to get away from you and your stinking gin that seems to be more important to you than either Daddy or me. I know he loved someone else but would never embarrass you with a divorce, even if it meant he'd be free to be with the woman who loved him."

Callie Jane stalked to the door of Cold Spring. "I may not have my father anymore, but I *never* had a mother."

Chapter 25

Posey

THE NEXT FEW days passed in a blur, a mix of trepidation and gin with a guilt chaser. Her only contact with the outside world had been a conversation with Brother Cleave about the arrangements and a call to Arden at the Blue Plate, asking her to come to the house and prepare a lunch after the funeral. She cradled a bottle of gin in her arms as she retreated to her room, unplugged the phone, pulled her curtains tightly closed, and crawled into bed.

··········

The morning of the funeral she stood before her closet, clad only in a satin slip, considering her options. The bruise on her shoulder dictated her outfit. The purple splotch would be visible if she wore her favorite black dress, a sleeveless cotton sheath with a satin bow at the waist. No, the short-sleeve one with the high neckline would have to do. As she zipped up, she surveyed her frame from every angle. Did any tattletale color give her away?

Judging by the smells curling up the stairs, Arden had arrived to begin preparing the lunch. Although Posey would have preferred to return to the comforts of her bed and bottle after the funeral, Southern custom dictated that friends came to the home of the bereaved to offer comfort, and further mandated that the mourners be fed. *Better see how that's going,* she thought dully. *Although it's not likely I'll impress anybody with my hostessing skills here at Cold Fish.*

She paused briefly at the top of the stairs. *In a few hours, the whole town will be here, poking their noses into every crevice and corner.* Just a few days ago she had made a valiant effort to keep the reunion-goers contained to the tent and terrace, but now she was too exhausted to even attempt coming up with a plan to corral the throng of mourners. She briefly recalled the long-ago snooping she had done at Frances's home, which had included opening drawers and browsing in her closets like a shopper making her way through the racks of a department store, but dismissed the image as not being comparable. She continued down the staircase and entered her kitchen.

Arden was busy winding plastic wrap around a platter of finger sandwiches. The Blue Plate's owner was a little odd, but at least she didn't join in the hateful gossip so loved by most of the ladies of Spark. "You are so kind, Arden." Posey cast down her eyes. "I've been too distraught to even think straight, much less plan a meal."

"I loved Vern, and so did every other soul in Spark," Arden said, gesturing to endless bowls and platters overflowing with fried chicken, green beans, mashed potatoes, seven-layer salad, turnip greens, and towering Jell-O salads studded with marshmallows. "People have been bringing food to the Blue Plate nonstop once they found out I was in charge of the lunch." She popped an ice cube tray into the freezer. "I need to go home and change for the service." She peered into a skillet of fried corn, replacing the lid before continuing. "One of my waitresses is coming to finish the last-minute details." She retrieved her purse from the kitchen table. "After the . . . I mean, later, you might want to have someone check your fridge. It's running way too cold." She took a step and then paused. "Brother Cleave said to tell you Grady and Hannah Neal will drive you to the church and to the cemetery afterward."

Grady parked in the gravel drive of Cold Spring and loaded Posey into their car. A pregnant Hannah sat in the back seat and patted Posey on her tender shoulder. Posey winced as Hannah's fingers drummed her bruise. When Grady pulled into a spot reserved by an orange cone marked *Bereaved*, Hannah choked back a sob. "We will miss him so much."

Vern had a standing-room-only crowd. Brother Cleave's sermon could not be called inspired, but he was able to hit the high points: a good man is a man who is good to all. Vern never met a stranger and was always the first to serve in anyone's time of need. Everyone was called to be more like Vern.

With Sheriff Ricketts and his wife, Barbara, leading the way in the squad car, the funeral procession rolled slowly toward Cedar Hill cemetery. When Mike turned onto Poplar Avenue, she realized they were passing by their old house. Vern's daisies were flourishing, and the hydrangeas' heavy blue mopheads seemed to be bowing to honor Vern's body as the hearse crawled by the home he loved so dearly.

As she exited the car at the cemetery, supported by Grady, she was surprised at the number of vehicles trailing behind them. *This whole town adored him*, she thought. A flash of jealousy coursed through her. *I wish I had.* She studied the crowd that gathered around Vern's open grave, scanning the teary, somber faces. *Why was I never able to feel what these people did?*

She wobbled to the small tent, casting about at the mourners' faces as she took a seat beside Callie Jane. Would his mistress be brazen enough to attend? How would she even know which one she was? She choked back a sob, prompting another painful pat from Hannah. A few rows of chairs had been placed on either side of the gravesite for the family and closest friends, but the others were left to position themselves as they could, awkwardly standing on plots. It had always seemed odd to her that the bodies destined for their graves were treated with such dignity, but once they had been committed to the earth, it was fine to trounce over their final resting place.

Darlene and Dewey, Queenie, Lurelle and her husband, the whole town was there. All the Humboldts were in attendance. Trace was accompanied by a plain-looking girl in a gray dress. *Who brings a date to a funeral?* She was startled to see all of Vern's Pennsylvania relatives. Callie Jane must have called them. If that sanctimonious gaggle of Jarvises so much as spoke to her, she would lose her religion. Shorty Strickland had shuttered his drugstore, and Bill Horton had closed up shop as well. She frowned as she remembered the exorbitant fee he had charged them to fix the kitchen plumbing after the faucet broke. She squinted at the man. *Apparently not enough to afford a decent suit.*

A glint of color flashed in Posey's eyes. She searched the crowd for the source. A woman in a black scalloped-hem dress passed her, wearing a rhinestone heart hanging from a delicate silver chain. The last time she'd seen that necklace, it had been in Vern's luggage, packed for the Poconos. Tina Anderson was its owner. Posey gasped. The identity of Miss Brass Button had been revealed.

The blistering sun had been assailing the canvas tent since their arrival, and what little air Posey was able to breathe

scorched her lungs. She shifted in her seat as the casket was lowered into the ground. Tina let out a sob, drawing a few stares.
You're the mistress, not the wife, so shut the hell up.

Her eyes rested on Mike Ricketts, who sat with Barbara on
the opposite side of the open grave. He was staring intently at
his wife as she talked. What news was that ninny relaying that
couldn't wait until Vern was buried? The casket landed in the
bottom of the vault with a *thud*.

Was Mike glaring at her, or just reacting to the harsh sun in
his eyes? No, he was definitely staring. *Damn it.*

A wave of dizziness made everything swirl around her head.
The earth slipped away, and darkness filled her eyes as she fell
toward the mat of artificial grass that surrounded Vern's grave.

Chapter 26

Callie Jane

AS BROTHER CLEAVE droned on, movement among the headstones caught Callie Jane's eye—a bluebird perched atop a rigid plastic blossom on a nearby grave. How had the bird been fooled by the imitation, as fake as the copy of Leonardo da Vinci's *The Last Supper* hanging in the Emporium? In a world overflowing with lush gardens bursting with every type of flower in God's creation, why had this bluebird chosen a cemetery as her home?

The *thump* of her mother's body hitting the ground startled everyone, including Callie Jane. Her mother's face was as chalky white as the funeral program Grady Neal was using to fan her. Grady scooped her up and set her gently in the rickety folding chair. As soon as her mother regained her senses, she jerked her arm to the upturned right sleeve of her dress. She frantically pulled at the fabric until it lay flat against her arm, only then dealing with the hem of her dress, which had ridden up her leg, providing too much information about her mother's undergarments. *Why didn't she fix that first?*

Brother Cleave didn't miss a beat. As soon as she was returned to her chair, he continued preaching, ignoring the hint that if the widow had fallen out, it might be time to wrap things up. After a final prayer, Brother Cleave approached, pressing his hands over first Callie Jane's and then her mother's, signaling the end of the funeral. After murmuring his condolences, he turned to the crowd. "Posey invites you all for lunch at the home she and Vern shared. You may offer your condolences to her and Callie Jane there."

Evangeline drove Callie Jane to Cold Spring. They pulled in directly behind Trace, who enveloped her in a bear hug. He tried to speak, but all he could manage was, "Oh, Callie Jane." He took the hand of a young woman he introduced as Laurie Anne and went inside.

Every inch of the dining room table was covered with a bowl or platter. The smells of the food—ham and biscuits, deviled eggs, macaroni salad, okra, plus a dozen more offerings—hung heavy in the air, nauseating Callie Jane. She watched from the doorway as people grabbed a piece of her mother's china from the sideboard, smiling and talking as they loaded their plates. This tradition of comforting the bereaved upon learning of the loss, then solemnly standing at the gravesite, stone-faced, to support the survivors, only to immediately be followed by happily gorging on all the food and exchanging the latest gossip, had always puzzled her, but some version of the same three-act play had been performed in Spark all of her life. She shrugged. *Guess people can handle only so much decorum before their true natures, or maybe their stomachs, take over.* She grimaced as Wasp Fentress helped himself to a drumstick and stacked it on top of an already towering mound of food.

She was headed for the door to the terrace, desperate to be outside, when she heard talking from the nearby catio that stopped her in her tracks. She slipped behind a bamboo screen to listen.

Rosalie King was talking. "Of course you don't see it 'cause he's your brother, but everybody knows Wasp is the best-looking boy in the whole county. Those muscles are to die for."

Linda Fentress answered. "Those muscles are why we *didn't* die. Ever since he was a little kid, he lifted weights to bulk up so's he could fight Daddy whenever he got drunk and came after us. Once Wasp was big enough to win the fights, the beatings stopped, so I will always love him for that, even if he is dumb as a box of rocks and mean as a snake. He even stole the ceramic angel he bought me for my birthday to get a refund. He said he didn't, but I saw it back on the Emporium shelf when I was helping Daddy pick up a table. He's not going back to school come fall, but I guess what you need to know about farming tobacco is taught in a field, not a classroom."

Rosalie said in a sultry voice, "I'd like to teach him a thing or two. And what I have in mind doesn't require brains or a civics medal."

Linda giggled. "You are so bad. Hush up."

"I hope his injury didn't take him out of the game altogether, if you know what I mean. I still can't get over a boy named Wasp actually getting stung *by a wasp* on his pecker."

Linda shushed her giggling friend. "Remember, that's a secret, so don't go blabbing. But it *was* hilarious. He had some weird allergic reaction and had to stay in bed a whole day, which meant I got stuck helping my daddy pick up a heavy table from the Emporium. That tale he told about a wasp flying down his pants was a hoot. I wonder what the real story is. Guess we'll never know."

The room was airless, leaving Callie Jane gasping like a fish thrown onto the shore of Flat Rock Creek. She dashed through the door of the catio and collapsed on the low rock wall surrounding the terrace.

Memories of that night assaulted her. The red wolf dream, the eyes staring at her as she slept. Muse growling and snarling. *Sweet baby Jesus.* Wasp Fentress *was* the figure she spotted outside her bedroom window that night. *I'll find the sheriff and tell him everything I saw.* It was too late for Wasp's latest victims, but she could make sure he was stopped from violating anyone else. A thought hit her hard enough to make her dizzy. *That means Wasp killed Daddy. And I'm the reason he's dead. If I'd been brave enough to name Wasp as the Creeper, Daddy would still be alive.*

She struggled to her feet and went back inside, intent on finding the sheriff. As she frantically scanned the crowded dining room, her mother took her arm. "You're as white as a sheet."

"I know who killed Daddy!"

Her mother's eyes flew open. "You *what?*"

"The Creeper shot Daddy, and I can identify the Creeper, so now I know who killed him." Her eyes searched the room. "Where is Sheriff Ricketts?"

Pulling her into the empty butler's pantry, her mother asked, "Who is it?"

"Wasp Fentress! I heard his sister talking, and she said something that made me realize he was the face in my window that night. I need to tell the sheriff."

Her mother had an odd look on her face, like she had just figured out who the murderer was on one of those whodunits she liked to watch on television. She spoke slowly. "I'm having trouble picturing the Fentress boy. Could you describe him to me?"

"Tall, about six feet, with red hair. Lots of red hair. He's in the dining room right now if you want to see him for yourself." She turned away from her mother. "I need to find the sheriff."

After a moment of silence, her mother spoke. "Let's go to the dining room so you can point him out to me, but make sure no one sees you. He can't know you've figured out he's the Creeper."

The pair walked to the dining room and Callie Jane nodded in Wasp's direction. Her voice shook. "Right there. He's got potato salad all over his face." She looked around. "I just saw the sheriff a few minutes ago. He needs to arrest Wasp."

Evangeline approached, keys in hand. "Let's go home, Callie Jane. You look so tired."

Before Callie Jane could respond, her mother spoke. "Evangeline is right. You've had a terrible shock and need to rest. Would you like me to tell the sheriff for you? I was just on my way to speak to him."

As soon as Evangeline had mentioned going home, Callie Jane was overcome with exhaustion. After a moment of hesitation, she nodded, tears dripping down her face. In her grief, her mother was actually behaving like a loving parent. *Maybe I've judged her too harshly.* "Thank you."

"I'll take care of everything," her mother murmured. She stroked Callie Jane's hand as she spoke in a soothing tone. "You just let Evangeline drive you on home and I'll tell the sheriff all about Wasp Fentress."

Her mother was already making a beeline for the sheriff. For a split second she thought of joining them to make sure her mother conveyed the message accurately, but when Evangeline took her arm and gently led her to the front door, Callie Jane went with her.

Chapter 27

Posey

POSEY SPED OVER to the sheriff. "Mike! It's urgent I speak with you privately."

Mike looked around the crowded first floor. "Where at?"

"Follow me." She led him into the secret office, not caring that he would see the paint cans or the mold. This was her big chance, and she wasn't going to miss it because of a reputation that was already in tatters. Once she had closed the door behind them, she announced, "I remembered something. I know who shot Vern."

Mike's eyebrows shot up. "You do?"

"As soon as I woke up this morning, I realized it." She raised her chin and spoke with a clear voice. "I opened my eyes, and the first thought in my head was that Wasp Fentress was the figure I saw running from Vern's body that night."

"Are you sure?"

"Yes. I was understandably in shock, but this morning I realized the truth. I couldn't get to you before the funeral to tell you." She tucked her hair behind her ears. "There's more. Callie Jane has just realized Wasp was the face she saw in her window. The Creeper—Wasp—killed my husband."

Mike said, "I'll need to speak to Callie Jane."

Callie Jane's part in all this is true, but why take a chance? "She's *so* upset, Mike. Please don't make things worse by making her relive that night. She'd tell you the same thing she just told me. She heard Wasp's sister talking about Wasp and realized he was the Creeper."

"Tomorrow morning, nine o'clock. Be at my office to give your statement."

· · · · · · · · ·

Posey needed a quiet place to gather her thoughts before she met with the sheriff. She pulled behind the Emporium and parked under the maple. Oddly, she found comfort occupying the spot Vern had used for years, like everything was back to normal and she was just running in for a moment.

The day was already stifling, way too hot for mid-May. She rolled down the windows and turned off the ignition, ready to face some ugly truths. CJ had never loved her and had used her as a tawdry distraction from his country club life. She meant no more to him than the cigarette butt he'd snubbed out beneath his heel. She had never loved Vern, but he had been a good husband and an excellent father. He adored Callie Jane and cared for her like she was his own.

Laying her forehead on the steering wheel, she cried. Her sobbing became wailing, and she rolled up the windows despite the heat, certain the whole town could hear her. After a few moments of racking sobs, she stopped, gulped for air, and searched for a handkerchief in her purse. Her hand brushed smooth metal. She had told herself no drinking until after she had spoken with Mike, but she needed to steady her nerves. Extracting the flask, she took a long pull.

Vern had married her at her lowest, saving her from a lifetime of shame. A fresh cascade of tears wet her cheeks. She could blame her actions on the disastrous reunion, CJ's rejection, Vern's painful words, or even her ever-absent father, but it didn't matter; she had killed her husband. Hell awaited her for sure, and prison if she wasn't careful.

She lifted her head. Vern was not an entirely innocent party, though. "Thou shalt not commit adultery" was chiseled just as deeply into Moses' tablet as "Thou shalt not kill." She had been a faithful wife, albeit not a loving one. Vern was the one who had broken their marriage vows. *"You're not good enough."* She'd seen only red that night, first from her own fury, and then from the blood that sprayed from Vern's body.

The pain of picking at a fingernail created a momentary distraction as she cried for herself. Spotting CJ at that estate sale all those years ago had destroyed her life. She wanted safety and security, money and social standing. Marriage to him would have brought all of that. But she could have dropped a dozen earrings into Frances's drawer and still ended up pregnant and alone.

Regardless of how hard she tried to shed the skin, she was still a Stadler, and those women would never forget it, no matter how many stories her house had, how many designer outfits were stuffed in her closet, or how much silver graced her sideboard.

The cruel comments about Cold Spring had been humiliating. Everyone had their share of odors and mold, but the women had carried on about her house like theirs were palaces. She banged her fist on her steering wheel and bowed her head. She had yearned for years to be mistress of a home finer than Eden Hall, but three minutes of overheard gossip took her triumph away.

After a moment, she raised her head with phoenixlike determination coursing through her body. *Save yourself and be strong, like you've had to do your whole life.* Posey pulled out her compact and examined her blotchy face. Choosing to forgo makeup in the interest of looking desolate had been a good call. Snapping her compact closed, she resumed her preparations.

Her account of what happened the night of Vern's death needed to be so convincing that no one would ever think to seek the actual facts. It had all happened so fast, though, that she was having trouble wringing the events of the evening from her soggy memory. Massaging the bridge of her nose, she reviewed what had transpired. Mike had found Vern's truck hidden in bushes by Nashville Highway in response to a possible Creeper sighting. She had been so proud of thinking to have Mike drive it to Cold Spring, stranding Vern miles from town as revenge. Had that been a mistake? Would that somehow implicate her? *Quit dreaming up what could go wrong and focus on how to make it right.*

Less is more. Say as little as possible, and don't deviate from the narrative. She raised a delicate finger as she reviewed each point in her story. One: She heard a noise, reached across the bed, and woke up Vern. Two: He took the gun outside to confront the prowler, presumably the Creeper. Three: The person overpowered Vern, took his weapon, and shot her husband. Four: She rushed to the window just in time to see a figure fleeing.

She waggled her pinkie finger. Was she leaving anything out? Ah, yes. Number five, the key to guaranteeing her exoneration: Not just any figure. Wasp Fentress. She allowed herself a tiny smile. Thanks to her daughter, she could name Wasp Fentress as the culprit. And she had Callie Jane's own account of seeing Wasp in her window to back up the story of the Fentress boy being the Creeper.

She twisted the ignition key and headed to Mike's office. Standing outside his door, she inhaled the oppressive air. *To get what you want to get, you have to do what you have to do.*

Mike's desk, chairs, and bookcase were all crafted from old whiskey barrels, smelling of cigar smoke mixed with the bite of decades-old liquor, bringing to her mind images of television westerns.

"Have a seat." Mike's voice echoed in the wood-filled room. She slid into the chair opposite the sheriff and willed herself not to quake. Setting her purse beside her neatly crossed ankles, she folded her trembling hands and waited. Mike cleared his throat and spoke. "I'm sorry for your loss. You understand, though, that I have a job to do, so I need to ask you a few questions."

She summoned the childlike whisper Jackie Kennedy had been so unfairly criticized for. "I understand."

He dragged a yellow legal pad across his paper-strewn desk and clicked his pen. "Start from the beginning, and don't leave anything out. The tiniest detail could be what breaks this case wide open."

She patted her eyes with one of Milbrey's linen handkerchiefs as she told her tale. She included good details but didn't elaborate too much. *Just a little more, Posey girl, then you can go home and have as much gin as you want.* "I saw that Vern was dead, but I rushed to him anyway. I held him against my body and sobbed, telling him how much I loved him, begging him not to leave me." She peeped through her lashes at the handsome sheriff. "And then I called you."

"What time did Vern get home that night?"

She had done her math homework, and it was time to turn it in. If the truck was found at twelve thirty, Vern had to be home at least a half hour before then. But not too much before, because the party didn't wrap up until after eleven. "Around eleven thirty, maybe a little later. I was asleep, but I heard him get into bed."

He nodded, then checked his scribbled notes. "Tell me again what you saw out the window."

"The man ran right under a floodlight, so I got a good look at him. Tall, about six feet, with red hair. Lots of red hair." She paused dramatically and then whispered, "Like I told you yesterday, it was Wasp Fentress."

"And why did it take you until yesterday to identify him?"

She was ready. "It was shock. My body's way of protecting me from what I've been through. But when I woke up the morning of the funeral, I remembered. Before I'd even opened my eyes, I remembered it was Wasp I'd seen."

Posey watched Mike write and then added, "And thanks to Callie Jane, we know he is also the Creeper. She was planning on telling you, but I said I would do it." Posey sniffed. "She's been through so much already, losing her father."

He resumed writing. "And you're sure of the time you saw the Creeper . . . I mean, Wasp? Three a.m.?"

"Yes. I looked at my clock when I heard the noise."

Mike stood. "Thank you for meeting with me." As he walked her to the door, he added, "Barbara and I give you our deepest condolences."

She stumbled to her car, exhausted. Slipping behind the wheel, she paused to dab her eyes before turning the ignition key. He was watching her out the window, she was sure of it. She dabbed again.

Chapter 28

Callie Jane

CALLIE JANE TRUDGED to the end of the driveway to retrieve the weekly copy of the *Gazette*, faithfully delivered by 6:00 a.m. every Friday. Reading the *Gazette* had been an enjoyable habit, full of lighthearted stories about a family welcoming a second set of twins or a resident winning a blue ribbon at the state fair. She hadn't stopped to think that this issue, the one printed a week after her father's death, was one she shouldn't read. The front page seared her eyes.

"Vern Jarvis Murdered! Killer at Large!" Below the giant headline was written "Posey Jarvis Stunned!" accompanied by a photo of her mother standing by an antique secretary. The caption read, "Posey Jarvis prepares to entertain the Spark High Class of '46 at her lovely home, Cold Spring, the evening before the murder."

She tried to push away the paper, but her eyes were drawn to the newsprint.

> Vern Jarvis, the proprietor of Jarvis Emporium, was slain in the early morning hours of Saturday, May 14. His grieving widow, noted Spark socialite Posey Jarvis,

reported to Sheriff Mike Ricketts that she heard a
noise outside and awakened her husband. Armed with
a rifle, he investigated. The prowler overpowered Jarvis,
65, and shot him in the head with his own gun.

A wave of nausea overtook her, and she began to sob. What
she wanted most in the world was the one thing she couldn't
have: her father. The closest she could get was going to a place
he loved with his whole heart, Jarvis Emporium.

· · · · · · · · · ·

Pulling into her father's parking spot felt invasive, like she was
taking something that didn't belong to her. Bypassing the light
switches, she collapsed into the tweed recliner by the office,
curled up in the massive chair, and cried for her father, who
would never cross the threshold of his beloved shop again. All
he ever wanted was to tend his garden, feed his bluebirds, and
visit with his friends when they stopped by the Emporium. She
added one more thing to the list: be a father.

Then she cried for herself. If she had never existed, he never
would have married her mother, ruining his life. And had she
found the courage to report her suspicions about Wasp Fentress
right away, her father would be alive, planning a Memorial Day
sale as he swapped stories with his customers. And maybe slipping out a little early to see Tina Anderson, whose weeping at
the funeral had unnerved both Callie Jane and her mother. Did
her mother know about Tina? She must have, judging by the icy
daggers she was slinging Tina's way.

Rising from the chair, she settled behind her father's desk. A
fresh wave of tears formed when she caught sight of the crayon

drawing of a bluebird she had made in second grade. Pulling tissues from a box, she blew her nose and surveyed the room, chock-full of china cats with clock stomachs, cast-iron skillets hanging from pegs, and neat stacks of dishcloths.

She sobbed, this time for all she had to give up. She had been so hopeful about her future, excited to begin a new life, but she couldn't deny her father his most fervent wish. California had been a pipe dream. Tears of sorrow and frustration coursed down her cheeks. She had finally committed to leaving town, but now she had to stay in Spark and run the Emporium to honor her father. They had both been buried this week—her father in Cedar Hill cemetery, and her in Jarvis Emporium. She returned to the recliner and wept.

Chapter 29

Posey

WHEN MIKE HAD called to say not that Wasp had been taken into custody but that he wanted to question her again, she had to fight to keep her voice steady. "Of course, Sheriff," she had purred. "Whatever I can do to help bring Vern's killer to justice." *As long as it's not me.* After hanging up, she made her way to the liquor cabinet. *Just one,* she told herself.

Glass in hand, she climbed the expansive staircase to prepare for Mike's arrival. She glanced longingly at her closet, overflowing with at least a dozen sleeveless dresses that would have been perfect had she not needed to hide the bruise that had blossomed to the size of a chrysanthemum, with streaks of green and yellow emerging petallike from the purple center. She chose a dress that would completely conceal her discolored arm and slipped it on, tugging at the long sleeves, wildly inappropriate for the predicted ninety-four-degree day, but she wasn't risking even a short sleeve after the near-disaster at the funeral. Her hands shook as she fastened the row of buttons that ran in a neat line from her neck to her waist, then descended the staircase to wait for the sheriff.

She paced in the living room as she practiced her story. *Keep it simple.* She peered out of the enormous library window and then at her watch. He was late. She stared wistfully at the gin bottles sparkling in the midday sun. *No more.* A tall glass filled to the rim would be her reward after he left. She searched the driveway again. No sign of him. She paused, frowning as she considered that Mike might be suspicious. *What had Barbara been telling him at the funeral?* She paced the length of her house in an effort to rid herself of the adrenaline surging through her body.

The deep, bonging chime of the doorbell finally pulsed through the first floor of her house. Running her hands over her hips, she grimaced in a hall mirror to check for any signs of lipstick on her teeth before approaching the door.

Mike shuffled his boots on the mat. "Wouldn't want to track dirt in," he said, smiling at her. He jerked a thumb in the direction of the plaque by the front door. "*Amor Vincit Omnia.* 'Love conquers all.' Nice touch."

How does a dolt like Mike know Latin? "May I get you some coffee or iced tea?" She bent her head down to hide her trembling chin. "Or maybe something stronger?"

"I'm on duty. Just some water. Hotter 'n the devil's doorknob out there."

"The library's right over here," she said. "Please make yourself at home. I'll be right back with our refreshments."

She returned carrying a silver tray with a pitcher of water and two of Milbrey's finest crystal glasses. "Would you like to sit down?"

He heaved his body into the leather chair. "I'm sorry to disturb you during this difficult time, but I have a few more questions."

She smoothed her dress and tried her best to look doe-eyed as she nodded.

"Did Vern have life insurance?"

Her mind flew upstairs to the sturdy oak cabinet containing her husband's generous policy. She had carefully read through it the day after the funeral and was planning on calling the insurance company as soon as a respectable amount of time had passed. And right after the check cleared, she was calling a pool company. "Vern took care of that sort of thing, not me. I haven't even thought about life insurance." She sniffled and mournfully added, "I can look in his file cabinet and let you know." Rivulets of sweat ran between her shoulder blades.

Mike pulled out his notepad from his shirt pocket. "You say Vern got home from the Emporium around eleven thirty."

"Something like that. As I said, I was asleep when he got into bed."

"When I called you that night, I asked if Vern was home. You told me to wait and then came back to the phone to tell me he was home but asleep. Were you checking to see if he was in the house?"

Oh Lord. That's exactly what I was doing. "Certainly not. I had to, well, visit the little girls' room. I hardly wanted to announce my need to *urinate*, Sheriff."

He scribbled on his pad and then shifted in his seat. "I hate to ask you this next question." He cleared his throat. "It has come to my attention that Vern might have . . . well, um, there might have been a lady in his life that, uh . . ."

She swallowed hard. *That must be what Barbara was whispering to him at the funeral.* Mike's pen was poised over that damn pad, waiting for her response.

Flicking her wrist dismissively, she said, "Oh, you mean Tina Anderson." She stood and walked to the window overlooking her vast estate. *Do not blow this.* Turning to face the sheriff, she added, "Men have certain needs that must be met." Her emerald eyes scanned the sheriff's body. "I'm sure you understand the male drive." She ran her hands along her hips. "I allowed it, and although I wasn't thrilled by my husband's choices, I accepted that his baser desires were being accommodated." She moved to the silver tray and refilled her glass. Taking a long gulp, she added, "Can that be off the record, Mike? I have a child to think of. Callie Jane is a sensitive girl, and there's no need for her father's reputation to be dragged through the mud."

"I understand. Are you aware that Tina Anderson rents a house near where Vern's truck was spotted?"

She lifted her chin. "No, I was not aware of that."

He hung his head. "Sorry, Posey." He rose from the massive wing chair and refilled his glass. "So you were okay with his cattin' around on you? You all hadn't been fighting about the affair?"

"I wouldn't say I was *okay*, as you put it, but I accepted my husband's indiscretions as part of marriage. For better or worse and all that. No, we didn't fight about Tina that night, or any other night."

"Let's see if I've got this right. Someone came to your house and stole Vern's truck shortly after Vern returned from a late night of"—he checked his notes—"bookkeeping. After stealing Vern's truck, this person hid it by some bushes outside of Tina Anderson's house, a good ten miles from here. For now, let's assume the person was the Creeper, because his intent was likely to peep through the window. When the Creeper was, ah, through at Tina's, he went to escape in Vern's stolen truck and found it gone. Next, for reasons we do not know, the Creeper returned to your house, where he had just stolen the truck from, presumably on foot, since he no longer had the truck, and once he got here made enough racket to wake you up, then shot Vern with his own gun when he came outside to investigate." Mike scratched his head. "That's a little hard to believe."

Fear twisted her stomach. "We don't know it was the Creeper, I mean Wasp, who stole the truck. Maybe it was someone else."

He cocked his head. "So we got us a crime wave. Some unknown person steals Vern's truck right outta your carport and abandons it at Tina's house, and then in an unrelated incident, the Creeper, Wasp, shows up at your house to spy on you and shoots Vern dead, all in a few hours?"

"You're the law, not me. I don't know what the criminal element is out there doing."

"So when they dust the rifle for prints, they'll come back as Wasp's?"

"I have no idea. Maybe he wore gloves."

Another notation in his spiral pad. "I don't think your story is working."

A chill passed through her body, despite the sweltering heat. She forced herself to steady her voice. "It's not a story."

"I'm seeing it differently," he said as he closed his notebook. Posey felt his eyes boring into her skin as he presented his theory. "I figure Vern was with Tina, not at the Emporium, the night he was murdered. While you were occupied with the reunion, he hid his truck in the bushes near her house and spent the evening with her. When he was ready to leave, he discovered his truck missing." He chuckled quietly. "Seems I drove Vern's truck out from under him. He must've gone back and told Tina, who brought him home, since it's too far to walk."

"Is there a question I can answer for you, Sheriff?"

"Yes. You said you heard a sound outside at 3:00 a.m.?"

"Haven't I said that I did?"

"See, that's another problem. You're sure of the time, but every Creeper report I've received places him at a bedroom window between"—he opened his pad and flipped back a few pages—"9:30 p.m. at the earliest and 10:30 p.m. at the latest." He looked up. "So why was he out at three in the morning? The Creeper was trying to see women undressing for bed. Wouldn't he assume you were asleep by then?"

The room spun. The *Gazette* articles had never mentioned the time of night, and Darlene hadn't said anything about how late the Creeper struck. *Damn it.* She licked her dry lips, desperate for the comfort of her gin. *Soon, Posey.* "The whole town knew of the reunion party at my home that night. He probably figured I wouldn't be going to bed 'til then."

He clicked his pen. "Another thing, the oldest victim was, let's see, twenty-three." He looked up from his notebook. "You're a tad older 'n that."

She bristled. "I am aware of my age."

He bowed his head slightly. "You say it was Wasp Fentress. Tell me again how you're so sure."

Panic rose in her throat as she realized she may have made a fatal error, naming Wasp as the perpetrator before thinking it through. What if Wasp had an alibi? She had seen Callie Jane's revelation about Wasp as the ribbon that would tie up her story into a neat package, but she was realizing that ribbon might just as easily become the noose that would hang her.

"When I heard the gunshot, I ran to the window." She couldn't change her story again, so she plowed ahead, hoping for the best. "I saw a figure running across our driveway." She was lifting her fingers as she hit each point in her story, then froze. Had he glanced at her hand? *Damn it.* She resumed her version of events, tucking her hand under her thigh. "When he passed under a floodlight, I recognized him. It was Wasp Fentress. That red hair is unmistakable." She swallowed hard. "I was in shock when I first spoke to you. The morning of the funeral, I realized who I had seen."

Mike's stomach rumbled. He checked his watch and said, "Getting to be lunchtime. Could I trouble you for a sandwich?"

"Of course." She hopped up, grateful for the interruption, and headed for the kitchen. "And I can do better than a sandwich. How about fried chicken, potato salad, and coleslaw left over from the funeral?" She looked at the sheriff, now sitting at her kitchen table. "Would you like sweet tea?"

"Yes, ma'am. Beholden to you." While she busied herself heaping a plate with food, he unfastened the top button of his uniform. "You know, solving this murder would be a real feather in my cap. Even the Nashville boys would be impressed if I could get this one figured out. Probably a raise in it for me, and a commendation from the governor." He interlaced his fingers and popped his knuckles.

Her knees quivered as she continued to pile food onto the sheriff's plate. "As soon as you arrest Wasp Fentress, all the glory you so richly deserve will be yours." As she deposited the plate and a glass of iced tea in front of him, she added, "I bet the governor will give you a medal."

His reply was hard to make out through a mouthful of chicken. "Nobody much cares for any of those Fentresses. They've been trouble long before any of this happened." He nodded at the mound of food, tapping the potato salad with his fork. "Nice and cold, the way I like it." He burped and continued. "I've always wondered if Hatch wasn't behind the theft of some farm equipment a coupla years ago." He shoved coleslaw into his already-full mouth. "Never could pin it on him, though. I felt like Hatch was laughin' at me, getting away with it. Arrestin' his boy could be a good way to even up the score."

She sat in the metal chair across from Mike. "Absolutely. And won't you enjoy watching Hatch's face when you slap those handcuffs on his son? Go arrest Wasp right now."

He sawed open a biscuit and slathered it in butter. "Cain't," he replied, stuffing it into his mouth.

"You're the sheriff. You can do whatever you want."

He grinned. "Glad you think so." He swallowed and wiped crumbs from his face with the back of his hand. "Here's my problem. We got a tip on May 11—that'd be two days before the reunion—that Wasp Fentress was most likely the Creeper. Seems Wasp was braggin' to a buddy of his about having a pair of Cheryl Ann Tisdale's underpants, and the boy got scared he'd be in trouble and told his father, who phoned me." Mike stretched his arms over his head. "We've had the Fentress place under surveillance since the call. My son's been out there every night." He held out his empty glass. "Could I trouble you for more tea?"

She crossed to her Foodarama, steadying herself for a moment on the long metal handle. Opening the door, she blessed the blast of freezing air she had so often cursed, now offering her a moment of relief from the heat, which was increasing by the minute. The pitcher of tea seemed as heavy as one of Vern's bowling balls. She filled the sheriff's glass, placed it by his plate, then returned to the counter to pour some for herself. Her hand inched toward the vinegar bottle. Blocking the sheriff's view with her body, she grasped the bottle and tipped it into her glass. After stirring her drink with her finger, she turned to face Mike.

"Maybe your son fell asleep and missed him sneaking off."

He nodded. "Could be. 'Course, Billy's a trained professional executing his sworn duty. He's a night owl too, always has been. Billy 'n me had a suspicion for a while it was Wasp, based on a couple of partial descriptions we kept out of the paper, but we didn't have enough evidence to nab him. I was pretty sure that call about the Creeper being sighted near Tina Anderson's house was a false alarm since we already had Wasp under surveillance, but I have an obligation to investigate any tips. For all I knew, there was a whole other crime goin' on." Mike took a long gulp of tea. "This morning an eyewitness came forward with information that confirmed two things for me. No doubt. Wasp's the Creeper." He scraped his plate with the side of his fork. "Billy'll sit out there until Wasp goes prowling again, which will be the final evidence we need. I was ready to arrest him after I talked to my eyewitness a few hours ago, but Billy wants to do things by the book and catch him red-handed, so to speak." He slowly dragged the fork from his lips and then studied the shiny tines. "That eyewitness was your daughter."

A lump the size of the buttermilk biscuit Mike Ricketts had crammed into his mouth formed in her gut. What had Callie Jane said to him? Posey had already relayed the information that Callie Jane knew Wasp was the Creeper. What else was there to tell? The room was airless, her wool dress was sticking to her chest and legs, and her skin was itching. "I need to excuse myself for a moment." She forced her legs to carry her to the powder room. Cranking the faucet wide open, she soaked a washcloth with icy water and ran it across her face, already glistening with sweat. After yanking the tight neck of her dress away from her skin, she dabbed at her chest. *Careful, girl, or you'll be trading your flagstone terrace for a cement cell.* She ran more cold water and soaked the washcloth again, rubbing the back of her neck and then her legs. *Pull yourself together.* She reached into a drawer for a tube of Scarlet Scandal. As she traced over her thin lips, she told herself, *You've been playing men all your life. Just do what you do best.* After smoothing her hair and dress, she opened the bathroom door.

Mike had left the kitchen and was back in the library. She wobbled to her seat, holding the massive wing chair's arm for support. "You've got a real mystery on your hands."

"Sure do." He nodded in agreement. "Got one more too."

Her ears were buzzing. "Another crime?"

"Nope, same crime. Here's what I can't figure out. I called you at twelve twenty, and when I asked to speak to Vern, you told me he was asleep. And then when I brought his truck here at twelve fifty-five, you said Vern was still asleep." He leered at her. "You were wearing a lovely gown, but don't worry, I didn't write that part down."

What is he getting at? "That's right. Vern got home and fell asleep right away."

"It could have happened that way, except for one thing. At twelve forty-five, Vern called my house to say his truck had been stolen."

She blanched. *Vern reported the theft.* When Vern told her he would take it up with Mike in the morning, she had assumed he hadn't said anything to Mike yet. But how could he notify Mike if Mike was with her?

"'Course, I was gone, investigating that possible Creeper sighting out on Nashville Highway and driving Vern's truck back to your house. My wife was woken up by the phone ringin'. It was Vern, sayin' he was calling 'bout his truck being stolen. He said he'd been working late at the Emporium, which we know to be a lie." He looked up from his notebook. "Barb knows to write down a message when a call comes in. She had it all there, with the time at the top, twelve forty-five."

He plopped himself in a chair and stretched his legs out. "During the funeral, she whispered to me it was a shame about Vern, that she had spoken to him just a couple of hours before he was killed."

Her body was petrified, but her eyes followed the sheriff's every movement. "When I got home that night, Barbara asked me what was going on, and I told her Vern's truck had been stolen but that I had returned it to him." Posey could feel the blood drain from her face. "She asked me if I had spoken with Vern. I said I had. Barb gets a little jealous, and I didn't want her all stirred up." He smiled as he said, "You lied to me that night, but I wasn't telling the truth either. Fact is, the missus doesn't much care for you. She's still mad about that little cloakroom incident in high school. I let you drive yourself all the way back drunker 'n Cooter Brown 'cause I couldn't risk her knowing you had driven me anywhere." He ran his hands through his thick hair. "Anyway, she didn't give me the message that Vern had called since I said I talked to him." He stretched his arms, seeming to consume all the space in the room. "Now how could Vern be asleep in your bed and on the phone to my wife at the same time?"

Should she tell the truth? Confessing that she had acted in a moment of passion might keep her out of the electric chair. *Manslaughter is better than murder. It might work.* She gulped. *And it might not.* The whole town would know she had killed Vern in a drunken rage. Long-ago words from her mother whispered in her brain. *"The truth is overrated."*

She studied the sheriff, recalling how besotted he had always been with her. Maybe she could make a deal they both would be happy with. Was it worth the risk? She considered her options and chose her path. Unfastening the first few buttons that ran down the front of her dress, she locked eyes with Mike. "I have a solution that will work for both of us."

He looked her up and down, lingering over her full breasts. His breath ragged, he stood, grabbed her from her chair, and kissed her roughly.

Posey slowly freed the remaining buttons, then slid her arms from her confining sleeves, causing the dress to fall to her waist. Mike's breath was hot against her skin as he traced his thumb along one of the petals of her yellow and purple bruise. The pain of his touch brought her to a sickening realization, and she grabbed her sleeve in an effort to return it to her shoulder.

Mike stopped her hand and took hold of the sleeve. "You have to hold a rifle in your armpit," he whispered. "Otherwise, this happens." He slipped her dress back onto her shoulder. "Come on, Posey. Time to go."

Chapter 30

Callie Jane

CALLIE JANE SAT at the kitchen table in her house on Stadler Court and thought over the events of the previous day. Unreal on one hand, but inevitable on the other. She had been honest and told the truth. The rest wasn't up to her.

From the moment her mother had offered to tell the sheriff about Wasp being the Creeper, something had not been sitting right with Callie Jane. She regretted not speaking to the sheriff the moment she realized Wasp was definitely the Creeper, and felt uneasy about leaving it to her mother to talk to the sheriff. Wasp had killed her father, and she needed to be the one to make sure he was brought to justice, not rely on her mother, like she was a child who couldn't speak for herself. After yet another restless night, she had woken up with a mission: to make sure her voice would be heard.

As she'd waited for Sheriff Ricketts to answer the phone, she thought about how often she'd silenced her own voice. How she had longed to object to participating in the Miss Tiny Tennessee pageant but had not wanted to rile her mother, and how she had allowed Mrs. Humboldt to mistake the beginnings of her *no* for a *yes*. She had a voice, and from now on, she was going to use it.

When he picked up, she said, "I want to tell you what I saw, who I saw, in my window."

"Sure, Callie Jane. Come on down to my office and I'll take your statement."

Once she was seated in his whiskey barrel chair, the sheriff clicked his pen and waited.

"Wasp killed my father, and I need to know I've done everything I can to make sure he goes to prison. That starts with me telling you myself about that night he came to my window."

"Your mama told me you realized right after the funeral that he was the Creeper."

"That's right." She explained her suspicions, and how she didn't mention anything earlier because she wasn't positive she'd seen Wasp that night. "But when I heard his sister talk about the wasp sting, I knew it was him." She stood. "That's all I wanted to say." Pausing, she asked, "You know who Wasp is, right?"

"Anyone in law enforcement 'round these parts knows Wasp Fentress."

Callie Jane picked up her purse and walked to the door leading to Market Street. With her hand on the knob, she added, "I figured everybody did, so it was weird Mama didn't remember him."

Mike's voice was sharp. "Say what now?"

"She said she couldn't bring him to mind and asked me to describe him."

"Sit down, Callie Jane." She walked back to his desk and sank onto her seat. "Are you saying your mother couldn't recall Wasp Fentress?"

Apprehension washed over her. "That's right. I had to point him out to her in the dining room."

Mike picked up his pen and clicked again. "Start again from the very beginning and tell me everything that happened."

Callie Jane launched into her account, being careful not to omit any details. "And after I heard Linda and Rosalie talking, and I realized Wasp *was* at my window that night, I told her I knew who the Creeper was. She asked me who, and I said it was Wasp." Callie Jane shifted in her chair. "She asked me to describe him, and then we went to the dining room and I pointed him out to her. Then she patted my hand and said I had been through enough, that she would make sure Wasp was arrested and that she would tell you what I had seen."

Mike stopped writing and looked up. "She told *me* that she realized Wasp was the person who shot your daddy the morning of the funeral, right when she woke up."

Callie Jane's voice quavered. "That doesn't make sense." The first cold wave of truth splashed against her heart. She spoke slowly. "When I told her about Wasp, she said she couldn't remember what he looked like."

"Are you certain of that?" His voice was steady but low as he repeated the information. "Your mother didn't know what Wasp looked like when you told her he was the Creeper?" As Callie Jane nodded, he leaned forward in his chair, frowning. "Will you swear to this in court?"

Her mother had lied, that was clear, but why? A wave crashed against her stomach. *Sweet baby Jesus.* What had her mother done?

"Callie Jane?" The sheriff was staring at her as he gripped his pen tight enough to make his knuckles whiten.

Her hands were clammy and her chest constricted. She'd never had a real mother, the kind she had so desperately needed, but her mother *did* care for her in the only fractured, inadequate way she knew how. As Callie Jane sat in the sheriff's uncomfortable whiskey barrel chair, she understood her mother could do no better as she attempted to raise a daughter she never understood. In those early years of Callie Jane's childhood, her mother had given all she was capable of, which could, with a kind enough eye and a generous enough spirit, be perceived as love. Somewhere during her mother's life, though, something had changed, something that could allow for the unthinkable, the killing of her father. She couldn't imagine such a thing, but all the evidence was pointing to exactly that.

The sheriff was waiting for an answer, one that would change both her own life and her mother's life forever. Did she love her mother in a way that could allow for claiming a suddenly foggy memory that was, in fact, as clear as a crisp Tennessee morning? And would the love she had for her father permit her to deny him justice?

The sheriff's voice was gentle, a rarity for him. "Do you understand what I'm sayin'? Your mother is the prime suspect in your father's murder."

The news was horrifying, but at the same time made perfect sense. Her parents never should have married and had been miserable their whole lives. She didn't think her mother hated her father, but instead hated everything about her own existence. Did she think taking his life would somehow make her own life better?

Truth and honesty joined hands and stood with Callie Jane as she used her voice to say, "Yes, I will testify."

She left the sheriff's office and headed for her old house on Poplar Avenue. Hannah answered when Callie Jane knocked on the door of her childhood home. Once she had explained her mission, Hannah, with tears in her eyes, responded, "Of course you can. Take whatever you'd like. They're his, after all."

As she stood before her father's garden, Hannah, waddling from the weight of her pregnancy, appeared with her father's cutting shears and a damp paper towel. "This should help." She smiled. "I know he loved these flowers. I've been out here every night watering. I promised your father we'd take care of the house and his garden, so that's what we're doing." A bit of breeze moved through the daisies. "When we confessed we couldn't afford the rent he was asking, he said, 'You've got a family that needs a house. I have a house that needs a family. If I cut the rent in half, would that help?' We were so embarrassed, but your father said knowing this house was filled with love meant more to him than money." Hannah wiped her eyes. "When we moved in, we found a package from your father. A baby rattle, with a note saying, 'Blessings to you and the little one.'"

Callie Jane choked back a sob.

Hannah walked two paces and then turned back. "I'm so sorry."

Callie Jane moved through the flowers, cutting the most perfect ones, swaddling the paper towel around the stems. She set the shears on the front steps of her old house and returned to her car.

Seeing the freshly turned earth at the cemetery brought her to her knees. With a keening cry, she sobbed for all she had lost. Tears she had been too numb to shed during the funeral flooded her eyes.

When she was too exhausted to cry anymore, she struggled to a sitting position and reached for the flowers that had fallen beside her. "I brought you daisies. They're from your garden." She arranged the flowers on his grave. "The one thing I'm thankful for in all this is that you never knew I figured out about Callen James Ryan. Don't worry, though. You'll always be my daddy." After a moment she added, "Hannah and Grady are taking good care of the beds. The tomatoes look great. They're watering every night, and I didn't see a single weed." She smiled. "The house is full of love again, just as you wanted."

She moved onto the stone bench she and her father had shared on their way to the appointment with Dr. Ryan. "You're getting something else you wanted, Daddy. I'll be running the Emporium." She gulped, which did nothing to dislodge the lump in her throat. "You always said I'd be a natural." Tears formed again in her already swollen eyes, and though the day was bright and warm, a cold darkness fell over her as she said, "I'll do my best."

··········

Callie Jane reopened the Emporium two weeks after her father died. On the day she was finally able to drag herself into the shop, she saw that someone had placed a black wreath on the Emporium's front door. She understood that no one would ever take credit for the act of kindness, just as she and her father never acknowledged they were the ones leaving brown paper sacks of tomatoes on neighbors' front porches. "That's one of the nice things about a small town. People take care of each other," she told Evangeline as she reported that night on her first day back at work. She suspected Evangeline knew the truth, that she was trying to talk herself into being okay with staying in Spark. Honoring her father's wishes felt noble, the right thing to do, but giving up on moving to California seemed like another death.

Wasp had been arrested and charged with an assortment of trespassing, loitering, and harassment misdemeanors, but as a juvenile, instead of a jail sentence, he got sent to a youthful offender program for the summer.

Her mother had been arrested too, and her charge was a single count of murder. She was being held in a women's prison in Nashville. Callie Jane had made no effort to contact her and was glad to let the sheriff be the one to deal with her. Maybe one day she'd be able to talk to her mother, or maybe even begin to forgive her, but right now she was focusing on herself, her future, and that did not include her mother in any way.

She met with Raddy Tisdale, who confirmed what her father had told her about owning the Emporium and their old house. And he told her two things her father had not. He had left her the money in his savings account, the cash he was going to use for retirement, and had made her the beneficiary of his life insurance policy. Now she had enough money from her father's estate to finance all her dreams—move to California, rent an apartment, find a job—none of which she could do.

On Fridays, Evangeline still asked her to have lunch on the Curly Q's back patio, but Callie Jane always declined. She'd quit making up excuses—too busy, too hot, not hungry—and just shook her head whenever Evangeline popped her head in the door. Trace had tried too, inviting her to supper with his family or to watch the Founders' Day fireworks with him and Laurie Anne, but without success.

Grady Neal got laid off from the factory in late June, and Callie Jane offered him a job as manager.

"*Being at the Emporium full-time would be a blessing to me and Hannah both, Callie Jane. People all around me were getting let go, and I knew my time was coming. I wasn't sure how I'd be able to support a wife and baby with only my part-time job here. I accept with pleasure and will try to do your daddy, um, I mean you, proud.*"

Callie Jane had answered, "*You've got a real knack with the customers, and while I'm not grateful you lost your job, I am glad the Emporium will benefit.*"

More than once she had to stop herself from calling out for her father when she heard Grady letting himself in the back door or rustling around in the stockroom. Grady talked with her about the relentless heat wave or the drought that had the farmers concerned for their crops, and Callie Jane always answered, but more often than not, silence filled the room when there were no customers.

She assumed her father's habit of driving to the cemetery every Sunday with a bouquet of daisies from his garden. Grady and Hannah finally had to tell Callie Jane to quit asking permission to cut the flowers, that they were Vern's anyway and to help herself.

Days turned to weeks. She stopped marking off the days until the concert on her calendar. *Why bother?* She had been so excited to see the Beatles, but now couldn't imagine herself doing something as frivolous as going all the way to Memphis just to listen to music. She'd spend way more time driving than she would at the Coliseum, not to mention the expense of the gasoline, food, and hotel room. The only event worth counting down to was the birth of Grady and Hannah's baby, and that was their life, not her own. She sighed. Her world was now selling thumbtacks and potting soil in Spark.

She held a Fourth of July sale but had cried so hard when she pulled out the red, white, and blue bunting her father always displayed across the front window that Grady had to gently take it from her shaking hands and hang it for her.

Gray Boy and Pearl still got their kibble, but even the sight of the two cats running toward her at the sound of Shelly's distinctive engine failed to make her smile. Her life was over in any meaningful way, and she knew it. She was as dead as her father, just without the funeral.

. . . .

Trace came into the shop one blistering August afternoon with a brown bag in his hands.

"Hey, Callie Jane. I brought you a present."

She opened the bag and pulled out a record.

Trace said, "It's the Beatles' newest release. You're still going to the concert, right?"

"No, I'm not. Seems like too much trouble for just a few hours of fun." She slid the single back into the bag. "Thanks for the record."

On the hottest night of the year, in her restless sleep, Callie Jane had a vivid dream. She was transported back to the day her daddy had removed her training wheels from the blue bike he had purchased for a dollar at a garage sale. She had been terrified to ride without training wheels, but at the same time was desperate to do so. When she had finally told her father she was ready, he had beamed at her. "I'm so proud of you, sweet girl."

When it was time for her first two-wheeler ride, she had panicked. "I can't do it, Daddy," she sobbed. "I'm too scared."

"It's okay to be frightened, but it's just as important to try," he said as he knelt beside the bike with a wrench. "You already know what to do." He rolled the bike toward her after he removed the training wheels. "I'll be right here."

Both terrified and exhilarated, she had first wobbled and then flown down Poplar Avenue, her blonde hair a bright flag flying victoriously behind her. She soared with the effortless joy of one of her father's bluebirds, the rush of freedom and success overwhelming her as she guided her bike back to her father, who was jumping and shouting, "I knew you could do it!"

As her dream self pulled to a stop beside her cheering father, she woke up, blinking as she looked around her room. Everything was the same, of course, but also different. And *she* was different, like a roadblock had been cleared.

The shrill ringing of the phone startled her. "Hello?"

"It's Grady. I'm at the hospital with Hannah. She went into labor last night, so I can't come in to work."

"How exciting! Don't worry for one minute about the shop. You just take care of Hannah." She scribbled out a note and left for the Emporium.

The black wreath, faded to a dull gray from three months of exposure to the relentless summer sun, slipped easily off its nail. She held the note in one hand and the wreath in the other, pausing to reflect on their meanings. Life and death, past and future, sadness and joy. She pushed the note onto the now-empty nail.

Closed for the Arrival of Baby Neal

She headed to Poplar Avenue for some daisies and then drove to the cemetery. As she approached her father's grave, she saw the bluebird again. At her daddy's funeral she had been so bitter, wondering why the bird was content to live among the dead. A new idea stopped her. Her daddy had said some bluebirds stayed in the same place their whole lives, but others migrated. Maybe the bird was just pausing to rest. Or maybe she was paying her respects to the man who had fed her and her kind for decades before she flew on to where she belonged.

A cool breeze ruffled the leaves and thunder rumbled in the distance as she stared at the heart marking her grandparents' resting place. "Beloved," the headstone said. "You *were* beloved, Daddy," she whispered. "And still are." Another sob choked her as she arranged the daisies on his grave.

She returned to the bench, recalling what her father had said about the inscription on his parents' marker. "Beloved *is an odd word. It means someone loved you, but it's also an instruction, to be loved. It's hard to figure out what that really means, but I know it's important.*"

Her father had loved her, of that she was certain. She was equally sure he wanted the best for her. When she had told him she was breaking her engagement, he had said, "*Never settle, Callie Jane. If you long for something with all your heart, then I'll be the first one cheering you on while you try your best to get it. But don't ever do something because you think it's what's expected of you, and not what you* want *to do.*"

She sat up. Was that what *be loved* meant? That you should follow your heart, with the reassurance that whoever loved you would also want for you what you longed for?

After her father's death, she had shunted her dreams aside, dismissing them as a childish fairy tale she had convinced herself could become a reality. But what if the best way to honor her father was to embrace those dreams and live the life she imagined for herself? Her future—her plans to see the Beatles in concert and then move to California—had brought her such joy and made her feel so alive. Her father would want those things for her, so shouldn't she pursue them?

She knelt at her father's grave and touched the earth covering his casket. "I finally understand," she whispered. "I am beloved."

A rumble of thunder, closer than the previous one, reminded her she didn't have much time. She stood and traced her steps back to her car, confident in her new understanding. What she wanted for herself was what he would also want for her, even if it was counter to his own desires. She would not step into her father's worn brown shoes and tick away the rest of her days behind the ancient cash register. She would follow her dreams—cheer as she watched the Beatles concert and then head to California—knowing she was beloved, and discover the life that waited for her there.

....

She had only three scheduled stops before she set off for Memphis, then California.

Her first stop was the Emporium. Unpinning the crude bluebird drawing from the wall by her father's chair, she smiled as she recalled him saying, *"A bluebird does what its heart wants and flies to where it's happiest. A good lesson for both of us."* She gently touched a wing and then carefully tucked the picture into her purse. As she closed the back door, she placed her palm against the old wooden planks and thanked the Emporium for all it had provided for her—a chance to spend untold hours with her father, a place to learn business skills that would serve her well, and a way to make the money she needed to buy Shelly and move out of her parents' home.

The Poplar Avenue house was her second stop. As she sat in the driveway, she could imagine her father tramping down the cement steps to greet her. She closed her eyes, feeling him surround her with love. She climbed those same cement stairs and knocked on the door, clutching a manila envelope. Grady answered. "Callie Jane! Come in."

Hannah sat in her father's old recliner, beaming. "We'd like you to meet Theodore Vernon Neal." She gently folded the blanket away from his body. "Theodore for my father and Vernon for yours."

Callie Jane dropped into a nearby chair, unsure of her ability to stand. "Oh, Hannah," she whispered. "He's beautiful." Tears pricked her eyes. "Daddy would be so proud."

She took a letter from the envelope. "I'm moving to California, but I have some things to wrap up first. Have you ever heard the expression 'good things come in threes'?" She held up the piece of paper. "This came in the Emporium's mail while you were in the hospital. It's from Little Lullabies children's boutique in Nashville. The owner fell in love with your work at the flea market and wants as many handmade items as you can provide. Blankets, sweaters, booties, the works."

Hannah's hand flew over her mouth. "What?" She gently laid Teddy in the Moses basket Callie Jane had given her. "If you hadn't suggested selling my knitting, this never would have happened. What a blessing." She crossed the room and hugged Callie Jane.

Grady turned to his wife. "I'm so proud of you."

After drawing more papers from the envelope, she handed them to Grady. "The next good thing is an offer for you to buy Jarvis Emporium. We can wait until you've been manager for a while to make sure you like it."

Grady whispered, "I don't know what to say." He looked at his wife, who was nodding. "Except thank you."

Callie Jane's voice shook a little, but she was smiling when she said, "And now the third good thing." She pulled a contract from the envelope. "If you want it, I'll sell this house to you. We can have an appraisal done, and that'll be the price. We could work out a rent-to-own deal with Everett Bradford at the bank, or you can just keep renting as long as you like. The main thing is, I would love for your family to be in this house for as long as it makes you happy to be here."

Shocked silence settled over the Neals. Grady whispered, "The house?"

Callie Jane moved to the doorframe of the kitchen and traced the wobbly pencil marks her father had made every year, with the date carefully recorded by each line. "It would bring me peace to know this home will be filled with love. My father always dreamed of a family bringing a lifetime of love and joy to this little house, but of course it's up to you."

Hannah scooped up Teddy from his Moses basket and stood beside Grady. She looked at him, and it was his turn to nod. "We accept, Callie Jane. All of it. You have blessed us more than we ever could have imagined."

She moved to gaze out the window overlooking her father's garden, his Eden. "Wonderful. I met with Raddy Tisdale yesterday, and he and Everett can handle all the paperwork." She picked up her purse. "I'll check in with you after I get settled in California. I'll want lots of updates, about the house, the Emporium, your knitting business, and especially little Teddy."

Tears slid down Hannah's cheeks. "I can't find words for all this."

"We're overwhelmed," Grady whispered. He sank into the chair Callie Jane had just vacated. "I don't think you realize what all this means for us."

"I hope I do. And I hope you all know what this will mean for *me*." Callie Jane's eyes were filling. "I'd better leave before I start blubbering."

The front door of the Poplar Avenue house, the one she had entered and left from for almost nineteen years of her life, looked the same, but walking through it this time would change everything.

As she hesitated, memories of life with her father wrapped around her like a warm quilt on a raw day. She grasped the doorknob. Was she ready? Her father's rich voice filled her head. *"You already know what to do."* His voice was so clear, she turned to look for him, as if he was standing beside her in his starched, short-sleeve shirt and clip-on tie, instead of lying in his grave. She stepped into the sun-filled afternoon and got into her car. One more stop.

· · · · · · · · · ·

Trace was carrying a bag of trash to the dumpster behind the grocery store. "Hey, Callie Jane," he said, opening her car door. "What's up?"

She gave Trace a big hug. "I'm getting the hell out of here. I'll write when I get settled." She frowned as the feral cats, attracted by the now-familiar sound of Shelly's engine, peered out from the woods, ready for a meal. "I hope Gray Boy and Pearl will be okay. Evangeline said she'd feed them for me, but she's gotten so busy at the Curly Q she may not have time."

"I'll do it."

"You'll take care of Trouble and Nuisance? Since when did your hatred of cats turn to love?"

"I've never loved cats, and I never will." He brushed her cheek with his thumb. "But I've always loved you." Kissing her forehead, he added, "And I always will."

....

Evangeline was slicing an avocado over a green salad. "I've made your favorite lunch." She sighed. "I'm going to miss you so much, but I'm so excited for you."

Callie Jane took a bite and asked, "When is Becky coming?"

"She should get here tonight."

"I'm glad. It makes me happy knowing you two will be here together." She paused. "I'm not really sure how to say thank you for all you've done for me, Evangeline. My whole life has changed because of you."

"You were my first friend in Spark and made me feel like I was going to be okay. I'm the grateful one." She added some crackers to Callie Jane's plate. "Harold checked Shelly, and you've got the number for my brother, right?"

Callie Jane grinned. "Yes and yes."

"And your concert ticket?"

"In my purse."

After finishing lunch, Callie Jane walked toward her bedroom, stopping to pat Muse. "I'll never forget how you saved me from Wasp." She kissed the Lab's head. "You're my hero."

As she made a final check for any items left behind, her eye fell on the *Birth of Venus* postcard and the Empress tarot card, still tucked in her mirror's frame. "Come on, ladies. We're heading to California," she said, nestling them beside the bluebird drawing in her purse. She took her Venus necklace from the top of her dresser and slipped it over her head. Grabbing her suitcase, she walked out of the house and tossed her luggage in Shelly's back seat, with Evangeline close behind.

"I'm so proud of you, Callie Jane. Hey, are you going to look for JJ at the concert?"

She turned to Evangeline. "If I see him I'll say hi, but I want this night all to myself." She smiled. "If that's possible in an auditorium with thousands of people. A long time ago I promised myself I'd see the Beatles in person, and I want to focus on having that experience." Tears blurred her eyes. "Take good care of yourself, okay? And write to me."

"You know it." Evangeline hugged her tightly and turned to go back inside the house, but not before Callie Jane spotted tears on her cheeks.

She slid behind the driver's seat of her car and cranked the engine. The lilting strains of "I'll Follow the Sun" filled the car. Patting the dashboard, she said, "Come on, Shelly. Time to go."

Epilogue

POSEY SAT IN the beauty shop chair, critically watching Denise as she put the final touches on Posey's hairdo.

"What do you think?" Denise asked as she windmilled hair spray over Posey's freshly styled beehive.

Posey patted the left side of her head. "Next time could you try to give me more volume? It seems a little flat."

Denise grimaced. "Sorry, Your Majesty." She handed Posey a mirror to inspect the back. "And speaking of next time, please reconsider letting me give you a Farrah Fawcett feathered style. I did one on Ruby last week, and she loves it. Updating your look might perk you up." Denise surveyed Posey's hair. "Maybe Princess Di? It would be nice to have you join us here in the '80s."

"I like the beehive. It suits me."

"Sure thing, Posey. Just thought I'd ask." As Posey walked to the door, Denise added, "Good luck on your parole hearing this afternoon."

Posey turned back around and snapped, "They've said no every other time. Why should this one be different?"

A Note from the Author

THE EMPRESS OF Cooke County was born in a doctor's office. I had taken my mother to an appointment, and while we waited for her name to be called, we were chatting about the legend in our family that we are descendants of Pocahontas. "Did you know she was called the Empress of Virginia?" my mom asked. Her name was called, and I was left in the waiting room to think about what a great title that would make. I started imagining an empress from my home state of Tennessee and then settled on a more manageable area, a county.

I Googled *empress* to make sure I knew the difference between an empress and a queen and found the Empress tarot card. I learned that when the Empress is pulled from the deck upright, she represents all good things, and when she is drawn from the deck upside down, the inverse meaning is true. Most of this story rushed into my brain in about ten minutes, about a mother and daughter who are opposites. I started writing that afternoon. The story is not about tarot, but it *is* about a mother and daughter who cannot for the life of them figure each other out. They both have goals and dreams and encounter obstacles as they try to attain them, but that's where the similarities end.

When I was filling out a questionnaire for my publisher intended to guide them as they designed the cover and planned for the book's release, I was asked: *What is the theme of this book?* Suddenly I was back in my twelfth-grade English class taking a final exam, and this question was worth 20 points. After an embarrassingly long time spent pondering and pacing, I had a Dorothy-in-Oz moment and realized the answer had been right in front of me all along. All I had to do was read the brass plaque beside the door of the house I named Cold Spring—love conquers all.

Acknowledgments

AUTHOR LEE SMITH was my seventh-grade English teacher. (I *know*. Even I can hardly believe that.) Although I was just a silly thirteen-year-old, I realized how lucky I was. Lee acting out a scene from *Jane Eyre* for our class is my favorite academic memory of all time. She told me I was a writer, and I believed her. She later read my manuscripts, and an email from her calling herself a fan of my work has been on my refrigerator since the day I received it. Thank you, Lee, for lighting the fire that has sustained me all these years.

Thank you to the incomparable Adriana Trigiani, who was an early champion of this story. I will always be grateful to her.

I learned a long time ago it's impossible to understand everything, but if you're lucky, you will have the right people in your life to ask what you don't know. As I wrote this book, I called on so many people to help me get the details right. Thank you to Vickie Hoffmann, who patiently answered my endless questions about running a hair salon. Thank you to Bobby Butler and Walter Smith for their expertise in an area I can't name without including a spoiler. Thank you to Robin Cohn, the inspiration for the character of Evangeline. Her insights and perspective helped me craft a character I am proud to have created. I also want to remember Gilford Walker, a wonderful man who generously spoke with me about tobacco farming. I am grateful for his wisdom and the time we spent together.

Thank you to Elizabeth Wafler, who served as a critique partner for an early draft of this story, and to Sheila Athens who edited an early version. Thank you to my book club, who read multiple drafts and gave me real-world feedback. Thank you to fellow writer Hope Gibbs Cummiskey, the best friend and cheerleader anyone could ask for. Thank you to the Women's Fiction Writers Association and the Nashville Writers Alliance. And thank you to Jackie Arthur.

And thank you to my stellar literary agent, Kathy Schneider at Jane Rotrosen Agency. Without her willingness to take a chance on an unknown writer, this book would not exist. She worked with me to polish the manuscript and expertly guided me through a surreal bidding war for this story, an experience I wish for every querying writer.

Thank you to my daughters, Mary and Claire, who are the greatest blessings of my life. Thank you to my mother, Clara Bass, who made a remark to me that formed the first idea for this book. Thank you to my sister, Ann, for talking through endless plot points with me, and thank you to my husband, Steve, for his steadfast belief in me and my story.

So much of writing a book is a solitary process, but publishing a book takes many talented people. From that first memorable meeting with the Harper Muse team, I knew I was in expert hands. My first thank you goes to Becky Monds, who plucked my manuscript from her vast slush pile and brought it to the acquisitions team. Her editorial vision has strengthened this book in ways I could not have imagined. Thank you to

Amanda Bostic, who leads the fabulous team of Kerri Potts, Nekasha Pratt, Margaret Kercher, Savannah Breedlove, Natalie Underwood, Jere Warren, Patrick Aprea, Colleen Lacey, Caitlin Halstead, and Taylor Ward, all of whom helped make this book a reality. Thanks also to Julie Breihan.

Lila Selle is the talented designer who created my cover. She captured Posey at the beauty shop so perfectly. Thank you, Lila!

Most of all, thank you to every reader who picks up *The Empress of Cooke County*. There is nothing like the joy of discovering a good book, and I hope each of you feels you have found that in this story.

Discussion Questions

1. Posey's mother says "the truth is overrated." Compare how Callie Jane and Posey view truth. Would your answer be the same if they were reflecting on honesty?

2. Why did the author set the story in the 1960s? Would the story have been similar if she had chosen a different decade?

3. Posey is nearsighted, always squinting. In what other ways is Posey not able to see?

4. How do each of the two women understand love? How did they come to their very different understandings of what love is?

5. Callie Jane and Posey say they love each other. Do you agree?

6. Posey abhors fairy tales and refuses to read them to Callie Jane. Is her own life a fairy tale she told herself?

7. Numbers associated with Posey typically add up to thirteen. How does her fear of all things thirteen manifest in the story? The Empress card is number three in the tarot deck. How does the author use the number three?

8. The plaque by the front door of Cold Spring is inscribed with *Amor Vincit Omnia*, Love Conquers All. How does this illustrate a theme of the story?

9. The word *beloved* is used in reference to Vern, Tina, Callie Jane, Posey's gin, and even the Creekside Crone. Does the word *beloved* have the same meaning for all the characters in the story?

10. Callie Jane hears three Beatles songs on the radio, "Think For Yourself," "Run For Your Life," and "I'll Follow the Sun." How do these songs mirror her journey through this story?

LOOKING FOR MORE GREAT READS? LOOK NO FURTHER!

HARPER MUSE

*Illuminating minds
and captivating hearts
through story.*

Visit us online to learn more:
harpermuse.com

Or scan the below code and sign up to receive
email updates on new releases, giveaways,
book deals, and more:

@harpermusebooks

About the Author

Photo by Jackie Arthur

ELIZABETH BASS PARMAN grew up entranced by family stories, such as the time her grandmother woke to find Eleanor Roosevelt making breakfast in her kitchen. She worked for many years as a reading specialist for a nonprofit, and spends her summers in a cottage by a Canadian lake. She has two grown daughters and lives outside her native Nashville with her husband and maybe-Maltipoo, Pippin.

· · · · · · · · ·

Elizabeth can be found at www.elizabethbassparman.com
Twitter: @e_parman
Instagram: @elizabethbassparman